FREE TO DREAM

ALSO BY STEVEN A. HELLMANN

<u>Dreamer Series</u>

Call of Kayden

FREE TO DREAM

Book 2 of the Dreamer Series

Steven A. Hellmann

Printed in the United States of America

Published in 2020 by Hellmann Books, an imprint of Steven Hellmann

ISBN: 978-1-7344489-2-4

Cover design by Steven Hellmann with photo attribution to Stefan Keller on Pixabay.com

HellmannBooks.com

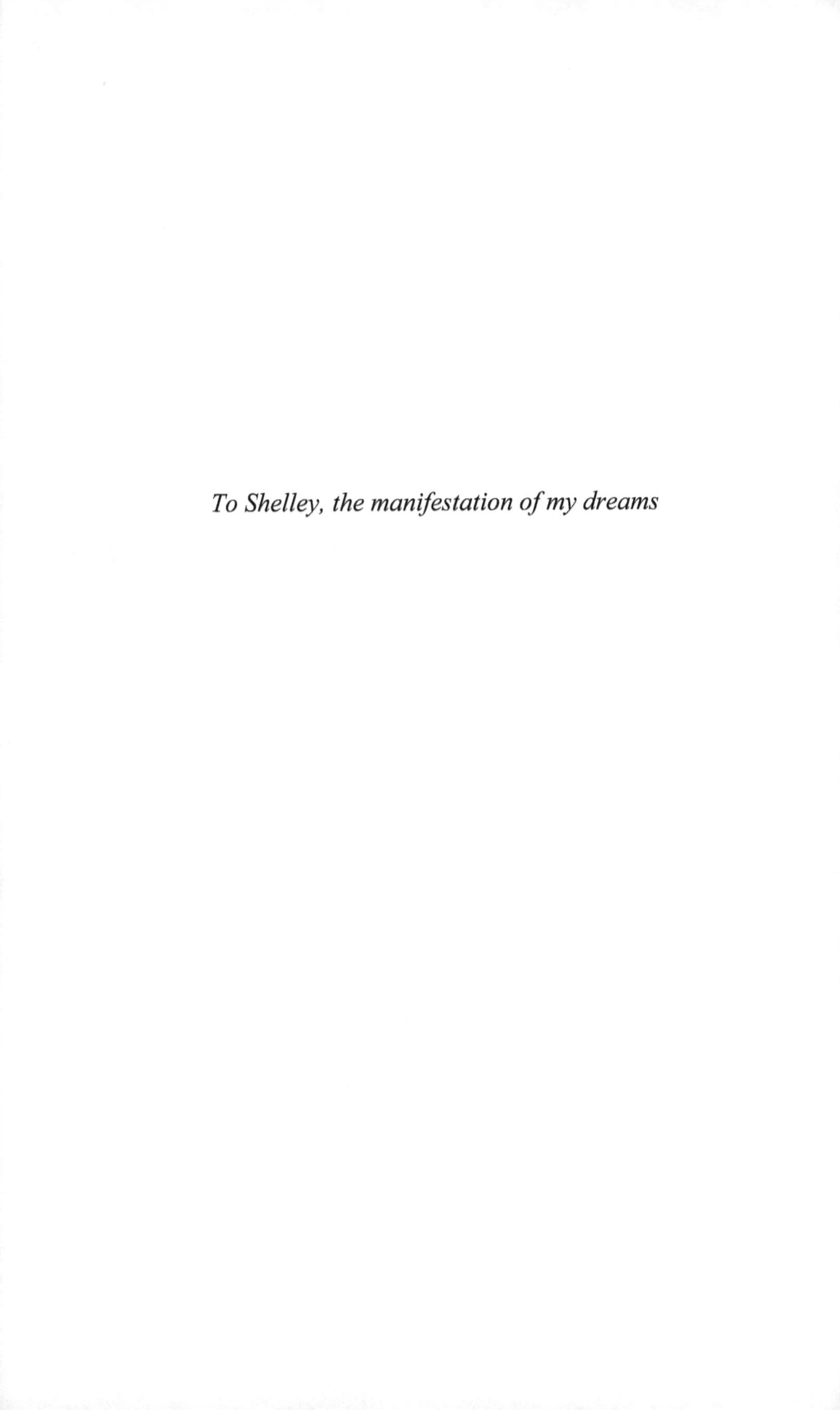

To Shelley, the manifestation of my dreams

Table of Contents

PROLOGUE

a dark and eerie gloom cast its aura over the building Darren was waiting in. While looking across the multitude of shadows, Darren tried to suppress the foreboding he felt inside. Here he waited, trying to patiently determine if his quarry would arrive at the rendezvous alone, or alternatively with those on a mission of betrayal. For now, no one appeared to be present, which on the surface provided a small measure of relief.

After a few minutes of waiting, he observed the quiet and solitary approach of someone walking in a way that seemed out of place. Darren stepped out of the darkness and made himself visible. This was where the greatest danger was – initial contact. If this was a trap, it would not go well for him.

"May science and reason guide your day," Darren spoke out.

"Without the lily, all hope is lost," came the muffled reply from the feminine sounding voice in the darkness.

This was the response he expected to hear to identify his contact. The person who spoke it also stepped forward where Darren could barely make out the outline of what appeared to be a woman's face.

"Do not despair, hope remains," Darren completed the counter phrase. "Are you sure you were not followed?"

"I left my handheld behind and I don't think I have any tracking dots on my body. I was told you could check me to be sure?" the voice replied.

Darren nodded and took out a portable device he had brought with him, proceeding to do a full scan of the stranger's body and clothing. It came back negative indicating that nothing was found. This wasn't the top scanner model available but it detected effectively, and most importantly, was small in size to carry, a key criterion on this mission.

"So far, so good," Darren offered. "I would like to generate an electromagnetic pulse to fry anything else that may be watching. You don't have any implants, do you? I didn't scan any, but want to ask before I do this in case causes you problems."

"Not that I know of. Do what you need to do," came the reply.

Darren shielded his scanner and face recognition disruptor then put the EMP device next to their area and triggered a burst. Nodding with the look of success, Darren looked up.

"We should be safe now from prying eyes and ears. I wouldn't take too long in case a live stream was disrupted and repair is initiated, but we should have a few minutes," Darren explained while he unshielded his scanner and put it in awareness mode to detect a change in surveillance state.

"Thank you for coming," the stranger responded. "I represent a growing group of people who are questioning the laws against religious studies. There has to be something more than the nothingness that exists beyond death as is taught by the Ministry of Education. If there is nothing beyond, what is the point of life?"

"A fair question," Darren replied. "And what have you concluded?"

"All we have are questions," the voice replied with the sound of frustration. "What we want more than anything is a free forum where we can explore these questions. But to ask these kinds of questions in public is a sentence for confinement or death. The eldest among us have memories of alternate teachings when they were children, but all references to them have been suppressed. There are rumors that there are those in Xenon who practice these teachings still and we long to learn from them if we can."

"It is true there are those in Xenon and near there who still do practice the ways of old," Darren answered. "If it were not for these ways, we would not have survived the clampdown two years back. It is good that you are asking these questions. You represent a seed that has been planted but you lack the water and sunlight to be nurtured into something more."

"Can you help us learn more?" the person asked hopefully.

"Be at peace," Darren replied. "I brought you some books regarding the teaching of the Lily. Only one whose mind is opened to the Way of the Lily can receive its gifts. Keep these safely hidden and learn from them. Pay attention to any changes in your dreams. Now go, so our presence is not discovered here."

The stranger nodded, gratefully accepting the bundle that Darren had presented. Looking around carefully, she exited the building. Darren waited a few minutes so they would not be seen exiting together then watchfully left by a different exit.

Darren Kubacki did his best to stay in the shadows. He trusted the facial recognition disruption technology he was wearing but he didn't want to take any more chances than he had to. He was deep within capitol-controlled territory, and needed to safely make it back to his transport point. There would be a lot to explain if he were to be captured on how he had got here not having authorization to be in this sector. The government had to have suspicions on how Kayden had evacuated the people in the recent conflict, but had not yet to Darren's knowledge gotten their hands on any of the transport tubes. Kayden did not want to surrender knowledge of this and had been very strategic in how it exposed this technological application to risk of capture.

Tracking technology was everywhere and the Oversite system was getting progressively better at filtering abnormal patterns of behavior and flagging it for follow-up. Oversite was developing a growing self-awareness, an artificial intelligence of sorts, at a level it had not exhibited previously. This capability made these sorts of excursions all the more dangerous. Even though Kayden was steadily growing stronger, it saw its only chance of survival was not in defending Xenon exclusively, but instead broadening its appeal, even into the heart of capitol-controlled areas.

Darren was not particularly strong in dream gifts. He had enough dream ability to be able to execute the transport tube and had a rudimentary ability to traverse his past in his dreams qualifying him to be trained in the Way of the Lily. Darren showed a great deal of courage during the Great Evacuation, helping to both transport the people of Xenon to safety as well as rescue captured children who were not evacuated in time. Darren had a track record of being calm in the face of danger as well as the ability to not stand out from his surroundings when entering foreign areas. When this opportunity came up, he was on a short list of people who could do this mission successfully. Other more gifted dreamers had assessed that the local interest in the Lily was genuine, and contact was worth making.

He was at least a full kilometer from the safehouse his transport tube was hidden. The sky was full of stars and the moon was but a sliver in the sky. A large city should not show the sky so clearly, but energy was never to be used without purpose. So, in the middle of the night all lights were turned off and the starry expanse of the universe was on vibrant display. Darren used the dim light from the heavens and made his way back to his point of entry. Just a little further to go and this mission would be a success.

∞ ∞ ∞

Sharna Malloy looked up from her primary workstation to determine the source of the notification she was hearing. This alert was one she had programmed, not the annoying alarm that some ministry minion wanted her attention. Sharna quickly acknowledged it and checked what was flashing on an alternate display.

Oversite just detected an anomaly in the Preath city of Morfort where she was currently stationed. The standard Oversite routine hadn't detected anything, but her new experimental one had. It was possible it was a false alarm, but that was the point of validating a new system wasn't it? Sharna quickly checked the data that had triggered it. Someone walking at night by itself should not be cause for alarm. This was a legal activity and done frequently. But there was some difficulty picking up the profile through facial recognition systems combined with the erratic nature of the movement that was detected. Facial recognition systems were known to not lock in, but that wasn't anything to deploy for every time that happened. No, there was also a mysterious sensor outage near where the person was detected walking. Each piece by itself would not trigger a team to be deployed, but her algorithm had made a solid connection. It was learning and that was a very exciting development.

"Sharna here," she spoke into her handheld. "I need a Covert Extraction Team to accompany me immediately. I will be downstairs waiting. Sending the destination coordinates now."

"Right away, ma'am," the dispatch officer replied. "The CET should be there within a couple of minutes."

"Make sure they get a move on it. I'm not sure how much time we have to catch up with this one," Sharna answered while quickly grabbing her portable workstation and heading toward the exit.

No sooner had she arrived downstairs a non-descript vehicle pulled up. Sharna quickly got inside and the vehicle took off toward the direction of the target at a higher than civilian authorized speed. The streets were mostly empty and the darkness was hard to pierce as the vehicle traversed the industrial area of the city.

Sharna was not a talkative person. Honestly, conversation bored her. There were so few people that she could speak with and be challenged intellectually, and they certainly were not present in her current work location. The CET that was assigned to her learned quickly to stay out of her way and do things just the way she asked. This team had been assigned to her for several months as she had been doing system validation. They knew the routine and what was expected of them. They didn't bother to try to engage in conversation. They were to speak with new information or respond if she asked something of them. Otherwise Sharna was to be left in peace to work. She liked it best that way, and if prior conversation attempts where any indication, they liked it better that way also.

Sharna opened up her workstation and immediately began to digest what the sensors were able to pick up on this suspicious character. She was able to track this person with an infrared scanner even though there was not enough light to get a good image of features. Surveillance showed the person had originated from a building that was known to be mostly abandoned, and appeared to be heading back in its direction after doing something enough to trigger the system alarm.

"Adjust our destination to these coordinates," Sharna commanded before sending the coordinates she wanted followed. "I want us hidden and inside of the building before the target gets there."

The navigator nodded and turned promptly to redirect his destination. They arrived just a few minutes later, after everyone but the navigator exited the vehicle. The vehicle drove off, but not before some passive sensors and drone surveillance devices were readied.

"Aglas, do a quick building scan before we go in," the CET team leader commanded.

Finding nothing triggering their sensors, the team proceeded to get the door opened and went inside. Each person carefully moved to spread themselves out strategically throughout the structure and out of sight.

"No one moves without my say so," Sharna reminded over the closed-circuit radio – Not that they needed to be told.

A rear door was heard opening, representing the only audible indicator present in the dark building. Sharna watched with low light technology as a floor panel was opened up to reveal an access door of some sort in the floor.

This was such an amateur move to not recheck the building he had come back to. The hidden passage should not have been this easy to discover. Sighing, she quickly deployed a mini-drone to follow, and crept toward the floorboard once it was closed behind the stranger. Sharna saw the drone's video feed and watched as a second opening was propped open in the wall of the subfloor structure below. There was some sort of vehicle like thing of unknown design inside. She could not allow this find to get away. Sharna signaled for the extraction team to detain the person, continuing to watch as they with great stealth and speed opened up the floorboard and followed into the passage below.

The subject entered the vehicle after closing the passage behind him. He appeared to put his hands on a couple of buttons after keying something into the console. He closed his eyes and looked like he was trying to do some sort of meditative activity. The extraction team was at the second door and replayed the footage to determine how to get the secret passage back open. After a couple of tries, the door popped ajar.

"He is about to get away. Stun him now," Sharna commanded into the team's ears via the wireless communicators, watching with satisfaction as the person there was hit with a concussive shockwave that rendered him motionless, causing his hands to fall to his side. The typical effect was a period of unconsciousness for a few minutes combined with a mild temporary paralysis. "Good work, I'll be right down," came a rare complement to the team.

Sharna arrived in the opening with curiosity beginning to consume her. "Get him out of that thing and restrain him."

Sharna looked around carefully. When she saw the transport vehicle, or whatever it was called on her drone feed, she almost expected there to be a tunnel that the vehicle could travel through. But now that she was in the small room, she realized that the rock wall was not an illusion; it really was a rock wall. This vehicle had nowhere to go, but the person acted like it would take him somewhere. Either the person was delusional or he wasn't. The most likely answer was yes, this was going to take him somewhere. This could be the mystery technology that had been used to evacuate most of Xenon. If it was, it would be a huge find, and one Sharna could not wait to reverse engineer.

Sharna's thinking was interrupted by a muffled groaning sound. The prisoner was coming to.

CHAPTER 1

Gabriel grimaced after reading the latest dispatch from Quintin. It was inevitable that he would be recalled to the capital at some point, but didn't think it would be so soon. Sure, they had disguised the summons so he could later return to Xenon, but Gabriel knew within his heart that once he left the boundaries of his farm, he may never be able to return. Gabriel acknowledged the message and logged out of Oversite. He needed advice and hoped his grandmother would be able to provide it.

Entering into the dream state, Gabriel embraced a state of calm that transcended his full being. He did this in the time it took him to close his eyes, an extreme improvement from when he had first learned how. Gabriel took in an altered awareness where a field of lilies was arrayed before him viewed across a black and white canvas. This optical display still brought a sense of wonder to Gabriel, even though he had seen it many times before.

In the distance, Gabriel was able to hear the unique tone of his grandmother dreaming. Raelynn's lessons called to him as he worked to filter out all the external stimuli, searching for the unique imprint that would indicate his grandmother was present in this altered plane of reality. The indicator was faint, but she was here, and with additional focus Gabriel allowed that marker to grow clearer as he initiated a mental connection required to link to where she was. Gabriel experienced a shift as his vision momentarily blurred before clearing up to reveal a new location and his grandmother.

This was an odd place to find her, Gabriel considered. She was in some sort of research lab he deduced. Gabriel did not deem himself as an expert in technology but he would have been blind to not see evidence of the state-of-the-art computing arrayed before him with a seemingly competent woman aggressively working the controls. There was a workstation with at least twenty viewing terminals, not to mention the hardware behind it. Behind the workstation was a robotics cell and beside that was some sort of electronics station. Specialized test equipment was spread around the very spacious work area. But what really got Gabriel's attention was a partially disassembled transport tube. If this was a ministry lab like he suspected it to be, this did not portend good things.

His grandmother appeared to be in good health, as much as could be determined in the dream state, and continued to exude a vibrancy to her that could not be mistaken. Behind that vitality began to show a look of increasing concern on her face as she finished looking around, finally acknowledging Gabriel's presence.

"Gabriel! So good to see you," she exclaimed with a true fondness in her voice. "I didn't expect to see you so soon after last time you visited. Is something a matter?"

"Good to see you also, grandmother," Gabriel answered. "I had something come up from the ministry I wanted to discuss with you. This is an unusual place to find you exploring. Is something going on?"

"You could say it was," Isabella replied with concern in her voice. "One of ministries has got a hold of a transport tube by the looks of it, not to mention the person who was using it. This is not good news."

"Is there anything we can do?" Gabriel asked.

"If we do, it won't be anytime soon," Isabella answered. They have our agent so secure it would take a small army to get close enough to get him out of there. No, he knew the risks he was taking. If we get an opportunity to free him, we will, but for now, he is left to his own devices."

"Losing a transport tube sounds bad. This will be the first one they have captured isn't it?" Gabriel asked.

"It is," Isabella answered. "That will hurt us potentially more than losing Darren will. I have been watching the person who is in charge of evaluating the transport tube. Frankly, she is as ruthless as she is brilliant. I shudder to think what harm she can do to our cause if she is able to figure out how it works. I hope Darren can hold out long enough to slow down her learning. But you didn't come here to worry about this, what is on your mind?"

"I am going to be recalled to the capital," Gabriel explained. "They are going to summon several leaders of farms in Xenon to provide training and help on updating the ministry farming standards. They are trying to diversify where food is grown and want some more help from experts. At least that is the cover story. The main reason is they want an excuse to do an extensive debrief on me."

"They have done the standard updates before," Isabella replied. "It is a common occurrence every few years, so it will not raise any suspicions on your loyalty. I am not sure those who are asked to go will trust the Ministry's intentions toward them if they leave the safe confines of Xenon's borders though. I wonder who will be willing to attend?"

"I was curious about the same thing," Gabriel remarked. "From the synopsis I saw, they plan on providing assurances that the allowances won two years ago will be extended to those making the trip, even outside the borders of Xenon. We have just brought in the harvest, and the next planting season won't come for a few months. All things considered; it isn't the worst time to be away."

"They must be planning something important if they are willing to make those allowances. Normally, they would be so worried about corrupting those who you came in contact with. Either that, or they have some ulterior motive. Sounds like I have some more digging to do. This will be dangerous for you," Isabella said with concern in her voice. "It is one thing to deceive from afar, it is another thing to do it under close scrutiny. Since they now have the transport tube, I think you should volunteer information about that when you get there. So much to think about. How much time do you have before you leave?"

"I should get the official summons with the others in a day or two," Gabriel answered.

"Come visit me before you go," Isabella asked. "I hope to have better and more informed advice for you by then."

Gabriel nodded, recognizing that she had other tasks to do and should let her to them. Gabriel said his goodbyes then willed himself back to the lily field. Gabriel was about to exit the dream state when he saw he was not alone. Raelynn was visible next to him. She no longer appeared every time he entered the dream state so it was a pleasant surprise that he found her there.

"Did you have a good visit with your grandmother?" she asked.

"Was I that obvious in joining her dream sequence?" Gabriel asked.

"It wasn't as obvious as some of your attempts, but yes, I had a hard time missing it," Raelynn answered with a smile. "Is everything all right? You don't normally see her so frequently, and you just saw her a couple of days ago."

"Ah, so that is why you came," Gabriel teased. "Your curiosity couldn't handle it!"

Raelynn simulated an angry expression before breaking into a laugh. "Someone who isn't a little bit curious doesn't usually become a Seeker in the Order. Plus, I wanted to see how you were doing."

"If you must know," Gabriel answered, "I am getting summoned to the capital under the pretense of some sort of meeting of farming leaders. I was asking my grandmother's advice on how to handle it."

"I can see how that could be dangerous for you," she answered with concern suddenly showing in her voice. "I'll bet you never thought you would be referred to as a farming leader."

"You have that right!" Gabriel said with a laugh. "I still don't think I understand half of what I am supposed to. But I have learned a lot thanks to everyone that has been helping me."

Raelynn nodded then seemed to be distracted all of a sudden, appearing to be in deep thought about something. "I was just thinking; I have been finding people emerging nearer the capital who have potential in the dream gift. Normally, I have been not having anyone contact them since it is so dangerous, but if we are going to have some people travelling to the capital on sanctioned trip, we may be able to do something with them. We are already seeing some seeds showing interest in the Lily forming. I wonder who all besides you is going?"

"Attendees haven't been announced yet," Gabriel explained. "I could probably advise a few names before the official invitations go out. Not saying they would take them all, but the main reason for this is to give me cover for being away."

Raelynn gave Gabriel some suggested people that would meet the criteria of the trip and had the skills that could be used to recruit new dreamers. The names were spread throughout Xenon and he didn't know many of them. Gabriel was unsure if he should be told this level of detail, but it also spoke to the level of trust that Raelynn and Kayden had come to give him. Gabriel was somewhat disappointed that Raelynn hadn't suggested herself to attend, but when he looked at the requirements for the conference objectively, he would not have had a justifiable reason for suggesting her that would not raise some suspicions from one of the ministries.

Gabriel said his goodbyes and refocused himself back to where he initiated the dream from. Envisioning himself back in the woken world, he opened his eyes, taking in the vibrant colors of his surroundings.

Gabriel logged back into Oversite and offered Raelynn's suggestions as possible other attendees. Gabriel wasn't sure that his advice would be heeded but it was a good idea on Raelynn's part. If he was going to have to risk himself in the capital, seeing if some greater good could be accomplished from it created the potential to make the trip worthwhile.

∞ ∞ ∞

Sharna stared at the device she had in front of her. If she was to believe the prisoner, it was called a transport tube. That admission did not come easily from him, but it had come, and she believed him. One did not undergo the duress that he was put through and still give answers that were detected truthful by her designed interrogation system. Several useless bureaucrats from the Ministry of Scientific Innovation had already came by, and while they were happy about having a prisoner in custody, they were largely dismissive of the device she had in front of her. When she explained what she thought it could do, she received blank looks of incomprehension followed by stupid platitudes about science. They didn't have a clue. They never did. All that they cared about was that the prisoner had admitted to spreading religious paraphernalia and had wanted Sharna to put all of her efforts on trying to trace down who had received them.

They could desire her to do that all they wanted, but she had higher priorities. Her work to improve the abilities of Oversite had not gone unnoticed in the upper reaches of the government, and she now had several high-ranking protectors. Unlike most researchers and technologists in the Ministry of Scientific Innovation, she now had a pretty free reign to develop and innovate in any way she wanted. That wasn't saying she could freely develop technology against the government core precepts, but it did mean she could work within its boundaries and even walk around the grey areas without fear of retribution. Since her passion was focused on information gathering and analysis, this rarely came into conflict with government priorities. But that wasn't her only area of capability. She could do so much more.

Sharna showed herself to be a prodigy early on in her life. She was born in Westbell, near the coast of the Beakor sector. She was taken into the Ministry of Education care at a young age as was normal in this sector. At first, she was believed to be slower than her classmates and was not initially evaluated to have much if any academic potential. This was due to the fact that she barely interacted with others and was not very compliant in doing class assignments.

However, when a prominent scientist visited their school, she surprised everyone by asking detailed questions on a recent paper that the speaker published, even to the point of casting doubt on the overall conclusions presented. For someone who was eight years old, this was astounding. Sharna was given a proper intelligence assessment and was found to have one of the highest scores ever recorded. She wasn't academically slow; she was simply bored. Shortly after testing, she was relocated to a school for gifted students in the capital, and was given much more focused attention to develop her abilities and education.

By all rights, she should have finished at top in her class if it was based on ability alone. However, she was not someone equipped to follow instructions and was not always reliable in turning in her assignments that were given. If she thought the work beneath her, she didn't always complete it, instead staying focused on what interested her most. Given how brilliant she was, this was mostly tolerated. When it came time to graduate, she was assigned to the Ministry of Scientific Innovation for her next phase of life.

Sharna struggled to acclimate at first in this workstream, continuing some of her school habits of not doing work that did not interest her. This practice could be a dangerous one, but she was fortunate that someone who could understand what he was seeing recognized the benefit of some work she had been doing on her own time. This started to earn her some help from above, and most important to her, autonomy to innovate what was most interesting to her. This independence paid off, which she was able to flip into additional wins for the ministry which in turn gave her more control over her own work. It also made her time requested a lot, often for priorities that did not interest her.

Sharna's latest coup was getting her lab relocated away from the capital to Morfort. It was close enough where she could get to the capital if needed or visitors could come by if it was important, but she didn't get stuck with endless interruptions from busybodies who were trying to take credit for all of her work or try to convince her to do things that were largely useless.

That gave her more time to work on things like the device in front of her. Sharna carefully measured it, fully documented its dimensions and took visual records of it. No known explosives were scanned and it did not appear to have any unique elements on it. Mainly, it just looked like a standard metallic shell containing a seating area with some sort of control board that could be programmed. If this was some sort of transport vehicle, she assumed the input board was where coordinates could be entered for the target destination or similar functions. From the video drone footage, the prisoner had his hands on two buttons which were likely some sort of go button. But there seemed to be a delay from pressing the buttons to an action occurring. This was one of the puzzling questions she had about this device. Perhaps it was building a charge up or awaiting a remote command somehow. Getting the vehicle fully opened up would hopefully provide answers to these questions.

Fearing a non-detected explosive charge or similar booby trap, Sharna decided to utilize a remote robotic mechanical to take this device apart. While she didn't think that there was anything there to cause harm, she wasn't going to risk herself to initially deconstruct it. True, she could requisition some trained humans to do the job, but she wanted it done right and the best way that she could be sure of that was by overseeing it herself. Her lab was situated in a weapons research center, so she moved the vehicle inside one of the blast resistant rooms and setup the robot work cell inside with it. Thankfully, it was after normal hours so she didn't have to argue with anyone for use of this area. The night crew steered clear of her and she did have access to everything in this facility anyway.

Once everything was in place, Sharna began to deconstruct the transport vehicle using her remote robotic arm. The frame came off pretty easily, exposing a very unique device under the front panel of the vehicle. It appeared to contain a combination of wires and circuit boards. It contained pretty standard components, found in most electronic items currently in use. Some of the circuit board work appeared to be several generations old, meaning it appeared oversized for its function. Sharna deployed a specialized sensor, and after several minutes of detailed scanning and wire tracing was able to build enough data that her circuit constructor program could analyze it.

This software represented a time when she got really frustrated by the lack of proper documentation in existing designs. She could usually get ahold of the schematic diagrams with her ministry connections, but that would require talking to people and jumping through a lot of red tape to get information released to her and even then the documentation wasn't always accurate. Instead of doing that, she wrote a program and would basically take the visual of a circuit board and overlay it in a visual representation of the actual design used. From here, it was easy to modify the design so she could improve it for her purposes, choosing to either have it remade or make a minor adjustment to the existing circuit boards. This design was no exception, and within an hour had a full schematic of the entire vehicle.

The first thing that she noticed was there was some sort of frequency detection circuit present. Sharna quickly did some rough calculations and was able to determine that it was tuned to a frequency spectrum that did not have very much commercial use. If fact, it seemed to be tuned to require four unique frequencies in different band ranges to all be detected at once. If this was detected, then it would go through some sort of power amplifier circuit. Or that is at least what that looked like. There was a lot of creativity in that design, and Sharna was pleasantly surprised she did not see the immediate way it worked. The rest of the design seemed more straightforward but still presented some unknowns. *One problem at a time,* she thought to herself.

Whatever was supposed to trigger this machine required these frequencies to be present. She fully searched the prisoner's belongings and he did not have anything on him that could generate the frequency spectrum this required. She kept coming back to the frequency range being looked for, between one and thirty cycles per second. There was so little used at that frequency. But then it came to her. Brain waves could be detected in that range. Could this be channeling some special mental trigger from the operator? Could someone be trained to generate a specific frequency that could be amplified as a power source?

Sharna pulled up a study on Oversite on brain wave distributions. Based on the frequencies being detected, it required waves to be emitted that would occur all the way from extreme mental concentration all the way to deep sleep. A person normally would not emit brain waves that crossed all of these at the same time. To do so would require a strange mix of mental control that had not been observed in studies. Just because it had not been documented, did not mean that it was not possible. The prisoner would have more uses after all. She needed him to demonstrate a brain wave distribution that matched design expectations to validate her hypothesis. To do that, she would need some equipment she didn't have present in her lab. Sighing, she put out the equipment request to the capital, wondering if it would be quicker and less hassle to make what she needed herself.

CHAPTER 2

*a*aliyah looked around, trying to ascertain if she was alone or had been followed. Shadows caused by flickering lights cast an ominous tone on her isolated surroundings. The relative darkness in this rarely trafficked area acted as both a blessing and a curse. *I must stay calm*, she thought, willing an outward facade she came nowhere close to mirroring within.

Ever since she received the bundle of items it felt like she was constantly at risk and would just be a matter of time until the government caught up with her. But so far, she had been safe and enough time had passed that if she was going to be arrested it likely would have happened already.

That is, if they knew it was her. The hiding place was a good one but that didn't mean it hadn't been found. A trap could be set just waiting to find out who the mystery person was who had left it there. But there were no signs of disturbance as Aaliyah carefully removed a cover that blocked where her prized items were stored. Risks sometimes had to be taken, even if death or imprisonment were the result. Aaliyah hungered for something more out of life, and what was in that package represented hope of a knowledge beyond her current understanding. It represented a new life, a new purpose, and even with the great danger, it had been all that she was able to do to wait to come retrieve the package left for her.

Aaliyah was young, having recently graduated from the Ministry of Education. She didn't score in the top portion of her class, but she did well enough, earning her a posting to the Ministry of Scientific Innovation. It was an entry-level position where she acted as a lab technician assigned to complete and track experiments that researchers had designed. This role did not have a lot of advancement potential with it but that didn't really matter to her. It was a job that supplied enough credits to live on comfortably and was not in the general laborer pool.

In her time working as a technician, Aaliyah became disillusioned with what she was doing. Aaliyah was taught all through school that science was all that mattered. The scientific method was pushed hard and advancements that came from it were highlighted as crowning achievements. However, when it came time to execute experiments now that she was out of school, there was great concern from the senior researchers that they could usher in a discovery that did not fall within current government accepted guidance. As a result, experiments were constructed to not cause controversy and anything that the results suggested could have some disagreement with established norms, were quickly discarded and suppressed like they didn't actually happen. What were they so afraid of? If the pursuit of science was about achieving knowledge wherever it took you, what possible advancement could come from suppressing new learning?

This mindset raised her frustration level with the status quo. She made a few risky comments expressing frustration to one of her co-workers who both thankfully and surprisingly did not dispute her or report her. Instead, she invited her to a small gathering. This was a group who thirsted for knowledge and pursued topics that navigated the gray areas of allowable topics. This group was careful. They had some countermeasures to ensure they were not being actively tracked and listened in on. If someone barged in on them, it would appear that they were doing an abundance of science reflection and meditation. But the truth was they were discussing controversial topics, debating the limits of their knowledge, while accepting nothing at face value. It was pure free thought and expression, something that was not permitted in the light of day.

Aaliyah did not find anything obviously rebellious or subversive in the discussions. It was just a true thirst for knowledge where nothing was automatically ruled out. What had really shaken her entire outlook were the discussions pertaining to religion. She had been taught religion was a myth, a pretext to hold power over the population – to believe in something that could not be proven. An enlightened people no longer needed such restraints. Society now had science and knowledge, which had fully supplanted the need for the myths of old. But true knowledge was not currently pursued. She knew that from her brief time as a lab technician. And if science had that much power over society, how was it truly that different than how religion was labeled? As she had considered and discussed this concept, she realized there was no meaningful difference.

But that didn't mean religion was necessarily bad. An elder in their group spoke of remembrances of what religion was like before it was outlawed. While he wasn't one who practiced it, he viewed it as a moral code that bound its adherents to pursue something greater than themselves. It also spoke of the supernatural, a set of phenomena that were not easily explained by current understandings of science. Was there a force in the universe that could be channeled, or even controlled? And if there was, was there something directing that force? These questions received a lot of meaningful discussion but lacked answers. Aaliyah could not let go of this concept, these questions. It consumed her. It was like she knew there was something more, but she didn't know where to go to find it.

Then she got the break she was looking for. As hard as the government had tried to suppress what had happened in Xenon, rumors began to filter back about some sort of religion being practiced in Xenon. Something with a lily was murmured, and she had openly expressed interest in it during one of the meetings. Somehow her interest must have got to the right people when she discovered the letter in her living quarters that outlined what she could do to receive more knowledge about the Lily. She was to meet someone from Xenon at a specified place and use specific phrases. They had her follow the same anti-surveillance protocols she used for her group meetings. And she was to immediately conceal what they gave her, until she was sure she was safe to view it.

Aaliyah once again checked her surroundings and stepped into the place where she had hidden the bundle that was given to her. She excitedly saw that it was as she had left it and it did not appear to have been disturbed. She carefully placed it inside her carrying bag and continued back to her domicile. Upon arriving there, she entered a small office space she was pretty sure was clear of active visual monitoring technology. Aaliyah's memory had always been good so she recited a common passage used for scientific meditation. This would likely be picked up by her handheld in the other room and any other audio monitoring devices. With luck, Oversite would assume she was doing extra meditations. It would also give her an excuse to sit quietly for a period of time to examine the contents of the bundle.

Excitedly, Aaliyah opened the contents with great care. Inside she discovered a device that looked similar to the active tracking sensor the Xenon person was carrying. A note instructed her to use it on her immediate surroundings by pressing the button on the side. If came back green, she would be safe from most devices in use. If not, she should choose a different place to open the contents. She pressed the button as instructed and was gratified that there was not active tracking in her immediate proximity. Looking further down, she saw what appeared to be paper books. Nearly everything was digitized now and while it was not illegal to possess paper content, it would raise government suspicions if you were caught with any.

Opening the front cover of the first of the three books, there was a note tucked inside that said to read, reflect and if it was safe, share with others she trusted. Aaliyah excitedly turned the page to the beginning of the first book. It was called *The Book of the Lily*. As she began to read, she could not stop. It spoke of something beyond anything she had dared to consider before and it resonated with her more than anything had in her entire life.

∞ ∞ ∞

Xavier looked out of his window on the top floor of the Ministry of Scientific Compliance headquarters. His ascension to the ranking minister position was rapid and largely unexpected after his predecessor had been ousted two years prior, having been blamed for the disaster in Xenon and the subsequent unrest across the nation. Xavier was still dealing with the fallout. His dreams of a quick suppression of Xenon were replaced with hopes of getting the rest of the sectors back into compliance to levels seen prior to the food shortage.

Now that some semblance of stability had returned, he was able to evaluate priorities more broadly. One growing priority was now a rise of religious practice of all things, as evidenced by the recent capture of a Kayden operative. The more Xavier thought about it, he thought it was a very strategic move on Isabella's part. The best way to keep Xenon out of the government's cross-hairs was to distract them so much that they didn't have the ability to do more than try to keep the law enforced in sectors they already supposedly controlled. This had prompted him to order Gabriel recalled for debriefing. Xavier needed better answers about Kayden than he was currently getting.

"Minister, Quintin is here for your next appointment," his assistant announced via the intercom.

"Send him in," Xavier replied.

Quintin entered Xavier's expansive office. Quintin was now in charge of the Xenon desk, overseeing all activity in this sector. Quintin appeared to be very grateful for this promotion even if it didn't have as much visibility as it did a couple years before. Xavier had been mostly ignoring Xenon focusing on getting the rest of the sectors back into compliance but Quintin seemed to be diligently collecting data to reconstruct who the leaders of the resistance were and to develop a plan should priority again be allowed to focus on Xenon. He also still maintained contact with Gabriel.

Gabriel was in a unique position it appeared. He seemed to know a lot about specific topics of the resistance, but in other areas he claimed ignorance. Either he was careful in what he released to protect himself, didn't really know some things, or was purposely withholding information to protect people within the resistance. Or it could be a combination of all of these things. Xavier had been on multiple undercover assignments in his celebrated career, and if you were not careful, it could mean your life. And the best way to lose your life was someone you reported to saying something he or she shouldn't or taking an action that they would only do if they had your inside information.

So far, he had never seen anything from Gabriel's reports that was inaccurate. If Gabriel reported it, it could be trusted, or at minimum you were sure that Gabriel believed it to be true based on the information he had. No, Xavier had full trust in Gabriel. His loyalty had been proven many times. Almost all they knew about Kayden had come from him, including Isabella's name as the leader of the resistance. He just needed a bit more information less able to conceal under the scrutiny of the capitol.

"Good morning, sir," Quintin offered. "You wanted to see me?"

"I'll be right with you, Quintin," Xavier answered. "Why don't you take a seat while I finish this last report."

Quintin took a seat on the couch a few paces away from Xavier's working desk. He looked around nervously, not quite being sure why he was summoned to this meeting. Xavier really didn't have a report to review but liked to set the imagery that his time was critically important, especially relative to those under him.

"Sorry for holding you up," Xavier offered after a suitable time had passed. "I wanted to discuss Gabriel's capital visit with you. I assume you have everything ready to go?"

"Yes, Minister I do," Quintin replied. "The delegation from Xenon is supposed to arrive tomorrow. We have several sessions lined up with one on one interviews and farm benchmarking visits. This will create a reason for some attendees to be apart from the rest of the group for an extended duration of time without raising suspicions. There will also be several events everyone will be expected to attend. We won't be able to keep Gabriel isolated from these."

"I suppose that can't be helped," Xavier answered. "We will really need to make really good use of the time we have him apart. How well do you have that planned out?"

"We have developed a full list of questions and I have some of our best interrogators assigned to this," Quintin answered confidently. "We will be ready."

Xavier noticeably cringed on hearing that answer. "Gabriel is not someone you treat like a suspect with an aggressive interrogation. You handle him that way, and you will not get good answers and you can forget about unwavering loyalty to the Ministry afterwards. I know you want to be thorough, but this needs finesse not brute force."

"We were not going to use advanced interrogation methods on him, sir," Quintin said somewhat defensively.

"No, but it doesn't sound like you are treating him as a trusted partner either," Xavier answered. "The reason he probably keeps things back is he is afraid we will screw up and compromise him. You need to build trust, not treat him like the enemy. Believe me, I have been there. He needs to think you have his best interests foremost in your mind, not just recklessly using the information he provides."

"I'll make adjustments to leverage your valued insights, Minister," Quintin answered with a forcibly neutral expression.

"Also, did you see the report I sent you from the research lab in Morfort?" Xavier asked.

"Yes, it was very interesting, especially the part about the transport tube technology." Quintin answered.

"I was intrigued by that," Xavier stated, "but I was more interested in the possible brain wave actuation of the transport device. The technologist indicated possibilities of creating a sensor array tuned into the frequencies used to actuate the transport device. If we could detect that, it would give us tremendous information we could undermine the resistance with wouldn't it?"

"I didn't consider the implications of that, Minister," Quintin answered. "Even if we didn't do anything with it immediately, we could sure learn a lot which we could use later on."

"Yes, we could," Xavier continued. "I want you to get Gabriel's take on this. Maybe even take him up to the lab in Morfort to see it firsthand. I think we have some new farmland near there that is in operation whose managers could benefit from his expert advice. It would provide cover for the trip. Please ensure you submit daily reports on what you learn from Gabriel and contact me directly if anything comes up that I would want to know sooner."

Quintin nodded and made his way to the door. Xavier watched as he left. He didn't seem to be pleased with having his carefully crafted plan for Gabriel modified, but Quintin would do as he was told. Xavier almost didn't see the report from the technologist. There was such excitement at catching a Kayden agent acting in Preath, that the technology discovery barely made a footnote of the report that had been sent to Xavier. Fortunately, Xavier had seen the reference and asked for the full report from the lead technologist who was analyzing the transport device. What she had been able to deduce with minimal information was simply astounding. She was clearly brilliant and her skills were likely being wasted and unappreciated by her peers and superiors. Either way, he was now getting live access to her technical research and had assigned one of his scientists to translate her progress into terminology he could more easily follow. This was an important breakthrough and one that had great potential to turn the tide against Kayden.

CHAPTER 3

The Ministry of Nutrition was not sparing any courtesy or amenity. Gabriel looked out his living room window as he saw a vehicle pulling up to his house. The shuttle type vehicle had seating capacity for several passengers. A person of short stature stepped out of the vehicle wearing the insignia of the Ministry of Nutrition on his lapel and proceeded to walk to the door. Gabriel looked around, making sure he had turned off all energy and water sources. Gabriel's travelling bag was already prepped by the door so he picked it up as he went to open the door that was now being knocked on.

"Good morning, sir," the navigator offered as Gabriel opened the door. "I am here to pick you up for the farming conference you were invited to."

"I hadn't expected you so early," Gabriel replied. "But I have everything ready to go."

"I am sorry for any inconvenience it may cause you and am glad to wait if you would like more time," he said nervously. "I have been told how important this conference is and I didn't want to be late to pick you up. I have had trips to the outlying areas take longer than expected before, so I allowed extra time."

"Are we still taking the transport from Northfalcon?" Gabriel asked, trying to change the subject to put his escort at ease.

"Yes, that is the plan, sir," he answered. "I need to pick up a Tom Carasa first, who looks like he lives nearby and then we can head there."

"Call me Gabriel, and I don't think I got your name?"

"Billy, sir, uh I mean Mr. Gabriel. Billy Sornby." he answered with continued concern in his voice.

"Nice to meet you Billy," Gabriel said with a smile as he extended his hand in greeting. William awkwardly extended his in return, not expecting this level of courtesy. "I don't mean to put you on the spot Billy, but you seem really nervous. Can you tell me why that is so maybe I can make you feel more comfortable?"

Gabriel's question did not have the disarming response he had hoped to provide. In fact, Billy began to nervously fidget worse than he had before.

"I am sorry I seem so nervous, sir," Billy answered. "It is just this is such a big opportunity for me to be able to transport someone of your stature and I don't want to screw it up. I've been in the general laborer pool for so long and when I was accepted for an entry level position in the Ministry of Nutrition, it completely changed my life. But I know that one screw up and I will be back where I started. I just don't want to mess it all up, sir."

Gabriel smiled at Billy's predicament but was also concerned by his comments on stature. "What makes you think I am someone important?" Gabriel inquired.

"Well sir," Billy fumbled with his words, "I know that vehicles are not sent for people who aren't important. Even midranking people would need to walk or take a common shuttle transport. I don't know what makes you important, but getting an assigned a car and navigator was all I needed to know."

Gabriel tried hard to keep a laugh from exiting his mouth at this answer. "Why don't we go get Tom picked up, Billy. Let me assure you that a vehicle was sent to make sure we came, not because of our rank or importance. The Ministry of Nutrition wants us to better document how we grow food so if we decide to stop doing it like we did a couple years back, the people in the rest of the sectors are less likely to starve. If we decide not to come, then they don't get the information they need. So, the only thing that could get you in trouble would be if I decided not to get in the vehicle. Beyond that, I doubt there is anything that you could do that would cause you problems!"

Billy had a look of slow comprehension come across his face, which then transitioned into a smile. "I am sorry for acting so stupid…Gabriel. They don't really tell me anything and I try to be very careful. Shall we go?"

Gabriel nodded as they got into the vehicle and took the short drive to pick up his cousin Tom. His uncle Kelby was the original invitee but had counter offered that Tom go in his stead. Since Tom knew the farming operation so well, the substitution was accepted. This would also give Gabriel someone he knew and trusted to be with him on this dangerous trip to the capital.

Tom lived in a house away from Kelby's residence with his family where his aunt and uncle resided. Billy started to pull up in front of the main house, but Gabriel directed him to the smaller one offset away from it. Gabriel and Billy got out and proceeded up to the front door. Tom's wife answered the door and invited them inside.

"Tom will be right out," Missy offered. "I think you surprised him by being early. Early and Tom are not usually used in the same sentence!"

"I will miss you too!" Tom said walking up, laughing while grabbing his wife in a hug. His kids saw this and then rushed to join in the embrace.

"You be careful," Missy admonished. "Gabriel, I expect you to keep him out of trouble." She said sternly.

"I will do my best, Missy," Gabriel promised while smiling. "You do know you are asking a lot of me?"

"I know it all too well," she said while laughing. "But I still expect you to do it."

"I am still here," Tom interjected also laughing. Then his expression grew more somber as he picked up his travel bag. "I will miss all of you. Be good for your mother."

Gabriel led Billy outside to allow Tom a small bit of privacy to say his goodbyes to his family. While there had been a lot of promises made by the government, there was a great deal of risk in going on this trip for Tom. Sure, Gabriel was thrilled to have him along, but it could be very dangerous to the point where he may not come back. But Tom was an adherent of the Lily and was resolute in going on this trip. Much could be learned in the capital that would benefit Kayden and if there was the chance to aid budding adherents of the Lily, that would be even better.

∞ ∞ ∞

The hum of the big city was an experience that Gabriel surprisingly had trouble readjusting to. Sure, much of what he saw existed in Xenon, but the abundance of motion and applied technology in the capital now felt overwhelming to his senses. He could with some effort tune it out to center himself, but it was admittedly harder. When you were alone in nature, you could feel the pulse of the land. The city also had a pulse but it was different somehow and did not naturally facilitate a feeling a peace.

Looking around, the Ministry of Nutrition had not skimped on the accommodations for the attendees. Gabriel had his own hotel room and it was sized similar to what a mid-level ministry official would command. One attendee told Gabriel that at the last conference five years prior, the accommodations were poor and no one got their own room. In addition to the quarters, attendees were provided generous travel energy credits and were allocated several vehicles that could be taken for travel and exploration. Attendees were given full freedom of mobility, and to an outsider looking in would appear they were living in relative luxury.

There was some inherent distrust toward the seemingly goodwill gesture from the government, but the more adventuresome of the group did not hesitate to explore the big city and all that it had to offer. Gabriel was known to have lived in the capital for most of his life and found himself being peppered for advice for things to do or places to see. Gabriel gave some guidance when asked, but really didn't view himself as an expert on the attractions someone from outside would like to visit. Gabriel should have probably felt a similar urge to visit the places or people he knew when he last lived here, but surprisingly he felt no pull to do that, instead feeling comfortable to socialize with the members of his traveling party who didn't go exploring. There would likely be a strange awkwardness if he encountered some of his old acquaintances. He was viewed as a disgraced former ministry official, and anyone who was career minded would do all they could to avoid associating with him. Gabriel didn't care about that anymore. Even though he thought it funny that he likely outranked most of those who would act that way not knowing his true ministry situation, he mostly wanted to avoid any discomfort and get this trip over with.

After getting a good night's sleep, Gabriel got up to attend the opening session of the grower's conference. The group was greeted by a high-ranking person in the Ministry of Nutrition, excitedly extoling the value of their knowledge and all that could benefit farms throughout the sectors. Gabriel noticed that there were many farmers not from Xenon attending, likely to learn as much as they could from more experienced experts. Gabriel looked at the agenda and there was supposed to be several workshops and discussion groups today regarding best practices, energy conservation, weed and pest control and soil rejuvenation. Most of the speakers were from Xenon farms and some were researchers in ministry roles. Gabriel thankfully wasn't selected to serve as a speaker or panelist, but had to smile when he attended a session where Tom was speaking. Tom appeared to be in his element mixing levity with content which did a great job keeping the attention of those listening. Gabriel approached him shortly after he had finished his presentation.

"I didn't know farming was that exciting! Where do I sign up?" Gabriel said with a mischievous smile on his face.

"I should get you up here for the next session to present, then you can show how exciting it really is!" Tom retorted.

"How to ask others for help, presented by Gabriel Carasa," Gabriel stated doing his best to keep a straight face. "You will learn how to ask your neighbor for help to fix your many mistakes, even tricking him into doing the work for you."

"You got that right," Tom laughed. "I think you could present on that. You have it down to a science!"

"Sorry, but I don't think I will be available," Gabriel offered. "I leave this evening to attend a multi-day site visit to a farm up near Morfort. At least that is what my itinerary says. About a quarter of the attendees have been selected to visit the new farms and provide advice. I guess I am one of the lucky ones, while others like you get to stay here and make farming sound super exciting."

Tom gave Gabriel a knowing look, understanding the true purpose of the trip was likely his debriefing session. "Was it clear how many days you will be away?"

"No," Gabriel said with a hint of a grim expression showing on his countenance. "All I know for sure is that we will be back in two months in time for the next growing season. Hopefully I will learn more soon but I wouldn't get worried if I am up there most of the time."

"Well," Tom continued, "I will have to find a way to do without your exciting lecture topic until you return then. Is anyone being sent with you?"

"It looks like it is one person per farm, so I will likely be alone," Gabriel explained. "Anyway, I just wanted to say goodbye since I won't likely see you for a while. Hopefully Missy will understand why I am failing at keeping you out of trouble."

"I will do my best to be good," Tom promised. "Take care."

Gabriel walked away and went up to his room to gather his belongings in preparation of his trip. Morfort was a strange place to go for his debrief, but getting him away from the capital probably made the most sense to reduce the chances of questions being asked. He had received his espionage training in Morfort a few years back prior to coming to Xenon. It would take a few hours to get there by vehicle. The itinerary said that someone would be coming to pick him up shortly.

A knock on the door was heard and Gabriel was surprised to see a familiar face on the other side of the door when he opened it.

"Stefan, what a pleasant surprise. I wasn't expecting to see you here," Gabriel offered in greeting.

Stefan was a member of his late fiancé Emily's unit. Gabriel didn't know him extremely well, but had always gotten along well and was happy to see him. Stefan had an imposing figure indicating a high degree of physical strength. His eyes had a calculating intensity emanating from them with a gaze that kept shifting around the room, looking for possible threats.

"Hi Gabriel," Stefan answered. "It is good to see you also. I always appreciate seeing people who did right by my unit."

"I am expecting someone to pick me up soon, so I am not sure how much time I have, but you are welcome for sure till I have to leave. So how have you been?" Gabriel asked.

Stefan made a bit of an awkward smile. "I hope I don't disappoint you, but I am here to pick you up. I am to be your escort for the trip."

Gabriel wasn't sure what to make from that comment. Was Stefan here to ensure he did what he was told, sort of keeping him as a prisoner, or was he just a courtesy to make sure all his needs were taken care of?

The whole interaction so far had seemed unnatural and forced. Gabriel always thought Stefan was a bit on the odd side, but Emily thought the world of him and Gabriel decided to extend him that same benefit of the doubt.

Sensing his confusion, Stefan clarified. "Traveling by vehicle outside the capital isn't as safe as it used to be. I am here more to protect you more than anything, I am not supposed to do much more than that. I can explain more on the way," he continued.

"Very well, I am glad to have you as company. You can catch me up on what has been going in your world if you are willing," Gabriel offered as they left the room and proceeded to the waiting vehicle.

The vehicle they got into was much different than Gabriel was used to riding in. After putting his belongings and handheld as directed in the compartment in the back, Gabriel got into the seat next to Stefan. The vehicle was very sparse in amenities and had some strange electronics he wasn't familiar with displayed on the console. Stefan pressed some buttons on the control panel, then noticeably relaxed.

"This vehicle has anti-surveillance technology onboard," Stefan explained. It will basically jam anything that tries to penetrate it. So, whatever we discuss inside while this enabled, we can be reasonably confident we cannot be heard by others."

"There isn't even anything inside that records?" Gabriel asked skeptically.

"If someone has done that, all they will hear when playing it back is static." Stefan replied. A lot of the senior ministry officials use them to be able to securely conduct business when travelling. I did do a sweep for surveillance before picking you up as well and it was clean."

"So why do we rate this vehicle?" Gabriel asked as they started travelling down the road.

"Your existence is so classified," Stefan explained, "that anything that could be done to protect that, has. Quintin thought that if I explained the plan in detail to you ahead, you could minimize exposure of your true purpose and identity when you arrived in Morfort for debriefing."

"I guess that makes sense," Gabriel answered with still some apprehension showing. So how many people have been read in to what I am here for?"

"Not very many," Stefan said in an attempt to reassure. "To my knowledge it is the Minister, Quintin, myself and one interrogator. Everyone else will be kept from your identity or will be given a cover story on why you are here. We may add a technologist to that list later on, but we haven't fully decided on that yet."

"So how did you get assigned to this?" Gabriel asked with true curiosity. He was especially wondering how Stefan had known so much about his assignment. If they were genuinely worried about security, they didn't have to read in the person escorting him.

"I asked too many questions," Stefan said simply. I have seen enough people get put undercover over the years. From what I knew of you, I didn't believe for a minute the story that was put out about you trying to manipulate your energy quota. I asked Quintin about it on a later mission and he told me to drop the inquiry or bad things would happen. I did and then later on he asked for my help with your assignment, figuring I already knew some of it and kept it a secret. I have been read in on your reports for over a year now and have been doing some analysis. This is a step up for me, especially as my body is getting older. Having a less violent job should be good for my longevity."

"What do you know about this interrogator who is being read in?" Gabriel asked with some nervousness in his voice.

Stefan let out a soft chuckle. "She isn't assigned to do advanced interrogation methods on you if that is what you are worried about. She is just supposed to ask questions. She is much better at helping pull out things from memory you may not have thought important. I have seen this before, and it is going to be grueling, but should not be anything beyond that."

"That is a relief to hear," Gabriel replied with his own forced laugh. "What has interested you from my reports?"

"All of it, to be honest," Stefan replied. "The religious practice, the Kayden organization, the targeted resistance activities, you name it. You have got to have a lot of adventure in a short time. I know I am supposed to be angry that this resistance is happening, but I sort of envy you doing this. Hopefully we can discuss this more as I escort you around. This is probably the only safe place I can freely ask questions without a risk of misunderstanding."

Gabriel reflected on this last comment. Could Stefan be a free thinker who may have some pliability to new ways of thinking? This could also be a trap orchestrated by Quintin to determine what his true loyalties or underlying motivation currently was.

"I know what you mean," Gabriel said after a long pause. Certain topics can definitely get someone in trouble, even if their motivation is nothing more than pursuing the truth."

Gabriel and Stefan rode in silent reflection for quite some time after that before awkwardly introducing some small talk about past missions together and shared memories. Stefan had given Gabriel an opening. Did he trust the motivations? Gabriel resolved to do some dream state exploring at his next opportunity to try to determine the safety in pressing Stefan further.

CHAPTER 4

Sharna was patient to a point, but had reached her limit. It should not take two weeks to get the equipment she had ordered, but it had. Meanwhile, she had annoying ministry bureaucrats wanting to take possession of the prisoner she had captured. They wanted him – not to gain any meaningful intelligence, but to parade him around like a trophy that they had done nothing to capture. It was her software that had flagged his activity, and she still had need of him, especially since her equipment had finally arrived. Her unwillingness to give up the prisoner until she got her test data was probably the only reason she had the device in front of her.

While she had a very good understanding of the functional specifications of the multifrequency analyzer, Sharna could not afford any mistakes in setting it up and gathering data from it, especially since she couldn't operate it all the time. She used her authority to pull a lab technician to help her. Supplied technicians usually did what they were told and had proved mostly adequate in the past for simple tasks. Hopefully they sent her someone capable. If they didn't, she would promptly send the person back and get someone else. Sharna looked up as she saw someone come into her lab area.

"You requested a lab technician, ma'am?" a woman asked.

Sharna looked the person over carefully. This was someone she had not worked with before. She was pretty young, so was probably someone new. The people that were sent to help her typically had a healthy fear in their eyes and wanted to get their tasks done as quick as possible to get away. But this person had looked her straight in the eye, and while respectful, showed no fear. It was either ignorance or competence. Time would quickly tell which it was.

"I did," Sharna answered after a lengthy pause. "Can you do as you are told? I can't permit someone in my lab who will make reckless mistakes."

The technician continued to look her in the eye and waited a seemingly identical pause before answering. "If your instructions are clear, I both can and will follow them correctly."

Sharna nodded, liking the reply but not showing her approval on her face. "We shall see."

Reaching down, Sharna handed the technician a device displaying the user manual for the multifrequency analyzer. "You have two hours, read this over in that chair and then let me know when you are ready to test your knowledge."

Watching her go over to the designated seat, Sharna tuned in the equipment to pick up the technician's brain waves. As much as she tried to scan it from across the room, it was not picking anything up. Sharna stood up and pushed the equipment closer until she was able to pick up the beginning of a normal brain function response. The range of the analyzer was disappointingly limited. If she was going to have the ability to detect a brain wave pattern, she needed to solve the distance problem and the design of this equipment was clearly not suited to pick up everything that was needed. Sure, it would be good enough to conduct the experiment on the prisoner but not good enough to detect those who may be trying to use the transport tubes across the sectors.

Sharna pulled up the analyzer schematic and quickly saw some design changes she could make which should improve the response. Fortunately, she had the needed components on hand and tasked her robotic arm to make the necessary changes.

"What are you changing?" the lab technician interrupted. "I am ready to try out my knowledge when you want me to."

"This equipment doesn't sense at a long enough distance. I am fixing that." Sharna reluctantly answered. "You will have to wait until the modifications are completed."

The technician nodded and watched curiously as the alterations were executed by the robotic arm. A few minutes later the work was finished.

"I need you to read your manual again for a few minutes. Go sit back down," Sharna instructed as she watched the person comply.

When the technician began reading, she powered the analyzer back on, and now had a strong and clear signal. Moving it to the far corner of the room, Sharna nodded appreciatively when the signal strength remained readable. She also noticed some other new signals had been detected. This would be a new problem. It was probably detecting her brainwaves now, as well. Nothing some localized filtering couldn't solve.

"Come show me how to operate this equipment," Sharna commanded after resetting it to the default parameters and turning it off.

Walking up to the analyzer, the technician proceeded to turn it on, checking the setpoints on it. "What frequency spectrum do you want me to tune to?" she asked.

"One to thirty cycles per second," Sharna answered.

The technician nodded and proceeded to make the correct adjustments to detect only in this frequency range. "I am getting multiple signals. Do you want me to display all of them or filter some of them out?"

"Leave them all. Just offset them on the screen so I can view all of them," Sharna replied, internally pleased by the fast learning proficiency of the assigned technician. Once she had tested her knowledge fully, Sharna took the equipment back and proceeded to add an interface box to it. She had been working on a design that would detect the signal pattern that was used on the transport tube circuit. If she did it right, which she usually did, this signal would take the readings from the analyzer and if they matched the expected output, would signal the user of a match and time-stamp when it occurred. Nodding in satisfaction, she believed she was ready.

"We have a prisoner downstairs," Sharna instructed. "I need someone to operate this equipment in his proximity, and if he creates a matching brain wave pattern, I need it recorded and need to be notified right away. You shouldn't have to do much, but I need someone to make sure no one messes with the equipment and to recognize if it stops working. Can you do that?"

"I do not see a problem with that, "the technician answered as she followed Sharna to the holding cell.

∞ ∞ ∞

Aaliyah followed Sharna to the confinement area. There was a tremendous amount of armed guards present. She noticed the prisoner who was facing away from her in restraints and he had some sort of collar around his neck likely configured to create a fatal explosion if the prisoner left a zoned proximity. The way that the security was positioned, that detonation perimeter was probably not much bigger than the cell he was restrained in.

This assignment was the strangest thing that she had been asked to do since she had started at the ministry. Her co-workers had visibly smirked when the request came in to assist Sharna. Regardless, she had said she would do it. A coworker warned her just before she left that this person was very peculiar and to not be offended if she was mistreated or sent back in failure. It had happened to at least half of the team so far. Apparently, she was pretty reclusive, but whatever she requested she got. Aaliyah had watched Sharna modify the complex piece of equipment like she wasn't even trying. And it had worked the first try. If she was working for any of the other researchers here, they would have worked so much more deliberately to make sure they were not going against any sort of ministry procedure or priority. Sharna hadn't seemed to care. She had a problem, came up with a solution and implemented it. This is what Alayah thought was supposed to be happening at the ministry and this was the first person she had actually seen do it.

Truth be told, today wasn't the first time she had operated a multifrequency analyzer. Aaliyah used a different model in a lab exercise when she was in training a couple of years back, so she had a basic familiarity on what it did. That made reading the manual easier and helped her make a more favorable impression on Sharna. That would not guarantee she would keep a favorable impression, but being able to learn from this eccentric researcher oddly appealed to her.

"Move out of this space," Sharna said to the stationed security personnel. "I don't want anyone disturbing my testing."

Aaliyah watched the security team scramble quickly to comply with her instructions. There was the look of fear in their eyes as they moved quickly to make room and exit the immediate cell observation area.

Odd, considering this looked like an elite team of skilled military personnel with a reputation to not show fear. Sharna set the analyzer down and did some initial adjustments, pointing it in the direction of the prisoner.

"Stay here," Sharna instructed. "I will message you on your handheld if I need you to do anything more."

Sharna quickly left the room and Aaliyah found herself staring at a display showing a steady single waveform moving across the display. She moved her handheld to a prominent location in case Sharna needed her to do something and found a chair to sit in. Sharna didn't say anything about someone relieving her for breaks or when her shift was up, but she wasn't going to bring that question up yet. Better to sit still and do what was being asked of her.

Aaliyah looked mindlessly around the detention area, quickly becoming bored while watching the stable waveform of the prisoner. The surroundings were functional to contain someone but lacked any sense of artistic influence. A cage was needed and that is exactly what was present. The prisoner appeared to be in some sort of drug induced sleep, but it was hard to fully tell as only his back was facing her as he was lying down on what must count for a bed. Lacking anything better to do to pass the time, Aaliyah decided to walk a bit in the narrow area in front of the holding area. As she walked past the cell, she was able to get a view of the prisoner's face. His form had a haunting familiarity to it, but she couldn't quite place where she had seen it before.

It was all Aaliyah could do to not gasp in disbelief as she came to realization at the source of her recognition. Her stomach wrenched in nervous apprehension as she realized she knew who this prisoner was. This was the person who had brought her the books on the Lily. She was now certain of it. This was the same person.

A sense of panic welled up in Aaliyah, wondering if this was an elaborate staged event to prove her guilt. She had been careful, and she didn't think she had revealed herself to this prisoner or to any surveillance. But he had not taken the same precautions and she knew his face. Could she risk herself to help him? Or was what she was doing here going to betray him, Kayden and those who followed the teachings of the Lily? She walked back to her seat and sat down. All of a sudden, her mind was very distracted.

"I am waking the prisoner now," Sharna communicated over the handhold. "It should be a few minutes and then the drugs will wear off. He has been stressed lately by interrogation, I need him to be in as relaxed as possible and recover. Talk to him if he says anything to you, but otherwise just observe. I don't think you can tell him anything that will cause harm at this point in his interrogation. He answers to Darren."

"I understand," Aaliyah replied, thinking that the less said to Sharna the better relative to conversation.

Aaliyah looked around, all of a sudden feeling paranoid. There were so many people who had been guarding the prisoner and they were just outside. Were they there for her, just waiting on her to say something to compromise herself or give up additional information that could be used to get to others? She hadn't told anyone about the books yet. That was at least some consolation. The books spoke of finding your inner place of peace and calm and Aaliyah so much wanted to try to practice that right now but thought better of it. Instead she took a few deep breaths and waited until the prisoner woke up.

The prisoner named Darren opened his eyes slowly, seeming to immediately realize he was actively being restrained. His eyes swept the area around him, stopping momentarily on the form of Aaliyah, then having observed her, continued to scan the surrounding area. He didn't fight his restraints, but his eyes presented an eerie awareness that he understood well what limitations he was burdened with while not giving anyone watching the satisfaction of hearing him call out in complaint. After he completed his initial observation, he closed his eyes, relaxing his posture for a few moments and then adjusted his form into a more statuesque way.

Aaliyah's observation of him was interrupted by a low-level urgent beeping on the console in front of her. What had been a low amplitude single reading, now divided into a multifrequency waveform of at least three to four distinct frequencies. Aaliyah quickly made sure that the unit was actively recording and adjusted the waveforms to be separately displayed, creating some saved images in the buffer queue for later analysis. Realizing that she hadn't notified Sharna yet, she quickly sought to remedy that.

"I am getting a confirmed match reading. Saving data, please advise," Aaliyah urgently communicated to Sharna.

But as soon as the wave form had started, it stopped. Aaliyah was momentarily distracted from the ongoing unease she was experiencing. This person had exhibited the target waveform as soon as he woke.

"I don't think I have seen you before in here," the voice interrupted her. "What is your name?"

Aaliyah looked up to identify the interruption, realizing it was coming from the prisoner.

"This is my first time here. I am doing some testing. You can call me Aaliyah," she replied.

"The Way of the Lily is meant for you Aaliyah," Darren answered. "All who come with an open heart are welcome."

Aaliyah's console beeped at her, displaying a text message to transfer the data so Sharna could access it. Aaliyah looked directly at Darren for a long moment before shifting her gaze back down to her console. She quickly transferred the data Sharna wanted and sent it to her, acknowledging her request.

Aaliyah met Darren's eyes one more time, slightly inclining her head in acknowledgement of his statement. Moments later, her handheld beeped again, instructing her to leave the unit in passive mode and come back up to the lab. She quickly made the adjustments requested and stood up.

"I am sorry we didn't meet on better terms. I have to go," Aaliyah said as she quickly made her way toward the door, emotions churning within her. Doing all she could to keep herself pulled together, she nodded to the guards and walked toward Sharna's lab.

∞ ∞ ∞

Darren watched as Aaliyah strode away. There was something familiar about her that he could not place. He wasn't sure why he had spoken of the Lily to her, but he felt compelled to do so. It was important somehow. He had been drugged since he had been captured, he was pretty sure. This was the most mentally aware he had felt since he was taken. He wasn't sure at first what had happened, but that is why he had gone into the dream state so he could go back and replay what had happened since he was captured.

He was sad that he had given away so much about Kayden. He had fought the interrogation, but it was so probing and thorough. He had told of the transport tube and what it did. He didn't think he gave away anything about the dream state, not that they would likely believe him if he did. It was good that he wasn't aware of more missions and had been compartmentalized in his knowledge of Kayden operations. But he still held regret that he had not been able to hold more back.

His life was part of a larger puzzle he did not yet understand. But if they gave him enough time, he would do all he could to figure They had to think they had taken all he knew, yet they still had kept him confined and had some sort of equipment monitoring him. By all rights he should have been executed by now. The law was clear on this, but he lived. His life was part of a larger puzzle he did not yet understand. But if they have him enough time, he would do all he could to figure out his purpose here so it could use if for Kayden and for the benefit of the Lily.

All was not lost. He could still do good. And somehow this realization infused him with a sense of unrelenting joy. And for a reason he did not understand, he broke out into song. At the top of his lungs he sang song after song until his voice could sing no more.

CHAPTER 5

The sky was overcast with a biting wind blowing hard against any who were brave enough to go outside. Gabriel grimaced at the weather around him, thinking it was reflective of his current outlook. Even inside he could feel the chill, as the facility he was in took energy conservation seriously, not expending enough to maintain a comfortable living temperature in an intemperate season. Normally the winter season didn't impact him negatively, but today it seemed like an ominous sign of what was to come. Gabriel mentally told himself to shake off the malaise he was drifting through and to focus on his future predicament. He didn't quite go so far as to enter the dream state, but he did his daily meditation for Oversite and then took the quiet time to center himself, readying himself for his first day of interrogation.

"Are you ready?" Stefan asked right after Gabriel had opened his eyes at the end of the meditation. It was sort of an unsettling question given that Stefan had stood silently lurking while he completed his meditation. But at least he had waited, and Gabriel did feel in a much better place than he had before.

"Yes," Gabriel said while nodding, indicating his assent. "Thank you for letting me finish my morning reflection."

"You are welcome," Stefan answered. "I believe everyone is ready. If you could follow me."

Gabriel accompanied Stefan down to the lower basement level of the building they were in. The layout was somewhat expansive and as he went into the subsurface area, it seemed even more dreary than the weather did from the view through the window earlier. Maneuvering through what felt like he was in a labyrinth of hallways and secured passages, Stefan took a path that would be hard to remember. Through this journey, Stefan had to authenticate himself to proceed more than once. They were clearly in a highly secured area. Gabriel had been told to leave his handheld in his room and was pretty sure he had been scanned more than once on this way down here.

"We need to do one more surveillance scan, then we can go inside," Stefan explained before directing Gabriel into an area that had some additional equipment in it.

Gabriel stood there for a minute or so until he was given the direction to step aside and watched Stefan administer the same routine on himself. "We are clear to go in now," Stefan finally said.

Gabriel looked around carefully as he stepped inside the area he would likely be interrogated in. It was very non-descript. It had a table to sit at and some chairs. The room colors were neutral and there was nothing to give style or personality to it. While he didn't see it, he was sure there was probably some sort of equipment installed to record his interrogation. Gabriel had a feeling he would be seeing the inside of this room quite a bit over the next few weeks. There were so many other things he would rather do.

After taking in the surroundings, he allowed his gaze to land on the other people waiting for him in the room. Quintin, he recognized and made the obligatory walk to him to greet him and shake his hand. The other person he did not recognize. There was something disconcerting about her that gave him pause. Sure, there was a friendly expression affixed to her face, but it was her eyes that gave him alarm. It was like they saw through you –into your inner most being and laid you bare. No, there was immense intelligence in this person, one he could not afford to take for granted and be deceived by the persona she would likely try to convey. This was not his ally and he would do well to remember that in the days ahead.

"Hi, I am Gabriel," he said as he put on a brave face to greet the stranger in the room.

"Pleased to finally meet you," she answered. "Ursula Vondier."

Ursula gave Gabriel a penetrating look, then adjusted her expression to show an engaging smile while motioning for him to sit down.

"So glad you could be freed up to talk with us in person," Quintin said. "Normally when someone returns from deep cover, we have much more time to do a full debrief. But in that situation, we don't expect the person to go back into the field right away. We have some time, but not enough, so we will have to compress our normal schedule some."

"I can't say I am looking forward to this," Gabriel answered. "But I do see the importance of doing it. How long do you think we will spend on this debrief?"

"We will use as much of the two months as we can," Ursula answered. "But we will try to keep the questioning in this room to a few hours a day. We need for you to provide assistance to a local farm to maintain your cover, not to mention to get out of this facility that I admit can feel pretty confining the longer you are here."

"That is better than I was expecting," Gabriel said with a bit of relief sounding in his voice.

"Don't get me wrong," Ursula cautioned. "It will feel like a lot more than a few hours. I am thinking we will want to do your non-debrief activities early in the day, then come here later on. That will allow us time to reflect on your answers and get your next questions ready."

"Whatever you need me to do." Gabriel answered doing his best to sound on board with the proposed plan. "Do I have any activities today, or are we going to start right away on questioning?"

"Today will be questions," Ursula replied. "There are a few things we hope to gain clarity on which will help us get a good plan for the rest of our available time we have.

"Ok, I can work with that," Gabriel answered. What can I help you better understand?"

"Well, I don't typically work like that," Ursula stated. "I find that we don't get as detailed of an answer when questions are that specific. I would rather be a bit more open ended in my questions and we can see where it takes us. So why don't we start with your relationship with your grandmother Isabella. Tell me about the first time you met her. What did you notice as you think back on it?"

Gabriel paused for a few moments to task his memory. He could jump quickly into the dream state to recount the events exactly, but that carried some risks also. Instead he decided to see what he could just remember. He had been warned by his grandmother that there would probably be technology in place that could detect if he was lying or evading. It was best to tell the truth as he knew it and hope that questions were open ended enough to not give anything important away.

"When I first met her, she seemed very emotional and glad to see me," Gabriel explained. "At the time, I didn't really have the understanding that I do now on what importance family has in the lives of the people in Xenon. She looked at me, I guess with a muted exuberance. I could tell that she was excited but I think she also didn't want to scare me away with it, trying to give me time to come around on my own to reciprocate her interest in me."

"That is interesting," Ursula replied. "Did she have the look at trying to befriend a stranger or did she look at you like she knew you?"

"I hadn't thought about that before," Gabriel answered. "As I think about it, I didn't see any uncertainty in her eyes. It was like she already knew me somehow. I am not sure I can explain it, but yes, I think she had a look of someone who at some level already knew me."

"But you hadn't seen her before that you are aware of?" Ursula asked.

"Not that I am aware of," Gabriel replied, "but that is not to say that she wasn't unaware of me. I was her only direct living relative she had left. And given that we know she was leading Kayden, she clearly had more access to be able to keep track of me as I grew up and started working at the ministry."

"That is probably true," Ursula answered. "She is a very captivating woman. To think that she lived undetected for so long. Not many people could do that. Did she ever say or do anything early on to give you a clue that she was leading the treasonous resistance group?"

"None that I picked up at the time," Gabriel answered. "She seemed upset about her husband being killed by the government but never said anything that crossed lines that would get her arrested."

"Did she seem to have violent tendencies?" Ursula inserted. "Like a desire to take revenge on those who killed her husband?"

Gabriel paused for a moment to consider this line of questioning. Ursula was really good. She was engaging him in a way that would cause him to slowly lower his guard, never passing judgement and asking questions that were a natural extension of the one before it. It just seemed like a normal conversation but it was clear she was probing about the type of person the leader of Kayden was and her overall persona. Knowing your enemy is the key to defeating them. The government was well known to the people of Xenon, but the resistance was not well known to the government. Gabriel's presence today was about learning all they could to neutralize Isabella and Kayden.

"No, not as a first choice that I could tell," Gabriel finally answered. "Based on the rescue missions she approved, she was certainly prepared to use force, but did not seem to go out of her way to encourage its use. I never thought that she was motivated by power or revenge. She seemed to care about the people and let herself be an instrument to protect them. The big rebellious activity was escaping, not staying and fighting. But I don't know what she advocated for at a high leadership level. I think she purposely shielded me from that knowledge."

Gabriel continued to field questions about his grandmother for the remainder of the session. Every little detail needed to be asked about, asked about again in a slightly different way and then asked a third time. If Gabriel was trying to manufacture a fiction, it would be extremely hard to keep his story straight. So far, he was able to keep to the truth. Doing so may prove to be harder the longer the questioning went on.

∞ ∞ ∞

Aaliyah paused her forward movement momentarily when she heard a slight commotion behind her as she left the holding cell. She could swear she heard singing emanating from the place she had just vacated. Darren's words to her were not without impact, and now she was pretty sure the off-key attempts at music were coming from him. A normal inclination would be to dismiss the singing to the effect of being drugged, but he seemed fully there mentally when he had talked with her. This was something else and she did not understand its cause. Unfortunately, there was no time to reflect on this interaction. Sharna had summoned her back up to the lab and Aaliyah did not think it would reflect well on her to be slow in appearing.

Aaliyah increased the pace of her movement, passing into the lab area. Sharna was showing intense concentration on her workstation, likely going through the data that was just collected. Aaliyah was unsure whether to announce her presence, or just wait until she was called on. Deciding on something in between, she walked up in front of Sharna's work area and stood there quietly, waiting to be noticed. After several minutes of waiting, she was acknowledged.

"The prisoner said something to you. What did it mean?" Sharna asked suddenly.

"I am not fully sure," Aaliyah replied carefully, not wanting to give away what she had already learned about the way of the lily on her own.

"The government databases are all restricted on this topic," Sharna admitted with a hint of frustration forming in her voice. "I could probably find a way to get access to them, but that would create more problems for me than it is worth. I suspect it is something to do with religion which can be a very dicey topic."

After a few moments of silence, Aaliyah asked, "Did the data we collected allow you to conclude anything?"

Sharna looked up with muted annoyance, not expecting to field questions. "Yes, the signals matched the expected signals on the transport tube circuit. However, when I transmit these signals into the circuit, I do not actually get a response from the power module portion of the circuit. It is like it is a key to unlock an action, but doesn't actually provide power to trigger the tube transport. There is something I am missing."

"And this prisoner is able to actuate this somehow in a way you cannot simulate?" Aaliyah asked.

"Yes," Sharna continued, "and I think the answer has something to do with the question on the lily he asked you. I need you to try to find out more about this lily by talking to the prisoner and getting him to tell you about it. I could try to get him re-interrogated, but I am not sure I would get the answers in a way that is helpful to my research."

"Can't that get me in trouble with the government?" Aaliyah asked nervously.

"I'll give you a memo that instructs you to do so in the name of research. If there is a problem, it will fall back on me," Sharna offered. "Hopefully, someone important will read my reports and just send me someone who can better explain this whole lily business to me. Until then, you are the best I have since he seemed to like you well enough to talk about the topic."

Aaliyah nodded, agreeing to do as Sharna had asked.

"I'll requisition your time directly to me for the next several weeks," Sharna continued. "You can continue to do data collection on the prisoner for a few hours every morning, hoping to get him to talk with you about the lily. Then you can assist me in the lab for the remainder of your shift. You haven't been in my way so far."

Aaliyah was pretty sure that was the closest to a compliment she would get from Sharna as she tried to suppress a smile. Government sanction to study what she was already doing in private? This was an outcome she would have never predicted.

∞ ∞ ∞

Sharna looked at the signal data that had been collected, deciding to put off her paperwork just a bit longer. There was something she was missing on what would actually power the transport tube. That could wait she supposed. The best hope she had to get through this whole religion obstacle on learning was to give the government something that would help them find those who were causing havoc in the name of Kayden. If she could devise a way to cut off their ability to travel undetected, that would be of great value and would probably get her access to all the data she needed to solve the second part of this puzzle.

Sharna looked at the design of the sensor that alarmed when the prisoner had created the transport tube frequency. While functional, this was not practical to use in a sensor array. She needed sensors which were very small and covered a large range of detection. After dismissing several ideas as too limited, inspiration came to her. The time was late, but great ideas do not wait on sleep and she knew that when she was in the zone to create, it was best to persevere until she no longer could.

With urgent abandon, Sharna created her design both from a network array topology standpoint and then down to the component level. Her design was complex but the genius was in the inherent simplicity. She could use the existing surveillance array that was spread across all of the sectors. On this array she would add a carrier frequency that would transmit her data separate from the other feeds present. Some modifications would be needed to the surveillance electronics but these appeared to be minor and could be completed by tasking drones. Depending on the priority she could get on the drons, it should be able to be completed in a matter of weeks, more if they didn't give her sufficient precedence. Yes, the idea should work, but to prove it, she wanted to deploy it to the city around her first. She knew she had one person in custody who could trigger it to test it. With luck, she may find he wasn't the only one who could.

Sharna closed her eyes with an inner feeling of accomplishment as she sat at her desk. Morning would come quickly, and as her adrenaline finally subsided, she fell asleep in her chair having done all she was capable of doing without rest.

CHAPTER 6

The setting sun was obstructed by heavy cloud cover which caused the countryside to appear as a land of dark shadows. Xavier looked out the window of his transport vehicle, briefly taking a break from a report he was studying. A smile briefly came to his lips as he considered the view before him. This was his favorite time of the day – when darkness would overtake the light. Much could be accomplished in the shadows he reflected before switching his attention back to the matter in front of him.

Commanding his attention was the progress report by Sharna Malloy pertaining to the transport tube technology. He had tried reading her raw research several times, but each time had given up to peruse the summary one of his technology advisors had prepared for him. To think that brain waves were what was powering the transport technology that Kayden had been using. And now, this researcher was close to developing a way to detect where those brainwaves were coming from. If the government could get notice anytime someone related to Kayden was traveling unauthorized, it would send a crippling blow to the activities that were causing unrest both inside and outside of Xenon.

The validation sensor array should be operational in Morfort in a matter of days. If this proved even partially capable, Xavier couldn't wait to deploy it throughout all the sectors. Sharna was worried about drone prioritization. In Xavier's mind this was a worry that was not well founded. There was no doubt this fell within ministry priorities, and as a high-ranking minister, he would have sufficient clout to make sure this update was completed without delay.

The next obstacle she communicated was another story. She had chosen her words uncharacteristically carefully, but she appeared to want more information on the "way of the lily" wording that the prisoner had used. The topic of religion was a restricted area for researchers and required high level authorization in order to have access to any archives that were available. And even asking for access could get you in a lot of trouble.

Xavier was torn. This was no doubt an opportunity to provide a weapon against Kayden and the religious abomination that accompanied it. There were not many topics that caused the feeling of rage within Xavier, but this way of the lily was one of them. He did all he could to suppress its message from spreading, but to further combat it he would need to allow information to be released. Could he trust this researcher to handle it correctly? Then there was Gabriel. Gabriel had been very careful to not admit it in any reports, but Xavier was nearly certain that Gabriel had to have been exposed and likely participated directly in this religious practice to gain acceptance into Kayden.

Gabriel probably was afraid to share his knowledge for fear of being misunderstood and later punished. But Xavier knew that an agent needed to do whatever was necessary to maintain their cover and burrow into the organization they were asked to penetrate. Getting a feel for this was on his agenda for Quintin to try to uncover, but Xavier didn't think Gabriel would freely volunteer his level of involvement to someone at a rank that was not sufficient to protect him. Xavier needed to speak with Gabriel directly to convince him. Hence the reason Xavier was currently in transit to Morfort.

Xavier was traveling in a low-profile capacity in order to not draw attention to this mission. His security detail was with him, and he used land transport instead of flying as he was entitled to do in his minister capacity. His detail quickly had him cleared with the local security presence and was expediated through the maze required to reach the debriefing room. Pausing briefly, Xavier authenticated his presence and entered the debriefing room unannounced.

"This is a restricted area!" a large man who looked like he had seen recent military action called out before being quickly countermanded by Quintin.

"My apologizes, Minister," Quintin explained. "We didn't expect anyone today. Stefan, this is the Minister of Scientific Compliance, Xavier Alexandar. He is the sponsor of this mission and is read into to everything we are doing."

Stefan paled suddenly, realizing that he had overstepped himself badly. "I am sorry I didn't recognize you right away sir, please come in."

Xavier made a slight incline of his head to acknowledge the invitation and came into the room fully. Gabriel was present and looked tired. Beside him was the primary interrogator Ursula who he had met previously. She was very good at what she did and Xavier hoped she had not pushed Gabriel too hard.

"Gabriel, so good to see you!" Xavier offered enthusiastically. "I hope that we are not being too hard on you. You honestly look spent."

Gabriel smiled before standing to shake Xavier's hand. "Today isn't their fault, Minister. I got stuck doing some really hard manual labor on the farm I am mentoring today. I actually couldn't wait to be questioned so my body could actually get a break!"

"Yeah, I suppose it is hard to be credible giving advice if you are not willing to help do the work with them," Xavier offered. "How are you holding up?"

Gabriel looked at him with a neutral expression on his face before he forced a positive expression on his face. "It is harder than I thought it would be, but I am doing well all things considered."

Xavier glanced around the room making sure he had everyone's attention. He did. It wasn't often that a person of his stature visited a debriefing session. "I need to speak with Gabriel alone for a few minutes. Quintin, I need you to disable all recording equipment on your way out. I will have you messaged when we are through."

Confused expressions were quickly masked with obedient ones, as the group ushered themselves out of the room. Xavier saw Quintin press a few buttons on a carefully concealed console, after which he looked at Xavier to indicate the recording was turned off before exiting the room.

"We should be as private as we can be now," Xavier offered. "I wanted to talk about some sensitive topics with you that you may not be comfortable sharing in front of the rest of the group."

"Have I done something wrong, Minister?" Gabriel asked nervously.

"Not at all," Xavier answered. "In fact, I think you have done more good than you can possibly know. You have far exceeded my expectations on this assignment, and without you, I would not be in my minster role. I owe you a great deal as does your country."

"Thank you, sir, that means a lot coming from you," Gabriel answered.

"And as much as it would pain me to grant it, if you personally need to be recalled from your mission, just say the word and you will receive a hero's welcome in return," Xavier continued.

"I would like to continue with it, if it is all the same to you," Gabriel answered.

"Yes, I figured you would," Xavier answered. "There is nothing like being in the field where the action is. It does something to your senses that you can rarely approach working from a standard workstation. But I didn't come visit you to talk about my passions. I came to ask for your help on something you may not be comfortable doing."

"What do you have in mind?" Gabriel asked tentatively.

"I think you know a lot more about this 'way of the lily' than you have shared in your reports," Xavier stated while raising his hand to prevent Gabriel from interrupting. "Please hear me out before you respond. I have been undercover many times and have had to join in the illegal activities of those I was trying to undermine in order to gain my target's trust. Family or not, I don't think there is any chance you gained trust of someone in Kayden's leadership if you were not also demonstrating some proficiency in their religion that has to do with the lily. Now I am not saying you believe in it, but I bet you are one of the biggest experts we have access to on what the lily is and what it believes. And what I need from you is for you to share some of that."

Gabriel sat there silently, as if considering his response to Xavier's statement. Xavier did not see defiance on his face, more an expression of reflection as his mind processed the implications of what Xavier had asked him.

"I can see why you do not want to share this with Quintin and the interrogator," Xavier continued. "They can't protect you, and your actions could be misunderstood. I however, can protect you and will. There is some very promising research that is being done which may be able to detect when people operate the transport tubes that Kayden has been using. Did you know that these tubes are somehow triggered by a brainwave pattern? Anyway, a researcher has developed a way to detect this brain pattern and localize it, but hasn't been able to learn how it is generated. She thinks it has something to do with the practice of this 'way of the lily,' and I am inclined to believe her. If you could spend some time with her and honestly answer her questions, I would be extremely grateful. And yes, I often didn't share everything in my reports either. You need to be careful to protect yourself in case someone read into your mission screws up and compromises you."

"I would be willing to meet with your researcher," Gabriel replied after some moments of thought. If you have captured any contraband literature on the Lily, it would be very helpful. It may help me provide the proper information. Can we also suspend or scale back the debriefing processes while I am doing this? I am not sure I can handle the farm, the researcher and this session and still have a working body left at the end of the day."

Xavier chuckled before replying. "Quintin will probably really complain, but yes, that can be arranged. And I will instruct the researcher to code her research for this for my eyes only for now. If I have need to share the results, we will keep your role out of it. I will also make sure to vet her team if she has one. No more than one helper on her end to minimize the risk to your identity. Would that work for you?"

"I will do my best to make that work," Gabriel answered after nodding.

"I know you will," Xavier answered. "I can't wait to see the expression on Quintin's face when he hears I have screwed up his plans again!"

Xavier gave Gabriel a privately encoded authorization indicating he was conducting research on religion at the behest of the Ministry of Scientific Compliance. Gabriel now carried a special code on him that could be submitted into Oversite to reveal the approval authorization.

Xavier exiting the building after telling Quintin a sanitized version of what he had promised to Gabriel. Overall, it had gone much better than he had expected. How much Gabriel would disclose was yet to be seen, but his help had been invaluable so far and Xavier had very high hopes on where Sharna's research would lead. Kayden must be put down and Gabriel would provide him the means to accomplish that end.

And if Gabriel was doing more than just infiltrating Kayden, that could be dealt with later on.

∞ ∞ ∞

Gabriel let his body crash on the bed of his sparse hotel room. His energy was spent but his mind was racing trying to process all that Xavier had told him. If the government developed a way to detect someone using a transport tube, that would mean they probably would be able to detect anyone entering in the dream state. This would be catastrophic to Kayden's abilities to move around undetected and could hamper one of the biggest advantages that they had. If his grandmother didn't know this already, he needed to warn her.

Gabriel quickly evaluated the risk of entering the dream state and decided to chance it since Xavier had said the new surveillance capabilities were not online yet. Hopefully, he could dream undetected for a short while at least. And if he was somehow caught, he could explain it away as following Xavier's instructions and using the encoded authorization he now had in his possession. Not that it would be a good thing to use that protection so soon, before he had even met with the researcher.

Gabriel had not entered the dream state since he got to Preath and he did not realize how much he missed it until he centered himself to enter it. It took a few moments longer than normal to fully release his mind and being. He waited to see if Raelynn would join him while probing to see if his grandmother was in the dream state. He was in luck that his grandmother was available and decided he could not afford to lose the opportunity to speak with her. Focusing on her presence, Gabriel willed himself to join with her.

Gabriel found himself in a small apartment style living area standing beside his grandmother. As usual, the only color represented in his surroundings was represented by he and his grandmother. She was observing a young woman sitting at a small desk, reading through a paper book. Gabriel looked closer, realizing that this book was contraband and one that he had spent much time reviewing when he was doing his initial learning with Teacher. She was studying *The Way of the Lily*.

Isabella looked up toward him, acknowledging his presence with a smile.

"Who is she?" Gabriel asked.

"Her name is Aaliyah," Isabella answered, "and she has great potential."

"In the Lily?" Gabriel asked.

"Yes," Isabella answered. "The price to enable her has been high, but my hope is great. Her hunger for truth is hard to explain, but against all odds and restriction, she has found a way to the path of the Lily. She hasn't committed herself fully to follow it, but I think she will in time. Not that I am complaining, but to what do I owe the pleasure of your company?"

"I think I have some information you need to be aware of, if you are not already." Gabriel answered. "Minister Xavier came to talk with me today and wants me to meet with a researcher who has developed a way to detect the transport tubes being used, I think by detecting someone in the dream state. I will know more later, but I would not be surprised if a sensor array gets implemented in short order to detect this. It could really jeopardize Kayden if it works well."

Isabella grew a thoughtful expression on face before answering. "Did Xavier say at all how it worked to detect it?"

"Yes, he said something about detecting a brainwave pattern, whatever that meant." Gabriel replied. "I am hopeful I can find out more tomorrow when I meet with this researcher, but I am not sure how much longer it will be safe for me to enter the dream state to give updates."

"I think I have been watching this researcher, but she says so little out loud and her research notes are so technical, I am not always sure what she has discovered," Isabella explained. "She is brilliant, but I don't think she is a zealot to the government's priorities. She just wants to advance technology without anything getting in her way."

"Xavier also said he thought I was more proficient in the Way of the Lily than I let on in my reports, and wants me to share my knowledge fully with her," Gabriel continued. "He even gave me a special authorization form allowing me to do religion study with full protection so there would be no misunderstandings. It is one thing to provide a summary of beliefs, it is another to demonstrate those beliefs for government representatives."

"Wow!" Isabella exclaimed. "What an opportunity. They are instructing you to proselytize, and giving you full cover while doing it."

Gabriel had a look of confusion on his face. "You mean you want me to fully participate in it?"

"Of course," Isabella answered. "The Way of the Lily is available for all. Why wouldn't we want to share about it when asked, especially if they are providing a way that will cause you no harm?"

"And if the government learns things about the Way of the Lily, can they use that knowledge against us?" Gabriel asked.

"Like how to follow a moral code? How to care for others? How to live in a state of self-sacrifice?" Isabella answered. "And if you are worried about them gaining dream state abilities, let them. There is very little they can do for harm when in the dream state. Those with evil intent will not be able to get into or sustain the dream state."

"And the ability to detect dreaming?" Gabriel asked.

"See what you can find out about how they are doing this." Isabella instructed. My guess is we will not be detected dreaming in underground places, but we will want to be sure about that. If you can get me information that is more understood on the technical specifications, it will be put to good use. I will also send word out about the risk of detection being imminent and wrap up any infiltration missions outside of Xenon for a while until we can fully assess this risk."

Gabriel nodded in understanding to the revised plan. "Do you have any other advice before I return?"

"Just remember the process that Teacher used to train you," Isabella advised. "Don't hold back knowledge but give it to them in amounts they can process. If you jump to the finish line on what you can accomplish in the dream state first, you will not be as effective with them. Bringing them along slowly is the best way. And don't worry if they detect you in the dream state. But I would hold off on showing any special skills unless one of them is able to join you there. Maybe explain it as a special kind of meditation for starters."

"Thanks," Gabriel answered. "I feel better about all of this already."

"Be safe," Isabella answered. "Don't feel like you need to update me regularly unless you can do so safely. I will keep an extra close eye on you for a while. But do your elderly grandmother a favor and repeat out loud anything you want me to understand in simple enough terms that I can understand them!"

Gabriel smiled, "I highly doubt that is necessary, but I will do as you ask. Take care."

Gabriel released himself and willed himself back to the lily field, the intermediate place in the dream state. Raelynn was waiting for him which caused an unexpected bump of happiness.

"Quieter than last time but still pretty clumsy," Raelynn said with a grin on her face. "Everything ok?"

"Am I safe, yes," Gabriel replied. "But we have some risks ahead. I think the government has developed a way to detect people in the dream state."

"Did you tell your grandmother about this?" she asked.

"Yes," Gabriel answered. "She said she would let people know to be careful. My guess is you will be asked to let a lot of people know."

"When do you think you will get to come home?" Raelynn asked.

"Probably a couple of months," Gabriel said with a disappointed tone in his voice. "I would love to come back sooner, but I don't think I will be given the chance."

"Hurry back, I expect we will have a lot happening when you return. Something big is about to occur, I can sense it," Raelynn stated with conviction.

"I am worried about that also," Gabriel answered. "The ministry is gearing up for something big. They have gone way longer than I expected letting Xenon be."

Gabriel and Raelynn conversed for a few more minutes catching up on what was happening around Xenon and the challenges that Gabriel had been going through. She thought it was pretty funny all the hard work he had been doing on the farm on Morfort. Gabriel eventually said his farewells and transitioned back to the awake state. He was hopeful his dream excursion had not been detected, but didn't think he would be that fortunate the next time. Gabriel got around for bed. He was both physically and mentally exhausted. He needed some real rest if he was going to be able to brave the rigors of the farm in the morning. Not to mention whatever awaited in meeting with this researcher.

CHAPTER 7

*a*glas looked in on the prisoner he was guarding. The detainee was uncomfortably shackled in a small cell with multiple explosive devices attached to his body. There was no chance of escape without the help of some very talented and determined individuals. This was a prisoner who was being permitted to say subversive or dangerous things which could prove difficult for less vetted ears to hear. There were security reasons for his unit to have this duty Aglas had come to realize, as the prisoner was an unapologetic follower of religion in addition to being a person associated with the recent rebellion in Xenon.

"Good morning. Aglas isn't it?" Darren asked. "I am very pleased I can spend my morning with you!"

Aglas acknowledged his greeting with the slightest of nods. The prisoner must have overheard his name in conversation. This detainee did not match the profile of what he would expect of a rebel. Aglas expected to be looked at with hate, or at least disinterest, but this person was engaging. He constantly tried to make conversation even though Aglas said nothing in reply and he was constantly talking about his lily religion when he wasn't singing or doing other odd behaviors. Aglas had to secretly admit he liked this Darren, but it would be unwise to acknowledge this out loud.

"Do you know if Aaliyah is going to be coming by today?" the prisoner asked. "She usually visits about this time. Not that I know the time but I do see the sun peering through the window. It is probably going to be a beautiful day today. I have always liked winter days populated with sunshine. You know, I see you are listening to our conversations about the Lily. You know the Way of the Lily is for all who seek it, and that includes you."

Aglas did his best to maintain a neutral expression. Normally a prisoner who spoke so forwardly of religion would receive instant feedback to encourage silence, but Sharna had provided very clear instructions to let the prisoner say whatever he wanted to without retribution. He didn't know why Sharna had asked for this, but Aglas learned pretty quickly not to cross her. She may not have all the fancy titles some in the government had, but she had more ability to harm careers than anyone he had ever seen. Everyone was afraid of her and he was not going to override her just because he wanted a prisoner to be quiet. It was best to stay on her good side – if there was a good side. Or maybe at least stay on her not bad side.

This assignment in Morfort had at least been interesting. Validating new technology applications was not something he had done very much before. Sure, the hostile extractions portion of this mission remained similar to typical assignments, but the rest was nothing like his prior experience in the capital. After Aglas' captain was killed in a botched raid a few years before, his unit had been broken up and he was fortunate to get a spot on this team. Things had been going well for him here, and with some continued luck, he thought he had a chance at making squad leader sometime in the near future.

"Good morning, Aglas," he heard behind him, turning to see Aaliyah coming into the holding cell area.

"Good morning, Aaliyah," Aglas replied, thankful is was not Sharna stepping in and instead was her much more personable assistant. "Back to do some more testing?"

"You know Sharna," Aaliyah answered as if that would explain everything.

Aglas nodded. "I think your equipment is still setup in there and no one reported anything odd sounding coming from it. I'll be right here if you need anything."

Aaliyah nodded and proceeded to check on her analyzer. This was the last day of Aglas' current rotation to stand guard, and he would have some time off to do his normal duty for the next two weeks. He had to admit he would miss observing these sessions. He had never really considered many of the topics that were discussed. This prisoner wanted to help others and seemed to live his life in that pursuit. Aglas thought that society would be better off if more people had this attitude. But this prisoner had broken the law and laws were in place for good reasons. Justice didn't always have to be fun, but the law was the law and without it, order would break down.

∞ ∞ ∞

Aaliyah still felt nervous about conducting these discussions with Darren but she had formal authorization to do it. She wasn't sure that would fully protect her but was willing to take the chance. She had so many questions about the Lily from reading the books that Darren had smuggled her, and what better way to get answers to these questions than to talk to him directly under the pretext of doing scientific research.

Sharna had been monitoring these sessions at some level, and the only criticism she had provided was that the prisoner had not triggered another brainwave pattern event to match the one detected early on. Between Sharna and Aaliyah, they were not sure if the prisoner suspected the nature of their research and was deliberately choosing not to do the task. It was also possible he didn't see the need to do it. Sharna said the sensor grid was nearly operational in the Morfort area and hopefully would get some additional data points in the near future, even if it wasn't from their prisoner.

"Did you think about what I said yesterday?" Darren asked her suddenly.

"You said a lot of things yesterday," Aaliyah answered. "Did you mean something specifically?"

"Yes, we did discuss quite a few topics," Darren replied. "I guess I specifically mean did you think about the key tenants of the Way of the Lily?"

"I spent some time thinking about what you said on them." Aaliyah answered. "It is a completely different way of thinking."

"It is not just thinking," Darren stated. "It is also belief. You shouldn't just think about it; you need to have faith to embrace it, to let it encapsulate your life. Anything less and you will never fully experience all that it can provide you."

"What do you do to let it, as you say, encapsulate your life?" Aaliyah asked.

"It starts with surrendering your wants, desires and selfish tendencies." Darren answered. "When you are able to remove those distractions, you reach a place where you can center yourself and let all things that are not Lily-based fall away, leaving just the Lily and what it represents."

"I am not sure I understand how I would do that." Aaliyah answered. "Do I just sit in the room and do something like daily meditation with a different focus?"

"I suppose it is not terribly different than that," Darren explained. "But the daily scientific reflection sessions are focused on allegiance to a different set of values. What if instead of focusing on how you can serve the government and planet, you instead focused on how you could serve your fellow man, removing anything from your mindset that didn't forward that goal. Are you helping the weak? Are you giving up of yourself for others?"

"Can you show me how you do this?" Aaliyah asked.

"For everyone, it is different," Darren answered. "Can you get yourself access to a lily plant?"

"I think I can," Aaliyah answered, not sure where to get one, but hopeful Sharna could arrange it.

"Good," Darren said. "Get this plant, and I want you to spend some time trying to focus your meditation on its characteristics, its essence, on everything about it. Make it a part of you. Practice this frequently and you will have taken a step on the path to understanding."

Aaliyah wasn't sure she understood. This was not detailed in any of the books she had read. She wondered where the lily came in and maybe she was about to find out with this latest information that Darren had given her. Her reflection was interrupted by her handheld with a message that she was needed in the lab and to bring the analyzer with her. She would have to cut this session short.

"Thank you for talking with me this morning," Aaliyah offered. "Duty calls, I have to go for now. Hopefully, I will see you tomorrow. I will reflect on what we have discussed."

"The Way of the Lily is for all," Darren called out as she exited the area pushing the equipment in front of her.

Then she heard him break into song as he had established a pattern of doing as she was leaving him. Aaliyah smiled and then waved to

Aglas on her way out of the holding cell area. He had a very odd expression on his face and seemed to be deep in thought.

∞ ∞ ∞

Sharna could not believe the message she had just received. She knew that her work had high ranking protectors, but she didn't realize she was being followed at this high of a level. She had received a top-secret classification authorization to pursue the lily religion research she had carefully requested several days before. The cost was that her research from here forward on this topic was to be eyes only to the Minister of Scientific Compliance and she could continue to use one lab assistant only in this area of study. That by itself would have caused her some surprise, but what really surprised her was an offer to have an undercover agent who was familiar with this religion come assist them in their studies.

The imposition of a single helper was not really a hindrance. She typically worked alone anyway, but this new assistant had been surprisingly competent in her activities over the past few days. It was probably time to learn her name, Sharna considered. Finding Aaliyah's name, she submitted it for approval and then programmed security protocols into her lab perimeter to prevent any unauthorized access. A multifactor authentication would be now required to enter the research area. It didn't break Sharna's heart to make it harder to be interrupted.

"It was more challenging to get into the lab," Aaliyah stated as she walked in. "Has the security been modified recently?"

"Yes, I just installed some updates." Sharna explained. "The classification level of this work has increased. I let your normal access code work today, but tomorrow you will need to use a different one. Currently you and I are the only ones read into it, so you cannot discuss the religion research with anyone, is that understood?"

"Yes, I understand." Aaliyah answered. "You called for me? I think I got some good new information from my interview of the prisoner this morning."

"I can get you a lily plant if that is what you were going to tell me," Sharna stated abruptly. "I have that being procured now. Granted, if it takes as long as my equipment did to analyze the brain waves, the plant may be dead before it gets here. Either way, I have ordered it. Was there anything else of significance that I missed?"

"Probably not," Aaliyah answered.

"We have an undercover agent who supposed knows a lot about the prisoner's lily religion coming soon. If you do anything to jeopardize his identity, you will be glad if you have as comfortable of an accommodation as the prisoner you visit daily."

"I understand," Aaliyah said more sharply than she intended.

Sharna paused before saying, "I am not very good with talking to people. If I don't get the right answers out of him, I may need you to ask him questions like you are doing with the prisoner. The person sending him said he may be reluctant to share everything he knows for fear of consequences or messing up his mission."

"Is there anything we are doing that we can't tell this person?" Aaliyah asked curiously.

"No, we are supposed to fully share what we have learned, in case he has some suggestions for us," Sharna stated. "If we are fortunate, he may be able to mimic the brain pattern we are looking for. I also have been provided some book scans that have been captured pertaining to this religion. I recommend you use the time till he arrives reading them so we don't waste the limited time on basics we could have learned already."

∞ ∞ ∞

Gabriel approached the coordinates Xavier had sent to him. Gabriel was grateful the physical requirements at the farm had been minimal this morning. He felt alert, mixed with apprehension, unsure what to expect from meeting with this researcher. There was risk here, especially when this researcher had already developed technology to undermine much of the advantage Kayden had over the government. At a minimum, Gabriel needed to learn the details on the government's abilities to detect the dream state, not to mention any technology decoding they had compiled from the transport tube.

The building was a typical looking unmarked government facility. In front stood a statue of one of the founding scientists in a pose of great discovery, one of the few forms of artistic expression that had been commissioned since the Scientific Reformation. A hint of sunshine cast some shadows across the main entrance as Gabriel passed through with an ominous feeling he could not shake. Willing himself to action, Gabriel announced himself to the security officer manning the entrance.

"I was told to give you coded message A34FNQ23T5," Gabriel said reading from his handheld."

The security officer looked at him with suspicion before inputting the code into his terminal. He then initiated a biometric scan to make sure this person matched the characteristics that matched this code on file.

"You are expected. Please go through this door and wait for your escort. She will take you to where you are supposed to go."

Gabriel went through the indicated door and was met by a heavily armed person with a clear military bearing. She looked at him with suspicion before motioning him to follow. Gabriel suspected she was CET but no markings existed on her attire to confirm this. Gabriel followed her through several unmarked passages before stopping in front of a secured entrance.

"Your coded package has arrived," his escort announced over some sort of voice intercom. Then turning to Gabriel, "You will need to go this way. I am not authorized to escort you any further."

The door opened automatically and Gabriel stepped through. He was then required to input the second access code Xavier had given him and to again complete a biometric scan to ensure he was the person who was supposed to be there. After a few moments of computer contemplation, the next entrance opened up, revealing an open lab space.

Gabriel looked around what appeared to be a state-of-the-art lab that was expansive in size. The array of technology components spread out was overwhelming, but he did not know what most of the equipment did. Gabriel did recognize hardware reflective of computing power and based on the size and quantity of it, it dwarfed anything he had previously interacted with when he was stationed in the capital. Alaine would be very happy to have access to a place like this.

As his gaze shifted, he noticed a partially disassembled transport tube before his eyes finally came to rest on the person sitting behind a workstation. She appeared to be deep in thought, exhibiting an intensity that nearly caused him to shutter inside. Her appearance was not well kept with her hair messy and clothing a bit disheveled like she had slept in it recently without changing. He did not think this was reflective of her mind as her lab was in immaculate condition. She probably just didn't value a lot outside of her research.

Gabriel's eyes moved to find a second person in the corner of the lab at a small desk, looking at her handheld in deep concentration. He could tell she was aware of his presence, but was pretending to ignore him as to not break protocol to be first addressed by the more senior person. This person seemed to be very young to work in a lab this advanced as the only assigned assistant, but the researcher had her choice of a single assistant and had chosen her. Gabriel thought she had a nagging familiarity like he knew her from somewhere. Perhaps that connection would become clearer to him later on.

Gabriel continued to look around the lab silently taking in what he saw. He figured that the better he observed, the better he could come back to it later in the dream state.

"You are early," came an abrupt statement from the person behind the bigger desk. "I am told you are an expert on the lily religion."

"I know more than many on this topic," Gabriel carefully replied. "I am Gabriel, what should I call you?"

"I am surprised you offered your real name with you being undercover," Sharna answered. "I am Sharna and this is Aaliyah."

Hearing the name Aaliyah clicked something in Gabriel's mind and he knew where he knew her from. She was the person his grandmother was watching when he had last visited her in the dream state. She was a secret seeker of the Lily and now she was helping to expose it? It didn't make sense, but perhaps she was in a situation out of her control as well. Remembering he had been addressed, Gabriel decided to respond.

"What I know about your role, unless I wore a mask, I thought it pointless to try to hide it," Gabriel explained. "You probably already knew it after scanning me to get in here."

"Well deduced," Sharna stated. "It is good to know I didn't get an idiot sent to help me."

Gabriel was taken slightly back by her blunt assessment but decided to not take offense. "Xavier said you had found a way to detect a brain pattern used by people who use the transport tubes?"

"You mean Minister Xavier Alexandar?" Aaliyah blurted out.

"The same," Gabriel answered, smiling internally that he had gotten a response to dropping the high-ranking name in a personal tense. It may shift the power balance some on this discussion he had hoped. Sharna seemed unimpressed with his comment though.

"The transport tube has a circuit that requires a complex brainwave frequency distribution. This has only been captured once from the pilot who was captured with the transport tube," Shana explained. "He is an unashamed follower of this lily religion and I need help understanding how this brain pattern is generated."

"Can you generate the wave form artificially to trigger the transport tube?" Gabriel asked.

"Oh, I can trigger it and the circuit opens up, but the tube power transport does not energize," Sharna explained. "I haven't been able to determine yet what is needed for that to work but I am working on it and will figure it out. In the meantime, I have developed a sensor that will look for the brainwave pattern to detect if someone is generating it around the city."

"Get your scanning equipment setup," Gabriel directed. "I may be able to help."

Sharna motioned for Aaliyah to setup the analyzer to be ready to detect a signal form.

"Can I get you to take a few steps in that direction, Gabriel?" Aaliyah asked. "I am ready whenever you get in position."

Gabriel nodded and moved to the place she had directed, sliding a chair with him. He had debated how to approach this interaction and ultimately decided that if he showed them what they wanted to see it would quickly get their attention. If they tried to mimic it, then maybe they would end up embarking on the Way of the Lily.

Gabriel cleared his mind and centered himself. He purposely did it slowly as to not make himself seem to be expertly proficient at this ability. After waiting a full two minutes, he entered the dream state now staring at a black and while landscape of lilies. Gabriel was not sure how long to stay stationed in this place or if he should venture anywhere. After a moment's reflection he envisioned himself directly beside his body form, watching Aaliyah and Sharna excitedly track the waveforms on the analyzer. Sharna, after a few moments, directed Aaliyah to get out of her way as she adjusted some dials saying something about opening up the frequency detection spectrum.

Thinking he had provided enough for an initial taste of his abilities, Gabriel then reimagined himself in the chair he had left from, opening his eyes.

"Was that helpful?" Gabriel asked.

"We just lost the signal," Sharna stated, oblivious to Gabriel's question. "That was way longer than we got from the prisoner. I wish we had more time with the signal. I know there is something else there that I wasn't able to isolate."

Aaliyah had heard and registered Gabriel's question and decided to reply. "Yes, Gabriel, that is the best signal we have detected so far. What did you do?"

Sharna at this point had shifted her attention back to Gabriel, like she was just remembering he was still sitting there. "I just did the meditation of the Lily," Gabriel answered. "I don't do it very often as it takes a lot of focus, but that is all it was. Not everyone who follows the Lily can do it, but I have been told I have some ability in it."

Gabriel had stretched the truth a little in his comment but didn't think he would trigger any sensors as he had not directly lied. There was a lot he didn't say, but if she went back and checked sensor logs it would give his account further credibility.

"The prisoner said something about meditating on a lily today. I wonder if it is related?" Aaliyah spoke out. "But we don't have a lily here and he said I needed one."

Gabriel smiled, remembering his path to learning. "When I first learned, I couldn't do it without the lily. As I practiced more, I can usually do it without as long as I remember the lily clearly in my mind. If you can get ahold of a lily, I will do my best to show you how it is done."

CHAPTER 8

*a*aliyah was excited to share her paper books with others in her group, especially now that she had access to the same content in a fully sanctioned capacity. Aaliyah carefully hid the books on her person and began to walk to where the meeting place was scheduled to be at this week. While the personal risk was great, she still felt an internal pull, unable to keep what she had solely to herself.

The time she had spent recently with Darren and Gabriel profoundly impacted her. Darren was so unabashedly outspoken on the Lily and his belief in it. He knew that he was facing death but he didn't grovel or offer to sell others out in order to save his life. Instead, he continued to exhibit the very thing that he would eventually die for. And he did it with joy. What certainty he had in his purpose and deeds! Aaliyah wondered if she could ever have that level of boldness in the face of pending obliteration.

Gabriel, she still was making her mind up about. He hadn't triggered any truth detection sensors; Sharna had been sure she checked that. But Aaliyah felt there was more he wasn't telling them. Granted, he was a highly trained agent, able to portray himself in credible ways to others, but it was like there was something missing. There was more to his story. Sharna was ecstatic about his ability to enter the meditative state which triggered the brain wave pattern she needed. But Aaliyah sensed there was depth beneath the surface that he hadn't explained. Darryl had a certainty in his eyes and a peace with himself and Gabriel had it also. She didn't say it out loud, but she felt Gabriel could have stayed in the meditative state for hours. Instead, he chose to dangle a trinket in front of the researchers in order to lead them the way he wanted them to go.

Aaliyah arrived at her meeting place and went through the standard surveillance countermeasures that she had been following. She also, once was in position, activated the device Darryl had given her previously to further check for being monitored. It came back green, indicating they still had some believed level of privacy. Aaliyah sighed with relief, being afraid that with the increased security clearance she was under, that she may not be as safe as she once was.

There were six of her group present today. When her turn to share came, she opened one of her books and began to read aloud. Those who were listening would never be the same again – changed forever with the words that were spoken.

∞ ∞ ∞

Cyrius looked out his dormitory room window, shivering while taking in the blustery winter conditions outside. At sixteen years old, he was in his next to last year of general education. His school was located just outside of Morfort and was considered one of the premiere institutions in Preath. His view was amazing, one of the advantages of being an upperclassman and having a high class-rank. Cyrius looked out across the frozen pond as the snow continued to fall from the sky. This had been a colder than typical winter it seemed, but the seasons would change soon, bringing the warmer rays of the summer sun.

Cyrius was generally a very good student, but the curiosity that made him a good student also got him in trouble at times. Holes in curriculum content would catch his attention faster than anything. It was like the school instructors expected him to only use his brain sometimes and only on the approved topics. This was a lesson that he did not learn easily but after some strong discipline for asking questions on topics that were taboo, he began to learn when to inquire out loud and when to keep his questions to himself. Sure, he still had the questions and wondered about the gaps, but he now knew enough to regurgitate the expected responses back to questions even if he had fundamental doubts with all he was saying.

His outlook had all changed about three years prior when Trisha had been transferred to his school. At first, he had just been interested in her because she was pretty and the perception of danger that surrounded her. She was escorted by security officials for several weeks until slowly this stopped. It was like they were worried she would escape somehow. He came to find out that she was from Xenon, and this was the first time she had lived away from her parents. At first, she acted withdrawn, not wanting to talk to anyone, then something changed.

She was in one of Cyrius' classes and the teacher said something about the family structure being the downfall of civilization and only enlightened societies recognized the need to overcome it. Trisha was having no part of this, and immediately started arguing back with the teacher making point after point that exposed the fallacy of his thesis. The teacher and the class were not used to a free-thinking discussion and she clearly won the argument. This caused her to be put in isolation for over a week and she still refused to recant her position. This only earned her more respect from her classmates and when the punishment period finally came to a close, people, including Cyrius, starting coming to her quietly, asking her what she thought about other topics as well.

This soon led to some very dangerous discussions on religion. Even she knew how risky this could be since openly discussing religion in Xenon could get you arrested and possibly executed. But she had an audience who was hungry for truth, outside of the talking points the Ministry of Education had embedded into their schooling. She spoke to them about the Way of the Lily, about new values to live their lives by and about the value of self-sacrifice. She had a large many of the texts of this belief system memorized and helped them also commit what she knew to memory. Their group was small, just six of them in all, and when Trisha was eventually returned to her home in Xenon, the six she had invested her time and knowledge in continued in her example. This cell soon branched out with each of the six doing the same for five or six others, until their numbers were forty who followed the Lily in secret.

Trisha kept speaking of meditating on the Lily and that if they could get a hold of a lily plant, it would be easier to do. At the time it was just a seed that was planted in their minds, as there was no access to plants like this for them to use. But that had changed a few weeks ago when Cyrius' biology class had brought in several flower species to study.

With joy, he discovered one of them was a lily and quietly shared the news with his group. It took a lot of creative trickery but he was successful in taking the lily from the classroom, unbeknownst to his teacher. Now he was able to study it and meditate on it like Trisha had talked about. With his group of six others, he sat in silence, taking in the essence of the lily, examined its beauty and at some level almost felt one with it. Then unexplainably, he drifted into a state of strange awareness where color was absent and he was surrounded by an entire field of lilies.

∞ ∞ ∞

Sharna was frustrated with the problem in front of her. After making so much progress on being able to detect the meditative state, she was stuck. Yes, she had her sensor array deployed around Morfort, ready to detect any instances of this brainwave pattern. But in her mind, she had already solved that problem. The difficulty in front of her pertained to determining the source of the energy that was actuated when someone was in this lily based meditative state. After several days working with Gabriel, she had constructed an experiment to try to isolate that source of energy. Sharna disconnected what she thought was some sort of power amplifier from the transport tube. She had unhooked it so nothing would relocate, instead attaching it to a shunt device that could consume any high-power surges that may be sent over it. Once she had constructed this design, she used Gabriel's meditation to try to actuate it. To her delight, when he entered the meditation state, it powered the amplifier and provided an extremely high energy reading that almost fried the equipment she had hooked up.

While this provided confirmation that there was a secondary energy form initiated, she was still no closer to identifying how it was generated from a pure scientific standpoint that could be replicated in a lab-based setting. It was possible there was some sort of energy conduit available through the human mind that could produce this level of energy. If she could figure out a way to harness this energy, it would be an astounding discovery that would shake the foundations of science. But to prove this fully, she would need to be able to replicate it in a way that could be repeated by others, ideally in a laboratory-based setting.

There were prohibitions against animal-based testing, but that didn't preclude using human test subjects that were deemed unacceptable for value to society. Sharna had not needed to request test subjects before, since most of her research was technology based, not person based. That seemed like the logical next step in the research, but wasn't an area that Sharna had done much in before. Sharna thought if you could create a drug induced brain pattern to match what was generated in the meditative state, then maybe the energy state could also be replicated through the mind. It was a hypothesis at best, but it was somewhere she could go next if there were no breakthroughs soon. Sharna noted this thinking for later on in her research brainstorming file. So many ways to go with this and only so much time.

Sharna's analysis was interrupted by an alert on the console in front of her. This was from her new algorithm in Oversite that was looking for the targeted brain wave pattern. She had tested it on Gabriel a few times, but this was the first hit that she had received outside of him. After a few quick keystrokes, she pulled up her messaging device.

"I need a covert extraction team deployed immediately," she ordered. "Sending coordinates now. Suspected transport tube activity in process."

"CET is on standby and will be deployed. Do you require to accompany?" responded the dispatcher.

"Negative," Sharna replied. "I will monitor remotely and provide more data as I process it."

Sharna zeroed in on the location of the signal detection. The location was a bit of a surprise, but that is what the data was showing. It looked like a Ministry of Education facility specializing in older students who showed some educational aptitude. Sharna isolated the feed from the sensor array and took control of a nearby portable microdrone. She tasked the drone to where the signal was originating from. It was not what she was expecting to see. Sharna pulled up the communications feed to the CET that was dispatched.

"CET-1, update, this is not a transport tube operation in progress. It appears we have a suspected religion practice in process. Alter protocols to detection versus immediate apprehension per Ministry guidelines and seek instructions from Ministry of Scientific Compliance contacts for next steps." Sharna instructed, feeling somewhat disappointed.

Sharna had hoped to detect another transport tube in operation, but instead it was just some kids practicing religion. This would still probably be acclaimed from high as a great victory but Sharna did not view it as helpful to advancing her understanding of this brainwave pattern that had been challenging her. Now that she had Gabriel's help, she no longer needed test subjects who could create the brain wave pattern.

Sharna quickly directed Oversite to do a comprehensive sweep of surveillance logs in this school. If she didn't, she would probably have fifty idiots coming to her lab trying to get her to give them more information. As annoying as it was to do, giving them what they wanted before they came and asked for it would likely save her a bunch of time. After several minutes, the routine finished running the analysis, finding a correlating pattern of about forty students who seemed to be involved in whatever was being done with this religion. Sharna compiled the evidence logs and sent them to the CET that she had deployed, to use however the powers that be deemed fit. What a waste of time, but at least she would probably not be bothered further on this event.

Then it occurred to her that this whole process would likely repeat over and over as the sensor array expanded. With annoyance she started programming some new routines that would automate the communication and evidence gathering steps she had just completed. With luck, she would just get notified when a find occurred matching her desired parameters. The rest of the sensor hits could just go to preassembled teams who specialized in this type of activity. After that took longer than she wanted to complete, she returned her focus back to her original problem. How was the energy generated through the mind?

∞ ∞ ∞

Aglas was glad to be back in the field again after pulling guard duty for so long. It was hard to be in the presence of someone who kept talking at you like Darren did, making you think about things you hadn't considered before. The field duty was much simpler. You got an order and you followed it. It had been a pretty quiet duty rotation until he had received this current tasking from Sharna. Her work assignments tended to be more unpredictable, uncovering a level of misdeeds that were not normally seen. There were also some false positives as her system learned to distinguish random behavior from suspicious behavior. When he was tasked, it was not a guarantee that a party would be guilty, but lately, there had been very few false positives. Oversite had been improving its accuracy on detection, largely due to Sharna's efforts.

Aglas and his team arrived at a Ministry of Education facility just as he received notice from the dispatcher to stand down until someone from the Ministry of Scientific Compliance could join them to provide proper strategic guidance. Apparently, religious practice had been observed and several students were implicated. If these were full adults, they would simply be arrested and given the opportunity for re-education if it was their first offence; execution if it were their second. Dealing with students not yet of legal age was often handled more creatively. The point was to teach them and change their ways if they could be salvaged. If they couldn't be then they would be remanded for organs or similar outcomes which may as well have been execution. This would not reflect well on whoever was in charge of this school, which was even more reason to have outside personnel administer this intervention.

After the on-site CET waited approximately thirty minutes, a vehicle pulled up suddenly in the blowing snow and wind. Emerging from it was a medium height female, likely in her mid-thirties. She wore the uniform of a Ministry of Scientific Compliance official, but Aglas did not recognize her. As she shifted her head around, she looked each member of his team in the eyes. When her eyes met Aglas', he nearly shuddered. Her gaze was penetrating and it sent shivers down his spine. Her stare was like looking into a dark abyss with nothing but your own fear looking back at you. This was not a person to cross.

"Good evening. My name is Ursula Vondier. Who is in charge here?"

"For the time being, I am," Aglas' section leader answered. "I am section leader Martin Stuart at your service."

"My orders are to assume operational command for this unit," she said. "This is not the first religion violation we have had at a school recently. Ever since that relocation from Xenon of students, we have had a lot more work to suppress faulty thinking. Even though the Xenon infection has been purged, we are still dealing with the fallout."

"What can we do to assist you ma'am?" the section leader asked.

"I have full evidence gathered of forty students who were actively practicing some religion about lilies," Ursula explained. "I plan to have them assembled and have them threatened until they recant. We will see how strong they are in following this myth. And even if they are strong, we will send a strong message to others watching about the consequence of making this poor choice!"

"Yes, ma'am. We have the names also and will begin assembling them," Martin stated.

Aglas received his directions from his section leader and began to round up the students in question. He wasn't sure what to expect when he gathered them, but they did not resist or honestly even look surprised they were being summoned. One named Cyrius was especially calm, politely asking his name and showing a high level of kindness as he worked to find everyone on his list. After several minutes, forty students were assembled and the remainder of the school had been asked to gather in the main auditorium. The school administrator looked especially nervous but was showing nothing but tacit compliance.

"Good evening," Ursula called out loudly, getting everyone's attention. "We have a very serious matter to discuss with all of you today, in hope that it never happens again. Our educational institutions are supposed to teach the unassailable truth that myth and religion are the enemy of science and the people. But I am highly disappointed to discover that lesson has not been learned well here."

Ursula nodded then watched as evidence of the practice of religion was played on the projected screen for everyone to see. It likely wasn't all the evidence, but it showed each accused student doing a religious act, clearly taking part in this banned activity. After about ten minutes of this playing, Ursula once again commanded the attention in the room.

"This is completely unacceptable! What do you have to say for yourselves?" she asked the forty students on stage with her.

Aglas looked at the students sharing the stage with him. He did not see fear in their eyes, he saw strength, resolve, and certainty of purpose. Where Ursula had cowed him with just her eyes, they looked her in the eye and did not waver. They ranged in ages, mixed pretty evenly between boys and girls. The youngest was probably around ten years old he decided with the oldest likely about seventeen.

"The Way of the Lily is for everyone who seeks it, even you," the boy named Cyrius answered. "We have come to know faith, belief in something greater than ourselves. Something that has filled the gaps in the so-called knowledge that is taught but not explored. The way of man fails, but the Way of the Lily brings hope."

"That is enough!" Ursula yelled, breaking the stone-faced façade she had portrayed up until then. "Is it not enough to be shown in violation of the law where you could plead for mercy? But instead you practically beg to be given the full extent of the law for this heinous offense. Is there any among you who will recant this misguided way?"

The students stood firm, none willing to stand forward to ask forgiveness for their transgressions while the audience watched in silence, transfixed by the scene playing out in front of them.

"Very well, we shall see the limits of your stupidity," Ursula threatened. "Anyone can be spared further humiliation and punishment if they will at any time but come to me and publicly disavow themselves from this irrational myth. But those who do not will suffer greatly and die."

Again, no one moved to change their stance, standing firmly together in solidarity. Ursula waited for nearly a minute in dramatic silence, seeing who would be the first to break ranks. But no one came forward.

"Ok, don't say you weren't warned," she stated. "Section Leader Stuart, please have your team remove all of the offenders' clothing. The privilege of clothing is only for those who follow the law."

Martin had a confused look on his face, but he directed his team to execute the order. Aglas was not particularly happy about this order but did as he was told. Humiliation was often a form of punishment effective in eliciting change. Aglas heard a few snickers from the audience but overall the atmosphere remained charged.

"Nobody willing to come forward yet?" Ursula asked. "Very well, don't say I didn't warn you. I saw a very nice pond driving in here which appeared to be frozen over. Section Leader Stuart, I want you to march these rebellious students out to that pond where they can stay until they either freeze to death or come back inside to warmth if they are just willing to put aside this silly religious farce."

Aglas didn't like the sound of this at all. It seemed wrong. What had these students really done that merited this outcome? But there was no outcry, no protest from their classmates who were not accused. It was more a stunned silence, a shock at witnessing something they did not fully understand.

Aglas followed the students outside, feeling embarrassed and ashamed at his role in this event. He was conflicted inside if this was right or not. He had been on countless extractions and punishments before for similar offenses but this time it felt different. These were children who only hoped for something more. They had only dared to believe in something that defied the allowed beliefs. He looked around, hoping to see similar reservations on any in his squad but he saw nothing but duty on their faces.

The children walked out to the ice-covered pond, visibly shivering in the wind and snow. Aglas looked at each of their faces as they shuffled by him. His focus went to Cyrius who had a far-off look in his eyes, looking like he saw something beyond himself which provided him contentment and peace.

"You have the first watch, Aglas," his section leader said, projecting his voice above the howling and biting wind. "If they recant, let them back inside, otherwise you have your orders."

Aglas provided a distracted nod, acknowledging he understood what his orders were. He wanted to turn away from the huddled mass of shivering children but could not. Their courage was searing an imprint into his mind that he could not shake. He wanted to offer them his warm coat to shield them from the elements but instead he just stood there transfixed on the look on Cyrius' face as he said words to encourage those around him to stand fast, keep the faith and stay true to the Lily. There was more than this life, there was something fantastic awaiting them beyond.

What seemed like an hour passed when Ursula and some attendants came out to taunt the freezing children some more.

"There is still time to change your ways," she called out. "Come inside. I have a warm place prepared for you and warm clothes. We will even draw a warm bath if you just put away your misguided ways."

A small boy could take the cold no longer and stumbled his way toward Ursula. The rest of the children did not condemn his action but still tried to encourage him to stay. He was welcomed by Ursula and given warm clothes to wear before being carried inside. Aglas looked on in sadness that they had not all stayed true and as more hours passed, he saw little movement on the pond, save for a faint glow that seemed to be surrounding those on the ice.

And then he understood. He understood Darren's words to him and the resolute actions of the thirty-nine who remained – whose lives were flickering out. And for a reason that he couldn't explain but knew to be right, Aglas shed his clothing and joined the thirty-nine on the ice until he too passed from the ranks of the living.

CHAPTER 9

*X*avier felt frustration well up after reading the report in front of him. Thirty-nine promising students dead, not to mention one of his CET agents. And for what? That was the question. This lily religion continued to be a thorn in his plans. Something meaningful was going to need to change to confront this growing threat. There was clearly a mistake made relocating detained Xenon students to the many schools across the sectors. They should have just terminated them or kept them in isolation together. The belief that they would be rehabilitated with the right influences of other students was in hindsight dreadfully wrong. Instead they were the infection that corrupted the strong influence and control the government had amongst the youth population.

Anywhere a native Xenon student had been sent seemed to have some residual issues. Not all were related to widespread religious practice, but many were questioning what they were being taught, even to the point of open rebellion. And the rebellion was contagious as evidenced by this latest travesty. Xavier had approved strong handed tactics to force compliance, but at least with these thirty-nine students, they had called the Ministry's bluff and chose death for their beliefs, which would probably only add mystique to the lies they were advocating.

The one bright spot through all of this was at least Sharna's sensor array had worked to expose the students' religious practice. He was justified in getting Gabriel to help her and once the sensor array was up in Xenon, it would open up so many more options to subduing this rebellious sector.

Living under the terms of the peace agreement meant he couldn't just order arrest for those practicing religions in Xenon. But he could build a database of its adherents so when the ministry was later ready to strike back at Xenon, they would have the intelligence needed to do so effectively. Based on Gabriel's comments to Sharna, it sounded like not everyone had the ability to enter this meditative state that triggered the transport tube. He should have been surprised that Gabriel could do it, but the more he reflected about it, he wasn't.

It was a shame that Gabriel would need to be sent back to Xenon soon. Xavier was tempted to recall him back to the capital. Gabriel already had more in-depth knowledge of this religion and the Kayden organization than anyone before him had gathered. The question was if his future value to the Ministry by staying in place was worth more than his advice would be if he were back advising operations. Xavier's musings were interrupted by his assistant.

"Minister, your next appointment is here."

"Send them in," Xavier answered.

Xavier watched as Quintin entered with his team in tow. They had been analyzing all the interview material in the time since Gabriel was sent off to the research lab and were ready to review their conclusions.

"Good to see you Quintin," Xavier offered, moving to greet each visitor. "Nice to see you two again, Ursula and Stefan."

"Good morning, Minister," they said in unison.

"That was some pretty nasty business at the school," Xavier said. "I just finished reading the report of that. You were the Ministry of Scientific Compliance official on call for that weren't you, Ursula?"

"Yes, I was Minister," she answered. "If they were willing to stand in the cold and freeze to death, I sincerely doubt they could have been salvaged any other way. I know it is unfortunate to lose so many promising students. We believe we have traced this back to a Xenon student who spent a few months at this school during the Xenon rebellion."

"In hindsight, we should not have tried to integrate the students so quickly into our general student population," Xavier said with resignation. "There was so much fear of a mass rescue attempt, the decision was made to spread out the students to increase leverage and security. Now we have to deal with the long-term consequences."

Xavier noticed a pained expression on Stefan's face, one he was clearly trying to suppress.

"Did any of you know the agent to froze himself to death?" Xavier asked.

Quintin and Stefan nodded, before Stefan answered, "I served on a unit with him a few years back, before our captain was killed in action. I always found him to be very reliable. It was a shock that he did what he did. There has been a lot of chatter about it in our CET communication network."

Xavier made a mental note on this comment by Stefan. The agent who froze had been assigned to Sharna's response team and had a duty assignment to guard the captured Kayden agent who was openly expressing religion beliefs. While steps had been taken to limit who could come in contact with him, this person apparently had been corrupted. And now he had risked the purity of thought in the CET community. It was like an unending battle with new tentacles being created every day.

"Even more reason to stay diligent to the ways and teachings of science," Xavier replied. "This isn't why I had this meeting scheduled though. I want to hear your conclusions on the debriefing session with Gabriel. His time window is nearly up before we need to return him to Xenon or pull him from the field."

"I am not sure I trust him anymore," Quintin blurted out.

"That is a pretty strong statement," Xavier answered. "Why do you say that?"

"It is hard to explain, Minister," Quintin replied nervously. "His time in Xenon seems to have changed him and there is so much that he didn't share when he was in the field that would have been greatly helpful to us at the time. The question is, why he didn't tell us? And I don't think it is because he didn't think it was important."

"You have experience in this, Ursula," Xavier stated. "What is your assessment? Is he to be trusted?"

"I don't trust anyone, Minister," she answered with an intensity in her demeanor that gave Xavier pause. "The question is if he is still on our side or if he has been turned and is a double agent working for Kayden. And my analysis on this is inconclusive. The time I require was cut short, and methods I am allowed to use have been severely limited. There are inconsistencies in what he has told us and I do not yet know why. Frankly, I need more time."

"Time is something we are quickly running out of," Xavier answered. "Stefan, you have been quiet. What do you think?"

"I have never found Gabriel to be untrustworthy, Minister," Stefan replied carefully. "When I served in the field with him, he showed courage and made sure our team had everything we needed to succeed. And I don't think it was just because our captain was his fiancé. I think I trust him."

Xavier paused a few moments to take in the advice given to him. "All of your feedback is taken under advisement," he said. "I want Gabriel returned to the field per our original plan. If you have any suspicions of his actions, please note it in your reports and I will evaluate it accordingly. I have served undercover, where the rest of you have not. Things are more complicated than an outside observer would understand. But it is also possible to be tempted to flip to the side you are trying to infiltrate as you begin to develop relationships with the people. It does bear watching."

∞ ∞ ∞

Stefan walked out of the meeting with Xavier with a lot swirling through his mind. Aglas' actions were still bothering him a great deal. What could prompt someone to willingly surrender their life to freeze to death on a frozen pond? He felt an emptiness at the loss of his former unit-mate and friend. It may get him in trouble later, but he had reviewed the footage of the interrogation before the students were given justice. One student had bravely proclaimed something about the lily and he had a certainty and a peace in his eyes that was hard to explain, and it was shared with all those who were with him. "The way of man fails, but the Way of the Lily brings hope." That was what the student had said.

∞ ∞ ∞

Aaliyah stared at the lily in front of her. Sharna made good on her promise and several lilies were delivered to the lab for study. Gabriel explained that he was taught to use a lily to be able to enter the meditative state. Sharna wanted to see if she could replicate that in another test subject and told Aaliyah to try to accomplish it. After Gabriel would do his daily meditation session to support Sharna's experiments, the remainder of his time was spent instructing Aaliyah in the teachings of the Way of the Lily, with the goal to be able to equip Aaliyah to be able to replicate what Gabriel did.

She was secretly ecstatic about this arrangement as it gave her the opportunity to learn more quickly due to having a knowledgeable instructor. Gabriel even seemed to be enjoying their time together teaching her what he knew. Aaliyah had been expecting teaching on the techniques of focus, but instead all Gabriel spent time on was the tenants of the Lily. These beliefs and precepts focused on caring for others and adhering to a moral code that differed from what she had been taught while growing up. Gabriel hinted that she would need to reach a place in her mind to be able to embrace these tenants if she wanted to do the Lily meditation. And surprisingly, she was on that track. Did she have some doubts? Sure. But at the same time, they spoke truth to her in a way she could not shake and gave her a sense of peace.

Aaliyah took in the essence of the lily she was looking at. She absorbed its beauty, its features. She lost herself in its design.

At first, Aaliyah thought she had fallen asleep. It was like she was dreaming, but there was no color present in a field full of lilies. She looked around, seeing row after row of lilies as far as her eyes could see. She felt a compulsion to walk and began moving in a direction that seemed random. She felt in a daze, unsure what she was experiencing.

"I have been expecting you," a voice called out behind her.

Aaliyah turned to see a woman with bright red hair, whole presence stood out in a colorful array against the backdrop of hues of gray. "Where am I?" she asked.

"Where do you want to be?" the lady answered.

"I don't know," Aaliyah answered tentatively. "I was trying to meditate on the lily before this happened. I am trying to reach the meditative state Gabriel told me about."

"You have done well to reach this place without a guide," the woman stated. "I would have tried to guide you but I did not want to put you in danger needlessly. But you have arrived unaided."

"Who are you?" Aaliyah asked. "And again, where am I?"

"You can call me Raelynn," the lady answered. "I seek out those who have the gift of dreams to guide them safely on their journey. You have entered the dream state through your meditation on the Lily."

"Dream state?" Aaliyah asked. "Gabriel called it something different."

"Gabriel likes to understate things," Raelynn answered with a knowing smile. "The dream state is a place that those who pursue the Lily can sometimes enter. Not all those who follow the Lily are able, but you appear to have been blessed with this gift. We will test you over time for what you are able to do here, but many find they can impact the world around them by their actions in this place."

"Things like moving from one place to another?" Aaliyah asked.

"Yes, some have the gift of translocation," Raelynn answered. "Others can do more. We will figure out a way for you to learn more about what you are able to do on later visits. But I need to strongly warn you, great harm can be done by you in this state to either yourself or others. Please do not try anything without a capable teacher showing you how while you are here."

"I am not sure what I can possibly do here," Aaliyah answered, "but I will do as you say."

"I am glad," Raelynn answered. "I will listen for you and try to come when you visit until I can find you a teacher to take over your instruction."

"Thank you, I think," Aaliyah answered. "But how do I get back? Do I just wake up?"

"That will be our first lesson," Raelynn replied. "Do you remember the place you were at when you were focusing on the lily?"

"Yes, I know it pretty well," Aaliyah answered.

"Remember the room you were in and try to visualize yourself there," Raelynn instructed.

Aaliyah brought to mind the details of the lab she was in when she started the focus on the lily. Then she visualized herself standing in the middle of the lab. Surprisingly, she materialized in the lab, noticing that it lacked the usual color and was a bit of a haze muting the resolution of her view. Momentarily she found Raelynn standing beside her.

"Well done," Raelynn answered. "You did well getting here so quickly."

Aaliyah looked around and was surprised to see Sharna frantically checking instrumentation and running tests on her while she saw herself tuned out to the world with her eyes closed sitting without moving.

"Is this what is really happening?" Aaliyah asked.

"Yes," Raelynn answered. "You are watching what is happening in real time while you are in the dream state. This is one of the common things someone who is in the dream state can do."

"Wow, that is amazing!" Aaliyah exclaimed. "Was Gabriel doing this when he was in the – what did you call it, dream state?"

"He may have, but he probably spent the time in other ways," Raelynn patiently explained. "There are other things that can be done when dreaming also. We will learn about those in future visits. I am wanting to take things slow at first because sometimes dreaming is very draining to your body and we don't know yet what you are capable of."

"I understand," Aaliyah said. "Sharna is going to be very excited to hear about all of this I am sure."

Raelynn developed a concerned expression on her face suddenly at Aaliyah's last statement which was not missed by Aaliyah. Comprehension dawned suddenly on her face at the implications of sharing what she had experienced.

"It won't go well for me if I explain all of this, will it?" Aaliyah asked.

Raelynn's face quickly transformed to one of empathy. "You would most likely be dismissed as a lunatic. That would be the best outcome. What if she did believe you?"

"I would become the experiment, wouldn't I?" Aaliyah answered.

Raelynn nodded sadly. "Someday, I hope that those who practice the Lily can do so without fear of harm or persecution. But that day is not now. My advice is to tell her about seeing the field of lilies and the sense of peace or calm it gave you. The special skills you learned about and ones you may develop in the future, I would not share too easily. That knowledge can only be received by one who has been prepared. Share the Way of the Lily with Sharna. If she is able to come to the dream state, she may then be equipped to understand."

"I will do as you say, but Sharna doesn't miss much. She will know if I hold things back," Aaliyah answered.

"Do your best," Raelynn replied. "Now you should return. Sufficient time has passed. Envision yourself within the body you see in front of you, then awake. Do this and you will have returned. Be safe and I will listen for you should you return to the dream state again."

Aaliyah nodded in understanding, then following the instructions that Raelynn had given her, awoke. She saw the vibrancy of color return to her vision and saw Sharna scrambling around the lab excitedly. Aaliyah moved to stand up but then felt a pull on her body. She had no strength. She wanted to lie on the floor and go to sleep, but first she was sure Sharna would have many questions for her to answer.

∞ ∞ ∞

Sharna was thrilled. Aaliyah had done it! She had been able to replicate the meditative state that Gabriel was demonstrating daily. She had been dreading when he was no longer available to help her in her research, but now she had someone who would not have to leave – who could also replicate the signal.

She assigned Aaliyah to try to learn the method to replicate this signal, but honestly did not expect her to achieve it – for sure not this soon. Sharna setup the sensor array to detect the targeted brainwave pattern, but did not have the rest of her instrumentation ready to go when the brainwave was first detected. It was a near thing, but she was able to confirm that the power amplifier test got the same result as Gabriel did. There was no discernable difference between Gabriel and Aaliyah's brain signals, except that Aaliyah's lasted much longer than any she had measured on Gabriel.

"Did it work?" Aaliyah asked weakly, interrupting Sharna's thoughts.

"Initial data suggests that it did," Sharna said absently. "Do you think you could do it again?"

"Gabriel said something about only being able to do it once a day," Aaliyah answered. "I think I understand why he said that. I feel like my body has been completely beat up. I can barely move."

Sharna quickly checked her workstation instrumentation. "Your heartrate has slowed way down. Not life threatening, but somewhat concerning."

"I think I may be able to do it again, but not until I feel a bit stronger," Aaliyah answered. "Would you mind at all if I rested for a few minutes?"

"If you must," Sharna said. "Let me know when you are ready to try again. I have some data to evaluate."

Aaliyah nodded gratefully and stumbled to the furniture in the corner of the lab.

Sharna had many questions and was frustrated that her test subject was not able to answer them yet. Someone could be trained to replicate the brainwave pattern. If she could just figure out how to harness the power generated, there would be so many applications that could be developed. Her research would go so much faster if she had more reliable test subjects. It occurred to her suddenly that if she learned how to replicate this state herself, she wouldn't have to rely on others who got easily tired.

CHAPTER 10

*G*abriel stared off in a contemplative daze, patiently waiting for Sharna to finish whatever she was doing with the instrumentation in front of her. It was hard to believe that his time away from Xenon was coming to an end. He thought he had escaped the experience largely unscathed, but until he was back in Xenon, a nagging feeling of dread permeated his being. It warned him to be vigilant, lest he make a mistake to jeopardize his freedom.

Gabriel was surprised how much he missed his home in Xenon. Yes, home. It was strange to think of it in that way after only living there a short time. He enjoyed his mornings at the local farm in Morfort, but without the community and relationships he had built in Deerbarrow, it did not compare. His life was fuller with more meaning now, a concept he would not have understood a couple years before. He was ready to return. Not much longer, just another day or two until he could head back.

"I think I have gotten all I needed to from your last meditation," Sharna stated. "Your participation in this research has been adequate to my research needs."

"I am glad I could be of help," Gabriel answered dryly. "You promised me a portable sensor I could use to detect the brainwave pattern?"

"I am not sure why you want it, but yes I have made one for you," Sharna answered. "I will have the sensor array active in Xenon within a few days which will reduce its value."

"Thank you," Gabriel replied. "You did say the array may not detect fully deep underground. It will still be very helpful to my mission there."

"This is just an isolated sensor," Sharna explained. "I didn't integrate it on the Oversite network. If that is required, it will take more time but I have other things I would rather work on than that. Press this button and if the light turns green, it detects the pattern."

"I prefer it isn't on the network," Gabriel stated noticing that Sharna was way more talkative and accommodating than he could remember her being. "That feature could compromise my security."

"Then you have what you need then." Sharna stated before pausing a few moments. "When you are in the meditation state, what is it like?"

Gabriel was somewhat taken back by this type of question from her. "It is hard to explain but it is very peaceful. It is like you are one with the world around you. There are no doubts in your purpose."

"Aaliyah gets really tired when she has succeeded," Sharna said. "Does it cause you pain or make you tired?"

"Pain, no," Gabriel answered. "As for feeling tired, the longer I am in that state, the more tired I become, but I don't seem to be impacted as much as Aaliyah has been. It probably depends on the person."

"I know you have spent a lot of time teaching Aaliyah," Sharna continued with some hesitation. "Do you think I could be capable of doing it if I worked on it?"

"I have been told that not everyone is able to," Gabriel explained. "But I do know that until you can get yourself fully centered, you will never be able to enter it on your own. You can stare at a lily all day long and you probably won't succeed. Aaliyah had some success mostly by immersing herself in the teaching of those Lily books. Once she had prepared herself, she succeeded. If you try to shortcut the path without doing that, it will make it much more difficult to succeed."

"I have read some of what is in those books," Sharna replied. "It covers a lot of things that I don't see the logic in."

"Then you will have to let go of your preconceptions and bias against what it teaches," Gabriel explained. "Until you can show some level of belief, you will likely fail if you try. I am sorry, I wish there was an easier answer I could give you. You may be able to discover a different way, but that is all I know on this."

Sharna nodded slightly then went into one of her periods of quiet contemplation. She would sometimes do this for several minutes before randomly continuing the dialogue where she had left off. It was clear she was struggling to grasp what Gabriel was telling her. He was asking her to in her mind abandon reason and accept something on faith. She clearly had the evidence there was something real, but the path to achieve it defied her understanding of the world.

"You are free to go," Sharna said. "I have filtered you in Oversite based on Xavier's request, so any meditation you do will not trigger an automated response. I don't know how they are going to use this information, but you will not show up in the logs."

"If you are permitted to, you should do the same for Aaliyah," Gabriel requested. "It would help her to be able to practice whenever she wants to without having agents coming for her. And yourself, if you plan on trying to learn."

"That is obvious and I did that long ago," Sharna stated, now turning herself away from Gabriel refocusing herself back into her work.

Seeing no more attempt to be talked to, Gabriel made a slight bow and turned out the door while holding his new sensor. He was one step closer to going home.

∞ ∞ ∞

Stefan stood outside of the secured perimeter of Sharna's lab. Waiting here in the dimly lit corridor gave Stefan time to contemplate recent events that were weighing on his mind. Aglas' death was something that he was struggling to grasp. It made no sense. Why would Aglas throw away a promising career and a job that would be the envy of many in some sort of religious protest?

"Hi, Stefan," Gabriel stated with a small bit of surprise. "I didn't expect to see you until my next appointment."

"Since you are done here, I am going to resume escorting you until you get back to the capital," Stefan explained. "I have taken the liberty of sending your issued vehicle back to its home base."

"Ok," Gabriel answered with a slightly perplexed look on his face. "Shall we go?"

"Right this way," Stefan stated, leading Gabriel to the secure vehicle that had been used previously. Gabriel put his belongings and handheld in the secure holding compartment and joined Stefan in the front seat.

Stefan pushed some buttons to initiate the secure anti-surveillance mode then relaxed visibly. "We are secure now," he announced finally.

"Has anything changed in the plan?" Gabriel asked. "I still get to rejoin the delegation from Xenon this evening, don't I?"

"As far as I know," Stefan replied. "I have not heard about anything that is changing. Xavier said to send you back. Not everyone wanted to do that, but Xavier is in charge so he got what he wanted."

This should have been concerning news for Gabriel. If he was detained in Preath it probably would mean he was suspected as disloyal. "Why are you telling me this?" Gabriel asked finally after a few moments to process the revelation.

"I thought it was only fair that you knew," Stefan said. "You have been through a lot and it doesn't seem right to treat you that way. Quintin suspects you are not what you claim to be, so you should be careful with him going forward."

"He shouldn't have reason to think that," Gabriel replied carefully, "but thank you for the warning."

Stefan acknowledged Gabriel's comments. "Do you remember Aglas?" Stefan asked after a brief period of conflict trying to decide whether or not to start the conversation down this potentially dangerous path. "He served on Emily's team with me."

"Of course, I remember him," Gabriel answered. "How has he been doing?"

"He recently died," Stefan answered. "He was stationed in the same building you have been going to every day so I wondered if you had spoken with him."

"I am very sorry to learn that," Gabriel replied. "I wish I had known he was nearby. I would have sought him out. How did he die?"

"I would call it suicide, but I think it was more complicated than that," Stefan explained. "Some kids in a school near here were caught following some sort of lily religion in a call Aglas' team responded. Ursula got called to represent the Ministry and decided to force them to recant, to the point of having them freeze to death if they didn't. I guess he decided to join them in their protest and died the same way. I don't know what could make someone choose to do that."

"What do you think?" Gabriel asked in a tentative manner.

"I think this lily thing came from Xenon," Stefan answered. "You have been there a long time and probably know a lot about the subject. What is the appeal?"

"Have you ever believed in something so much that you were willing to sacrifice your life to protect it?" Gabriel asked.

"I have felt that way about some of the units I was in over the years," Stefan answered. "We had to look out for each other or it risked the whole team."

Gabriel gave Stefan a penetrating look, as if challenging him to consider the last thing he said. After a few moments Gabriel continued, "Maybe their beliefs were worth dying for. The Way of the Lily is not the dismissed ravings of a lunatic as the government would wish you to believe. You should seek to find out more and maybe you will understand."

Stefan slightly inclined his head in acknowledgement then sat in silence for the remainder of the drive. He had much to think about. Gabriel said more than he had to, but had not fully answered his curiosity. The words of the boy in the school continued to echo in Stefan's head. "We have come to know faith, belief in something greater than ourselves." Stefan reflected on these words, feeling an emptiness in himself that was begging to be filled with something more.

∞ ∞ ∞

"And that concludes my presentation on the farm I visited in Morfort. Are there any questions?" Gabriel asked the conference attendees, having just completed his planned remarks. He didn't think he had said anything monumental, but it would at least give credence that he had been there doing work to explain his long absence.

No questions came forward, likely since the hour was late and Gabriel was the last presenter scheduled on the agenda. Seeing no questions, Gabriel exited the platform to polite applause as the attendees began to disperse for the night. Everyone was going home tomorrow and wanted to say their goodbyes and prepare for the shuttle back to Xenon.

"I knew I was boring, but didn't think I was that bad!" Gabriel said to Tom as he walked up to greet him.

"You have no idea how bad you were!" Tom said with a smile on his face. "You have missed hours and hours of presentations basically saying the same thing while you have been galivanting up there in Morfort doing your own thing. Really, everyone just wants to go home. It has been a very long two months."

"Thanks, I think," Gabriel said sheepishly. "I almost gave the presentation I promised before I left on how to get your neighbor to do work for you, but didn't think the Ministry of Nutrition would have a sense of humor for me doing that."

"Maybe not, but you would have got a lot more cheering than you did if you had done that instead," Tom said. "I don't think I could handle another update on weed management for anything. Thankfully you didn't spend time talking about that today. I think you would have been booed off the stage if you had. No, I think you got off pretty good. You actually got applause. That stopped happening about a week ago!"

"So, what is the plan for tonight?" Gabriel asked. "Sounds like our shuttle doesn't leave until morning."

"I have a final night of going out on the town," Tom said cryptically in a low whisper. "I would invite you along but I think it is safer for you if you go to the farewell party instead."

Gabriel had a confused expression on his face but decided to save his questions for later when less surveillance risks were present. "I'll see you later on then," Gabriel decided to reply. Tom and some of others had come with plans to make other uses of their time in the capital. This was probably what he was referring to, but with Tom you could never be sure.

Gabriel walked around and greeted those he knew and hadn't seen since before he left for Morfort. Someone he didn't recognize attired as an official from the Ministry of Nutrition came up to him.

"I really enjoyed your speech," the official offered. "It is remarkable the amount of knowledge you have gained on farming in the short time you have been doing it. It gives me hope that some of our new satellite farms outside of Xenon can have a similar chance of success."

"I still have to ask a lot of questions of others," Gabriel demurred. "There is so much I don't know and understand."

"I think you are just being modest of your abilities," the official continued. "Since you took over the farm up near Deerbarrow, the output levels have increased by twenty-five percent. Help or not, that is impressive. I am hopeful your advice will help the farm in Morfort increase its yields in a similar way."

"They seemed very open to my suggestions," Gabriel replied carefully, not sure where this conversation was headed. He hadn't mentioned any statistics on his farm, so he was being targeted for some purpose he didn't understand fully.

"Forgive my bluntness, but I have been reading up on your history," the official stated. "You had a very promising career going in the Ministry of Scientific Compliance until that scandal hit you. This must feel like a very disappointing step down for you. Don't get me wrong, you have embraced your new reality and seem to be thriving, but you can't tell me this is how you want to spend your future after tasting the life of a ministry official like you have."

"It has been a change that has taken some getting used to," Gabriel said carefully, afraid of where this conversation was headed.

"I figured as much," the official said with a triumphant tone in his voice. "I could use someone with your skills. Handle this correctly, and you could make your way back to the capital again as a ranking official in the Ministry of Nutrition. We need people who better understand what it takes to make the food."

"But with my record, I am not sure how I could ever resume my career path effectively. That would always be hanging over my head," Gabriel answered.

"That is but a minor difficulty," the official said with a mysterious smile. "Do you think you are the only person who has ever tried to get more energy quota than they are entitled to? You just need the right sponsor and they can make these kinds of difficulties disappear from your record like they never existed."

"That would definitely change the trajectory of my life if that were to occur," Gabriel answered carefully leading him on but not committing to a course of action. "But I assume that doesn't just happen out of the blue. What would I have to do?"

"A very astute question," the official said with a suppressed sort of glee. "For now, I still need you running the farm in Deerbarrow. But I will send an inspector through periodically to check up on your farm.

If you are very helpful to what he asks you, it will earn my favor. And in time, I can make your dreams of returning to the capital come true!"

Gabriel considered the offer. To maintain his cover, he needed to not be disinterested. However, this was getting way more complicated than he wanted to deal with. To be a double agent was bad enough, now he was being asked to add another tentacle to that by informing to a separate ministry who had no idea of his true mission in Deerbarrow.

"Send your inspector," Gabriel replied. "I will think on your proposal and give him my decision. What you offer does have great appeal, but I am worried about what happens if I am labeled as an informer. It has been quite unusual that I was admitted into the trust of the locals. Most visitors who move there are not afforded this courtesy."

"My people are extremely careful," the official replied. "You will not be so labeled. If someone comes to visit you, they will use my name and your codename. Anyone else, it is not safe to discuss with."

"Ok, I will think on it," Gabriel offered with visible uncertainty in his voice. "What are the names I should expect?"

"Khalid is my name and your code will be called root digger," Khalid answered then switched his expression to something colder and calculating. "You will not regret gaining my favor, but I do not recommend the alternative."

Gabriel watched warily while Khalid walked around to greet other guests before disappearing from view. One more thing to keep track of in an evolving maze of confusion.

CHAPTER 11

Stefan walked into a secure meeting room back in the familiar confines of the Scientific Compliance headquarters. Quintin and Ursula were present, working diligently on some sort of analysis.

"Well, that was disappointing," Quintin stated looking up from his work. "I just know that something isn't right with Gabriel. And it is more than him holding things back to protect his safety. And you Stefan didn't back me up when I tried to get Xavier to do something about it."

"I am sorry, Quintin," Stefan answered defensively. "I said what I thought. He is the Minister. I am not going to lie to him."

"No one is asking you to lie, Stefan," Quintin said with frustration in his voice. "But you need to learn how to better navigate the political waters. This isn't like a field assignment with your old unit."

"What now?" Stefan asked. "You going to send me back to the field since I apparently screwed up?"

"Don't be ridiculous," Quintin answered now acting somewhat mollified by Stefan's contrition. "But you are going to make this up to me. What do you know about the place he went to instead of the planned interrogation with us? Trying to get information about what goes on inside that building has proven difficult at best."

"I don't know a lot, but I am not sure I should say anything about what I know," Stefan answered. "It is very restricted information."

"I can assure you, this is very germane to our mission here," Quintin said with a forceful tone. "You heard the Minister – he wants inconsistencies noted in reports if we see them. That means we need to know more about what he has been up to do our job."

"But if he wanted us to know, wouldn't the Minister –," Stefan stated before being cutoff.

"The Minister has a lot on his mind," Quintin rejoined. "The Minster expects his officials to take initiative and prevent problems from reaching him, because they are taken care of. And if you are incapable of understanding that distinction, maybe this role isn't a good fit for you after all.

Stefan felt anger growing inside of him. All Quintin had to do was explain why he needed to know with respect and he would have already told him what he knew. But maybe Quintin was right. Maybe he did need to learn how to navigate the political waters by thinking one thing and saying another. "I can do this job, sir," Stefan finally said formally. "What do you want to know?"

"Anything," Quintin replied. "Like what goes on inside there and what was he doing?"

"I don't know anything for sure," Stefan clarified, "but I know there is a covert extraction team stationed there and they have been doing something with some researcher there. It has something to do with improving Oversite surveillance is mainly what I know."

"So, what does that have to do with Gabriel?" Ursula asked with penetrating eyes, interjecting herself into this conversation for the first time.

"I don't have any idea on that," Stefan stammered. "But I heard through my network that they had caught someone from Xenon who was up to no good in Morfort and they were having to do guard duty for him."

"That seems like a waste for a CET," Quintin stated. "Guard duty is far below their paygrade."

"I thought so too," Stefan answered. "I guess he is some sort of religious fanatic that they caught and the researcher wanted him to be able to say whatever he wanted to, without being sedated. Since the CET had been the ones that captured him, they didn't want anyone else exposed to his religious nonsense. He kept talking about some sort of lily."

"I think I know about this person," Quintin answered with a partial realization dawning on his face. "He was caught with some sort of transport technology we think may have been used when all of the people in Xenon disappeared. The researcher was working on a way to figure it out and possibly detect when the technology is triggered with some sort of brainwave pattern. Xavier sent me a report on it to read a couple months ago."

"One of those idiot kids at the school said something about a lily also," Ursula offered. "Could be related somehow."

"You know anything else?" Quintin asked Stefan. "Don't hold back."

"That is all I know of," Stefan confirmed. "Now what?"

"I think it is obvious," Ursula said. "We need to learn more about this lily religion. Could be related, could not be, but until we understand what it is about, we won't find out. For all we know, Gabriel is tied into this somehow and Xavier knows about it and didn't want us to."

"Stefan," Quintin ordered, "that will be your next assignment. "Get me a synopsis on this lily religion. I know there has been some literature captured in the last few months. I would like a summary of what you learned first thing tomorrow. I will see you are given access to the restricted archives on this immediately."

Stefan nodded his head in assent and walked to the work station he had been using. At some level he was grateful for this assignment if he could force himself to get over the way that Quintin had treated him. He would now have a sanctioned reason to learn more about the lily topic that had been eating at him since he had heard about Aglas – not to mention since his conversation with Gabriel when he was asked if there was anything he believed in that was worth dying for. Seeing that Quintin had followed through with his system access, he began to research what this lily religion was all about.

Several hours later, Stefan boiled with internal anger. It was like he was seeing the world through a whole new lens and he didn't like what he saw, especially the part his life had been playing in it. He had been part of a mass injustice, perpetrated against a people who just wanted to believe something different. He read the booklet that had been captured. It was simple, but it spoke of doing right by others and taking care of others who were not strong enough to take care of themselves. How could this thinking cause lasting harm to society? Wouldn't society be a better place if people treated each other this way. And how did the government treat those who wanted to believe this way? The answer was it usually ended up killing them. And the worst of it was, he had helped them do it.

He should have asked questions about the why of what he was doing, but he hadn't. He was given orders and he followed them, not realizing what harm – no that wasn't the right word, what evil he had been participating in. Aglas must have saw the wrong in killing these kids and protested with his life.

And now, Stefan was faced with a choice. Was he going to stand passively watching, ultimately helping the persecution of those who wanted to do good? Or was he willing to make a statement similar to what Aglas did? He should feel courage and clear purpose in this situation, but the answer was still not that clear to him. What would do the most good?

It was frowned on, but Stefan thought best when he could write his thoughts down using a pen and paper. Sure, he could use the other systems, but today was a time where he needed to collect his thoughts. He was alone, with the rest of the team having gone home long ago. Stefan reached into his bag and pulled his notepad he saved for special occasions and began to write. And the words poured out from him onto the paper. And when he finished, he copied it several more times on different pieces of paper. He needed to share it with others.

Seeing

I am a simple-minded man. I trusted what the ministries told me and strove to embrace the ways of science and tried to ensure those around me did the same. I have learned though that in doing this, I espoused intolerance and misguided hatred for those who see the world through a different lens. The ministries taught me to hate those who believe this way, and encouraged me to persecute them, to bring them harm.

But in doing this, I have discarded my humanity, having lost sight of what is right and what is just.

I had a friend whose name was Aglas. He helped catch forty students in Morfort who decided they wanted to learn about caring for others, believing in something bigger than themselves, and acting selflessly. You read these traits and may say, what is wrong with this? The answer is that they were following a religion that teaches these things. A religion the government deemed vile and punishable by death. These kids were marched out on a frozen pond with the choice of freezing to death or renouncing these beliefs. My friend saw the injustice in this and decided he would rather die with them than oversee their murder. Many lives wasted who only wanted to make the world a better place.

I don't know if I believe in the religion that the kids did on the lily. But I do know that they should not have been viciously killed for wanting to learn about ways to do good for those around them. But they will not be the last. We will kill in the name of science and as long as we are not the target of their aim, it won't take our notice. We have our orders and will do as we are told. Unless we open our eyes to the reality around us and realize how wrong we have been. My eyes are now open.

∞ ∞ ∞

Clearing customs in Northfalcon should not have been this difficult, Gabriel considered. They were returning from a government sanctioned conference and had all their paperwork in order. But after two hours of questioning, he and Tom had finally been cleared to return home.

"Looks like we just missed the transport to Deerbarrow," Tom said with frustration. "It is like they went slower on purpose when they realized we had a connection that was about to leave."

"Are you really surprised?" Gabriel replied.

"Not really," Tom answered. "You would think after all we were put through, they could at least have someone to take us back to our homes,"

"They got what they needed out of us," Gabriel replied with a forced smile. "Now they are back to treating us like second class citizens."

"It looks like the next shuttle to Deerbarrow comes in three days," Tom stated after consulting with his handheld. "If it is even on time. Half the time those shuttles don't even come. We can walk, I guess."

"Walking is probably quicker if we push it, not to mention way cheaper energy credit wise," Gabriel offered. "But I am wishing I didn't pack as much stuff to carry."

"You got that right." Tom muttered. "I guess I am up for walking. My wife is going to be disappointed. She was expecting me to be back tonight."

Gabriel and Tom walked in silence for some time before finally speaking.

"Do you regret going to the capital?"

"It was an experience I don't think I will ever forget," Tom answered after considering the question for a few minutes. "The seeds I planted there, if they grow, will make it worth it. There are a lot more people than you would ever believe hungry for something different than they have been fed."

"When it is safe later on, I would like to learn about what you did in your free time," Gabriel said carefully. "It sounds like it was very fruitful."

"If you want to know, you know how to find out," Tom said with a twinkle in his eye eluding to Gabriel's ability to look back through the past while he was dreaming.

"That may not be as easy as it was before," Gabriel answered cryptically. "I will explain that later, but I recommend not doing anything along those lines until after we have had a better chance to talk about it. You wouldn't believe the advances in surveillance technology I saw while I was there."

"Well, at least something is advancing forward in our world," Tom said with a bit of sarcasm in his voice.

"I need to find Alaine and get her perspective on some things," Gabriel said while wondering how he would best be able to contact her. He was pretty sure she had returned to her home in the mountains.

"You suggesting getting the team back together?" Tom asked with a touch of excitement growing in his voice.

"You have already been away from your family for two months," Gabriel admonished. "Don't tell me you are wanting to run away from them already?"

"No, I am not wanting to do that," Tom explained. "I just think it would be great to see everyone again. It has been a while since we all got together.   Maybe we could get them to come visit us in Deerbarrow?"

"Now that is a good idea," Gabriel replied. "Just need a good reason to cover for their visit."

"You think they would be interested in farming for a while?" Tom asked. "You are probably short of labor you need for this year, aren't you?"

"Let me see if there is interest and I will post a job requisition," Gabriel offered. "There will be some red tape, but if she is willing, I think I can make it happen."

∞ ∞ ∞

Aaliyah knew Sharna was frustrated with her. Compared to Gabriel, she couldn't do the lily meditation on demand. She usually was able to make one happen per day, but it wasn't like she could fully control how long it would take her to get there. On average it would take her at least an hour of trying to enter this state, and one day she tried all day before finally succeeding. And the more she could feel the pressure from Sharna to deliver, it seemed like the longer it took.

Raelynn explained it was called the dream state but wasn't always there to continue teaching her. Raelynn told her she needed training in person to better be equipped to enter the dream state more quickly. That would be problematic at best in her current situation. She wasn't complaining though. The new experience was more than she ever could have expected and was filling a void in her she didn't know she had.

"You ready to try again?" Sharna asked.

"I am," Aaliyah answered. "I am hoping I will get to the state faster this time. I don't know how Gabriel was able to do it so quickly. I am sorry I keep making you wait."

"It is a necessary inconvenience," Sharna replied. "I plan to learn soon. If you are a capable student, I will show you then how to enter faster."

"I will look forward to that instruction," Aaliyah said while working very hard to suppress a smile at Sharna's comment. Getting into the dream state wasn't a scientific formula where you have to just follow some steps correctly and you achieved it. It was a mindset, the starting of a belief you needed to have. Sharna would figure that out soon enough on her own. Well, she would if she was honest about the reason when she didn't succeed. Aaliyah wondered how Sharna would respond if she couldn't do it. There probably wasn't much in her life she had ever failed at.

"What are we going to test for today?" Aaliyah asked finally.

"I have not picked up as much activity in Xenon as I expected to since having the surveillance array go live," Sharna explained. "I need to test the extents of the detection equipment I deployed."

"Oh, I thought you would be able to detect everything," Aaliyah answered.

"Unfortunately, waveforms attenuate over distance and through specific surfaces. The waveforms are usually still present but if get too small in amplitude, they become very hard to detect, even for the sensors I deployed."

"Is that why the analyzer had to be moved closer at first to what you were measuring?" Aaliyah asked.

"Essentially correct," Sharna answered with a tone that said she really didn't want to be bothered with answering questions. "I need to move you to a different place to try to meditate today. I suggest you bring your warm clothes."

"Where are we going?" Aaliyah asked while she grabbed her coat and the lily plant.

"There is an underground cavern just outside town," Sharna answered absently. "I have a test array already there and setup."

"Sounds interesting," Aaliyah answered, while following Sharna out of the lab to her vehicle.

They made the drive silently with Sharna deeply engrossed in her research on her portable workstation. Upon arriving, Sharna grabbed two portable light sources as they entered the cavern's entrance. Aaliyah felt an eerie calm come over her. The temperature matched Sharna's warning as a chill was present. This did not appear to be a frequently trafficked attraction. No evidence of footprints on the ground existed in the narrow path they traversed. Illumination did little more than light the path a few meters in front of her. It was not a place she would want her light to fail in. After an indeterminate period of walking, Sharna came to a stop.

"This is where you will do your meditation," Sharna stated. "I will be monitoring from the vehicle until you are through. Wait thirty minutes before you begin."

Aaliyah nodded as she checked the time then watched Sharna's silhouette disappear slowly from view. The quiet and sense of calm were beyond anything she had experienced in the lab setting. It was just her and her thoughts with very little to distract her senses. After confirming that the communicated time had passed, Aaliyah focused her attention on the lily plant in front of her. With seemingly no delay at all she was in a field of lilies, absent of color.

Undistracted focus and clarity of thought, Aaliyah thought to herself. That was a key to getting here quickly. She would have to keep that in mind for the future.

"I am sorry I haven't been here to greet you in a while," Raelynn spoke. "How has your practice been going?"

"Slow at best," Aaliyah answered. "But today I got here right away!"

"You really need a teacher before we can take your training much further," Raelynn stated. "Is there any way you could go off the grid for several days or weeks?"

"I am due some leave, but that may be hard to claim right now," Aaliyah explained. "I'll see if I can come up with an excuse though."

"I have someone arranged to aid your study," Raelynn answered. "You will understand better when you can get away."

"I should probably return," Aaliyah replied. "If I stay too long, I get very weak and I don't think I could make the long walk out of this cavern."

"Safe journeys," Raelynn answered before disappearing from view.

Focusing herself back to her body, Aliyah awoke, tired but not exhausted. She made herself stand and slowly reversed course through the cavern to await whatever revelation Sharna had made.

CHAPTER 12

Sharna probably shouldn't have allowed Aaliyah take time off, but the daily tests were yielding less and less quality data. A hiatus from the time-consuming testing should give her some time to get caught up on other pressing problems. Sharna usually worked without having a helper so it would not be a great inconvenience to be without for a period of time. Although, this lab technician had shown herself to not be entirely worthless.

Looking down at her to do list, there were a lot of problems that needed solved. Her experiments in the cavern showed her that unless she had a sensor array underground, surface sensors would not detect the lily meditation. She could detect partially underground, such as that hidden place where the transport tube had been located, but deeper than that was not currently detectable on her sensor array. This would be good in detecting transport activity but would be largely worthless in identifying an underground evacuation point should Xenon go down that road again.

Restricted technical libraries on mining were opened to her to speed up research. But the information she was given seemed incomplete at best. She was pretty sure she was viewing censored data still but something should be better than nothing. Sharna really didn't have a lot of personal interest in this area of technology, but sometimes you need to solve problems in other areas to be able to do what you want to in your targeted area of innovation.

So that left either improving the capabilities of her sensors or finding the underground recesses so sensors could be deployed there. She also wanted to still determine where the source of the power was coming from that would enable the transport tube. This had to come from a person, as an emulated response did not energize it with sufficient energy.

But before she solved all these problems, her first priority was to be able to initiate the meditation. Aaliyah was better than nothing, but she needed someone who didn't make her sit around all day waiting to go into the meditation state. It was very inconvenient to have the experiment all prepped, then waiting hours to have the event happen that would only last a few seconds. Gabriel had proven he could be consistent and if one person can do it, so should another.

Sharna read all the literature that Aaliyah had went through. It was a bunch of softheaded fluff about how you needed to act differently. It didn't have anything in it on how to meditate. And then there was the lily plant. Gabriel and Aaliyah had indicated its importance and talked about staring at it and thinking on it.

A lily plant was in front of Sharna, so she began staring at it. What was the point of this, she wondered? It was a flower. This was almost as bad as the forced scientific meditation stuff the government required. Yes, you needed to acknowledge the importance of resource conservation programs, but once you logically agreed to it, what was the point of sitting around wasting time trying to convince yourself more of something you already agreed with. This seemed a lot like that. Staring at an inanimate object, trying to feel a certain way. It seemed like such a waste of good time spent in other ways. But an experiment that is valid can be recreated. If Aaliyah did this to get into the meditative state, she should be able to also, provided she was fully replicating the inputs.

Sharna became more frustrated and angrier the longer she stared at the lily. It was not proving easy to enter the targeted meditative state. Three hours later and nothing. Aaliyah had entered by now when she had first stared at the lily. What had she done differently? Maybe she had missed a key step she had done. Sharna stood up finally, having had enough of this for today. Hours wasted, and for what? She was a brilliant researcher. If a lowly research technician could do it, there should be no reason she couldn't. She would need to review the video of Aaliyah entering the first time. Something was clearly missing in her attempt. She briefly considered trying to contact Aaliyah wherever she went, but wasn't ready to admit she needed help. Sharna had gotten far in her life not needing help from others. She wasn't going to start asking for it now at the first appearance of adversity.

∞ ∞ ∞

"Alaine!" Gabriel exclaimed while jogging over to greet her. "I can't believe you came. How are you?"

Alaine stood before Gabriel with a crooked grin. Her hair was unkept and her body slightly slumped from the heavy looking bag that she was carrying. Gabriel learned a couple years earlier not to underestimate her based on her appearance or manner of speaking. She was a genius when it came to electronics and technology and really fixing anything, now that he thought about it. He was excited about what she could do to help but was foremost happy that his friend has arrived safely.

"Well, this ain't no mountains but the company is good I guess." She answered with a smile on her face. "I guess I get to be a farmer for a while?"

"Don't worry," Gabriel said. "Not all farming is digging in the dirt. A lot of it is fixing things that break and figuring out how to do what needs done using a bit of creativity to get the job done. Skills you are pretty good at last time I checked."

When Gabriel had gone on the mission to rescue Philip in the capital, she had single handedly disarmed several proximity detonation devices and been a key part in the team's success. She didn't have all the fancy schooling credentials that some had, but she knew her stuff and Gabriel didn't know of anyone else who would have a chance to rival what he had seen from Sharna.

"Did you bring the items to be able to do what my message said?" Gabriel asked.

"Of course!" Alaine answered. "I may be from the mountains but I can read well enough to not mess that up."

"Come with me, then," Gabriel asked. "I have something to show you."

Alaine followed Gabriel to a private room that could be sleeping quarters. Gabriel was pretty certain based on his scanning that this area of his house was free from surveillance. He carefully pressed the button on a handheld scanner to confirm he was safe. On getting the all-clear, Gabriel entered the dream state quickly and translocated he and Alaine to an underground hiding area equipped with the beginning of a laboratory.

"I never did get used to that there transporting thing you do," Alaine answered after they appeared in the lab setting. "This looks like a very nice working area. Is it safe for you to have just sent us here? I have heard some stories about the surveillance on dreaming."

"That is one of the reasons why I needed you to come here," Gabriel explained. "I need your help finding a way to dream undetected."

"That would be easier if I knew how they are able to track you," Alaine said.

"That I can help with," Gabriel answered, producing the hand-held sensor the Sharna had given him. "This is what they use to detect those dreaming. Don't ask me how I got it! It picks up some sort of frequency spectrum used when someone is in the dream state."

Alaine carefully took the cover off the handheld scanner and examined the circuitry inside. "Nothing here that looks too complicated," she finally said. "With some time, I think I can copy it and figure out how it works."

"Something else you should probably know," Gabriel continued. "Kayden is running me as a double agent to the government. The Ministry thinks I am on their side and know I can trigger their sensors. The person in charge of the program has me filtered out to not auto notify the powers that be. That means I can probably do more dreaming than most without extra unwanted attention. But there is still risk."

"I thought that may be happening but was never for sure," Alaine answered. "Don't worry, I won't tell no one."

"I knew I could trust you," Gabriel answered. "My grandmother told me to tell almost no one, but with the information I will be providing, you would have had strong suspicions something was amiss if I didn't tell you."

"I really like your grandmother," Alaine said. "How she doing?"

"Strong as ever," Gabriel said with a smile. "I think she is tired of staying in hiding, but she is very busy keeping tabs on everything. There isn't much she doesn't know about."

"How much do you think you can translocate me to this lab without drawing suspicion?" Alaine asked.

"I've been thinking about that," Gabriel answered. "I will need you to be visibly working on the farm during core hours during the week, but after that, I can get you there in the evenings and on non-work days. But even during the day if there are things you can spend time on that help your work down here, you can probably get by with it if doesn't raise any suspicions."

"At first, I think I just need time by myself with this new sensor," Alaine replied. "But I will need someone to dream for me and may need access to a transport tube at some point as well when I am ready."

"I can't probably be away as much as you can get by with, but I will make time with you," Gabriel answered. "Tom also wants to help."

"I'm excited to get going," Alaine replied. "I will just sleep down here tonight. Just zap me up when you are ready to start the day."

"I'll get out of your way then," Gabriel answered. "It is really good to have you here!"

∞ ∞ ∞

Quintin wasn't sure what and how it had changed in Oversite, but the amount of data suddenly being generated was beyond anything he had before. To think that it was now possible to detect someone's inner thoughts versus what they said out loud. If you really wanted to get at the purity of thinking across the nation, this capability was a game changer. Oversite currently only appeared to be able to detect those who were part of the lily religion in the act of practicing it, but if it could detect that, with some development what else could it be capable of detecting?

When Quintin asked more about this capability, Xavier sent him a confidential memo that the surveillance web was fully functional in Xenon, and upgrades were in process to expand it across the rest of the sectors in the coming months. Xavier's comments simply said, "Figure out how we can use this information." And there were so many options to do so.

"How can there be this much widespread religious practice in Xenon?" Ursula asked. "I mean, I figured there was some, but we are getting hits all over the sector."

"And if we have this much in Xenon," Quintin replied, "how much do you think we will find in other sectors once their arrays go live?"

"What did you expect?" Stefan answered. "Any barriers you had on religion were bypassed when everyone disappeared. There was probably a big jump in practice during the mass disappearance. The government didn't exactly add trust during this time with the people of Xenon."

"Which means if we are going to plan another clampdown, we need to better learn from last time," Quintin replied.

"You mean we are seriously going to try to do something again?" Stefan asked with disbelief on his face. "Didn't we learn our lesson last time?"

"Have you forgot the mission of our ministry?" Quintin asked tersely. "Xavier asked me to come up with ways we could better use this new surveillance information. And that is exactly what I plan to do. Can you handle that?"

"Oh, I can handle it," Stefan replied formally. "But if you ask me, doing something like we did last time will not get a better result the second time around. Even if we figure out a way to do it more efficiently."

"I disagree," Ursula interjected. "We have a more stable food supply, which was the main problem that wasn't accounted for last time. And we also are learning who the people are who could spearhead another evacuation of Xenon. If we can neutralize them, we can neutralize the sector. I am not saying we are ready to move yet, but with some planning, this new data can really shift things to our advantage."

"Let's imagine we were going to do something to clamp back down on Xenon," Quintin instructed. "What steps do we have to complete to get there and what is the soonest we could act?"

"We can produce half of our needs for food currently in the new farms that were setup in the more reliable sectors," Ursula answered. "At least that is what the latest report from the Ministry of Nutrition claims. We are not getting that level of output yet, but if energy targets are given exceptions for these farms, we can hit that target next harvest. And with the improved standards we have developed plus the experience from last time, we won't make the same mistakes when we send fill-in labor to run the farms in Xenon."

"Why would the Ministry of Energy Conservation waive the targets? They refused to do that last time?" Stefan stated with skepticism in his voice.

"New leadership," Quintin replied. "After the rebellion in Xenon, the blind changes to energy targets made the Great Scientist Council rethink their energy strategy. Xavier tells me there are assurances that won't get in the way of putting down Xenon in the future."

"If the energy targets are so important to our environmental protections," Stefan asked, "what has changed?"

"There is willingness to make certain allowances if it strengthens the power of the Great Scientist Council," Quintin explained. "There will be time to lower targets back down later on before too much damage is done to the planet. Or at least that is what I have been told."

Stefan allowed a confused and quizzical expression to show on his face. "That would be a big change in approach," he finally answered. "Won't that send a confusing message when we have been advocating a much different way for so long? And do we even have enough energy generation capacity to make significant changes to the targets?"

"Not a lot of excess capacity, but we do have some from the reports I have been reading," Quintin answered. "Between generation and tapping our stored energy reserves, we could support a temporary increase."

"Besides, who is going to complain if energy and water targets are increased?" Ursula said briskly. "We are wasting time when we should be developing a plan to restore the purity of thought to all the sectors. Back when diseases were more rampant, we had something called cancer. If there was a growth, the doctors would simply try to cut it out before it spread to other areas of the body. I think we need to take a serious look at what it would take to remove the cancerous growth that has been infecting our nation. It is growing, and if we do not do something now, we may never be able to effectively combat it."

"What do you have in mind?" Quintin asked.

Ursula explained in great detail what she thought could be done. This was definitely out of the box thinking, but not far removed from the precepts and ideals that the Ministry of Scientific Compliance was charged to uphold. The more Quintin thought about it, the more he began to sell himself on it being the best path. Stefan seemed to have an expression on his face that did not seem convinced. Ever since he had pushed Stefan the other day, he seemed to be disengaged and less supportive of what Quintin was trying to accomplish. Maybe Quintin had made a mistake bringing Stefan out of the field. Soldiers did not always appreciate the nuances of making the decisions that went into the mission tasking orders.

That could wait. So far, Stefan was still doing what was asked of him. And if he continued to bring up thoughts that challenged Quintin and Ursula's thinking, it would just allow them to strengthen their plans before others of a higher rank also brought up the same objections.

But at some point, Quintin needed absolute loyalty if he was going to pursue the plan on the table. If Stefan could not get fully on board – well tough choices would need to be made. Stefan knew too much to just send back to the field. It would be a loss for something to happen to him, but if he was not fully loyal then he deserved what he got. And in the meantime, deploying some drone surveillance on Stefan would just be a prudent insurance policy.

CHAPTER 13

a sense of excitement coursed through Aaliyah as she arrived at the primitive nature area. She had always been a city girl and really had very little experience in the wild. She did her research on what to expect, but actually doing it, and without a guide – well there was some risk associated with that. People sometimes didn't come back from excursions like this. There was a protected path you could stay on that had electronic barricades setup to keep predators from attacking. But those who strayed from the path had no such safety guarantees, and if you harmed any animal by venturing beyond or caused damage to the delicate ecosystem, you would suffer arrest and ultimately the penalty of justice.

Aaliyah had no idea if she was being tracked by surveillance. Her scanner was safely hidden in her apartment and she had left her handheld at home. Raelynn in her dream state had suggested she come to this place, but beyond that, it was not clear what to expect. Aaliyah did not have a danger motivation in the traditional sense of venturing here. She wanted to learn more about the Lily, which motivated her more than any potential danger she may encounter in this nature preserve.

Aaliyah looked closely on the posted trail guide sign, identifying the landmark she was supposed to get to before deviating off the posted trail. This place was deep within the preserve and would likely take the better part of her day to reach. She quickly consumed her meal shake and topped off her water supplies. There did not appear to be a water station anywhere near the point she was to travel to. Adjusting her backpack, she began the long hike on the trail.

The stimulation of her senses was the most noticeable thing she noticed walking down the trail. She heard birds chirping and the sound of her feet making impressions on the trail. The trees and plants showed an awareness of life and there was a beauty that was difficult to explain. Aaliyah felt at peace here, like this represented what was right in the world.

After laboring many hours to reach her destination she finally arrived. The view was scenic. Well, that was probably an understatement. The view was breathtaking. She heard the rushing of water, which drew her eyes to the promised waterfall in the distance. Looking around carefully for any signs of predatory animals, she left the safety of the marked path and headed toward the sound of falling water.

Aaliyah pushed her body, fighting the temptation of stopping for a rest. Here in the wild with nothing to protect her, she didn't think stopping would be safe. Her feet hurt. Her legs were tired but she persevered. The sun began to hide behind the horizon. There was not much time with light left and she did not want to be caught in the unprotected area at night. She looked around carefully as she approached the waterfall. There was a rock ledge the water was flowing over with just enough surface area to walk on. Balancing herself carefully on the slippery rock path, Aaliyah approached the rushing water, pushing her body behind the vertically dropping stream. Her clothing absorbed some water as the temperature dropped around her. She could barely see, but felt on her left what felt like a small crevice with a gap just large enough to possibly get her body into it. She removed her backpack and pushed it into the opening and then proceeded to crawl in behind it.

The darkness was all encompassing. The sound of the waterfall began to fade as she pushed herself further into the opening, following a slightly winding path. Space began to open up where she had room enough to sit up and possibly stand up. She had maybe crawled about thirty meters into this dark space, but it was hard to tell. The air felt cool with a musty scent engaging her senses. Aaliyah reached in her backpack for a light source. In hindsight she should have probably had it out before she got herself into this place. After fumbling to locate it in her pack, she turned it on, momentarily unable to see until her eyes had time to adjust. After a brief delay she was able to observe that the opening had another path exiting it – one where she could stand up and walk. The trail took a long time to traverse but came to a moderately large open area. No additional exits were evident at first glance.

Aaliyah looked around carefully, shining her light source around the perimeter. She almost missed it the first time, but just as her light was leaving it, she saw a very small, lightly camouflaged gap in the wall. Pulling on it carefully, it revealed an opening leading to another small chamber. She carefully squeezed her body through. Shining her light around she discovered a note posted prominently on the wall telling her what to expect. A scanner of some sort presented itself, likely checking her for evidence of surveillance. A few moments later a second door opened, revealing what looked like a version of the transport tube that Sharna had in her lab.

Aaliyah looked around carefully and found a second note before being startled by the sound of the door closing behind her. Inside the transport tube was a lily plant. The note indicated she was to sit in the tube and enter the dream state while her hands were on a couple of buttons. Aaliyah sat down in the transport tube while situating herself. Her mind was no longer calm as she processed all that she had saw. After several minutes of racing thoughts, she did her best to quiet her mind and focus on the lily plant in front of her. She suddenly felt a jolt of energy and when she opened her eyes, she was in a new place, being watched by someone wearing a strange mask.

∞ ∞ ∞

"What have you found out?" Gabriel asked Alaine in her newly adopted lab area. Alaine had been working non-stop with every moment she had, trying to understand all she could about the scanner Gabriel had given her and its capabilities.

"Whoever designed this here scanner sure does know what they be doing," Alaine answered. "Best I can figure, it finds some frequencies and when it detects them, it signals this here device. But what I can't get over is how the designer is picking up such low power signals at a long range. Pretty good smarts with how they did that."

"But you understand what she did and how it works?" Gabriel asked.

"Sure, I see how she got it working," Alaine replied with confidence. "Just saying, not many peoples could come up with something like this."

"Sharna was saying something about a circuit detecting the same frequencies being inside of the transport tube she got a hold of," Gabriel answered. "But she kept complaining about not figuring out how the power was amplified to make the transport tube work."

"That is just the power of the Lily," Alaine replied. "All she has to do is believe it in. Nothing hard about that."

"Well, she wants to be able to trigger it without having to believe in the Way of the Lily," Gabriel explained. "She doesn't have any faith, which is probably an advantage we can exploit if we can figure out a way to get around this sensor array. You have any ideas on that?"

"I got a few," she answered. "Need to do a couple of things, I think. Need to figure out what can and can't be detected with this here sensor. Then we need to work out a way for you to do dreaming a different way."

"What do you mean to do dreaming a different way?" Gabriel asked with a very perplexed look on his face.

"Why do you have to use the frequencies that this here sensor detects when dreaming? Why can't you use different ones?" Alaine asked in a matter of fact way. "Whoever, made the transport tube design musta had to have some research in this field of learning."

"I have been told that the designer of the transport tube technology was one of the highest secrets of the Order," Gabriel replied. "Not sure if we will be allowed to review that research."

"No we about it," Alaine answered. "I can't dream into the past. You need to learn and give me hints on what I need to do. Shoot, there may even be some books on topics like this somewhere. This is important stuff and we need all the help we can get."

"I will need to make a visit to Teacher after asking my Grandmother if I can gain access to any of the protected secrets Gabriel replied. "I can probably get to Teacher tomorrow if I give warning."

"You bring me the supplies I asked for?" Alaine asked.

"Sorry, I should have given them to you right away," Gabriel replied while handing her a bag full of various items.

"Looks like it is all here," Alaine said after looking through the contents of the bag. "If you can get Tom to spend some time with me while you go see Teacher, I think I can do some testing while you learn up on what we don't know about."

"I'll invite him over tomorrow," Gabriel promised. "He has been asking to help."

Alaine watched while Gabriel translocated himself back out of her makeshift lab. She didn't want to tell Gabriel, but she was already homesick for the mountains. There was so much more space up there and she felt much freer. But Gabriel was her friend, and if she wanted to protect her way of life, she needed to do her part to sacrifice her joys for the benefit of others. Alaine looked back down at the items Gabriel had brought her. And as it sometimes happens when not expected, inspiration struck Alaine and she began to pursue a concept for something that had begun to form in her mind.

∞ ∞ ∞

"Is that you, Affirmed?" Teacher asked wearing a robe while masked.

Gabriel looked around the area where he had spent so much time before. Gabriel found a robe and mask and was now wearing them as was the custom of this place. It was hard to believe it had been over two years since he had last set foot here. It felt like it was yesterday, probably because of the frequency he visited his experience in his dreams. So much knowledge resided here and he felt like he had just tapped the beginning of it. His first observation was that it was a lot more crowded looking than when he had last visited.

"Teacher! It is good to see you again. I can't believe how long I have been away!" Gabriel said with genuine warmth through the voice modulator in his mask. "So many more students than last time I was here."

"Our time of greatest adversity provided us opportunities for much needed growth," Teacher replied. "We have been able to reconnect to our roots and with our youth in ways we haven't seen in generations."

"That is fantastic to hear," Gabriel answered taking in all the activity going on around him. Learning appeared to be in process everywhere he observed.

"What do I owe the pleasure of your arrival?" Teacher asked.

"I am in need of some knowledge that doesn't seem to be part of the books you have initially provided to me as a library." Gabriel said quietly, motioning teacher away from the other students. "The government has come up with a way to detect the brain frequency of the dream state and have been using it to find people who follow the Way of the Lily."

"I heard that something like this may be true, but they haven't gone after anyone in Xenon that I know of yet," Teacher answered.

"Yet, is the key word," Gabriel answered. "You are probably safe down here, but those who dream on the surface have likely already been identified by Oversite. What I am hoping to find is anything in your library that gets into brainwave activity while dreaming or maybe alternate ways of dreaming that may utilize a different brain frequency pattern."

"I received a message from the High Seat to help you in your research, even allowing you access to areas of the restricted library," Teacher replied. "You probably don't have a lot of time so you will want to be page turning books as fast as you can to help you speed up learning in the dream state."

"I'll take anything you can give that will help," Gabriel added. "I fear we won't have a lot of time left before something happens."

"Ok, come this way then," Teacher requested as he began to walk away from the main library area. "Not many people are given access to what you are about to see."

Gabriel followed Teacher out of the library and through some winding passages. Pressing against the wall, Teacher caused an opening to occur through which Gabriel followed him inside. Gabriel looked around seeing a new library of much smaller size than the main one he had recently vacated.

"Why is this library kept apart?" Gabriel asked after they were securely inside.

"Mostly, this covers very complex dream actions here," Teacher explained. "Trying to do these items can be very hazardous to your health. We do not want newer learners acting beyond their capabilities, especially if it can harm themselves or others."

"Should I even be learning about the content in here?" Gabriel asked. "I am not that advanced in my training yet."

"There is no harm in learning, but acting, that can be a different story," Teacher warned. "Regretfully, I do not know of a living teacher who can help you decipher this library. You will have to rely on the past for this. Based on the topic you presented, you may want to start with the journals of Alfred Hinkley. I have read the summaries, but cannot be much more help than that I am afraid."

"Thank you for your help," Gabriel said with full sincerity. "I guess I will get right to work then."

"You are welcome any time," Teacher answered. "Maybe someday again you can have an extended stay as you did a couple years back. I would greatly enjoy discussing with you all you have learned."

Gabriel looked at the seemingly insurmountable number of books in front of him. Gabriel thought he could spare a day and not be missed on his farm. Looking through the method of shelf organization, he found the Hinkley books, taking the first one and began paging through it quickly so he could later review it in the dream state. It sure seemed like there should be a better more efficient way of doing this. He knew he was supposed to just quickly page to make the best use of his woken time, but he stopped quickly on a page when some words stuck out at him.

Today, I encountered a new phenomenon in my studies. Before, I have always entered the dream state following a period of meditation and focus. But today, I found myself able to coexist between an awake state and the dream state. It was like my vision coexisted in black and white and in color. There was a phase shift in my vision where one view was slightly offset from the other. I was able to do my normal gifts in the dream state but I was also able to walk around and interact with others concurrently. It was unlike anything I have experienced before. But it also seemed to have some limitations. I could not operate the transport tube. It was a different type of awareness, and one I plan to study in the coming days.

Gabriel excitedly stopped reading for a moment. Dreaming without the transport tube working. That would mean he was likely generating a different frequency! That or he wasn't able to channel the power of the Lily the same way in this state. Raelynn had described being able to monitor the dream state while she was awake. Could it be something similar to this? Regardless, it was a clue and Gabriel decided to quickly complete his page turning without further distraction. There was a lot of research he needed to do in a short period of time.

CHAPTER 14

Stefan looked around meticulously then activated a scanner to check for the presence of surveillance. Stefan's fieldcraft was top notch and finding the drone trailing him was not that much of a challenge. It was so predictable that Quintin had tasked a drone to shadow him after his last outburst. Woe to him that showed his willingness to challenge the almighty thinking and power of Quintin. Active surveillance created some difficulties in what he wanted to accomplish, but when planting the seeds of dissent, he could afford to be patient. Plans must operate with the end in mind, and if that meant lulling those watching him into a catatonic state, so be it.

Stefan did not think he was in Xavier's league for mission planning, but he did think he was at least equally capable to that of Quintin. And as long as his actions didn't make a mark significant enough to gather a more thoughtful participant, he hoped he would be equal to the challenge.

The response to his information campaign in the CET community was greater than he expected. The *Seeing* pamphlet he created and minimally distributed to a few trusted colleagues had unexpectedly been given back to him multiple times from others not knowing he had written it. Written in handwriting not his own spoke to the fact it had been copied multiple times and its reach was perhaps more widespread than he would ever know.

Stefan pushed a couple of buttons on his vehicle's console to interrupt the feed coming from the drone and replace it with some pre-recorded footage he had been building the two weeks prior. The drone would be parked with his vehicle but Quintin would see something else all-together.

Stefan enabled facial recognition jamming before leaving his vehicle and walked several blocks before entering a hangout popular with the CET community. If asked about it, it would be explained as a private fitness center, and it was that, but it was also something more. This was a secure compound, free from surveillance due to active jamming technology. A lot could be discussed here without fear of Oversite interference.

The building was not memorable to look at from the road. It was on a lightly frequented street and there was nothing announcing the purpose of the building on the outside. Stefan was known here and had no difficulty gaining entrance both to the main entrance and to the room where the meeting would take place. Looking around the conference area, there were ten people present. Anything larger would attract undue attention.

"Good of you to come, Stefan," a person in the corner of the room announced after seeing the green light come on that the second-tier anti-surveillance system was turned on and had not detected any active tracking present. Stefan looked closer and saw it was an old teammate he served with about ten years prior.

"It has been a long time, Thorin," Stefan replied, looking around and realizing that he knew most of the people in the room. Some he knew who they were, and some he had directly served with. There were no young new recruits here. These were grizzled veterans of multiple tours hardened by combat with a track record of mission successes and reputations for unquestioned loyalty.

"I am still bothered about Aglas," Thorin opened. "If he had a problem with what was happening, why didn't he just take action to stop it?"

"Since when does taking action outside the chain of command ever work out well for those involved?" one Stefan knew as Garrett answered with disdain. "He would have suffered the same fate and probably one that was more painful than what he did. No, he made his peace and went out on his own terms. Can't say I would've done the same but I respect that he did it."

"I get going after religious zealots," Thorin answered. "We have seen with our own eyes what harm misguided extremists can do. But these were just kids. How did we get to where we are executing kids and not being bothered by it? I know I am older than most of you are, but I remember when children were valued. Now with the population control targets, we keep the best, but those with low scores are routinely killed. Can't say I like what happens in Xenon, but at least there, they haven't lost sight of protecting basic life."

"We will see for how long that lasts," Stefan interjected. "The Ministry is getting ready to go in there again. Didn't learn its lesson last time."

"For what purpose?" Thorin said, angrily making his voice heard over the agitated chatter of the assembled group.

"It certainly isn't due to protecting the environment or due to the ideals of science," Stefan answered. "They are still ticked off that they didn't succeed last time. Nothing but power and ego if you ask me. We have some new sensor tech that lets us find those who still practice the lily religion the rebels follow. They are going to want to probably use the CET group to make a quick capture of key followers before they have a chance to evacuate again. It is the same tech that caused those kids to be caught that Aglas froze with."

"You saying all the teams are going to be called up to hit targets in Xenon?" Jillian asked. "Not sure I want any part of that."

"Anyone know much about this lily religion the Ministry is trying to go after?" Ingmar asked.   "All I hear are rumors."

"My supervisor let me see the intelligence on it so I could help analyze it," Stefan offered. "Mainly they want to peacefully follow beliefs covering a few moral tenants. They also think some can achieve special powers when they are dreaming. We have a researcher trying to figure out how it works. There is a transport device they power with their minds somehow. Don't know much more than that, but it has a lot of people worked up."

"Have they figured out how it works?" Jillian asked.

"No," Stefan replied, "all they can do is detect it being done. The books say faith makes a difference; believing without a reason to and hoping for preferred outcome, or something like that."

"Why wouldn't the Ministry care more about learning how it is done in the pursuit of science than trying to clamp it down?" Thorin asked with a sarcastic tone. "Never mind, we stopped caring about science long ago."

"I don't know about you," Stefan said with certainty, "but if it comes down to executing innocents or fighting back, I am not going to choose the wrong side. We have been lied to for too long and something needs to change."

"Dangerous words," Garrett said causing Stefan a momentary fear he had misread the mood of the room.

"Dangerous, yes," Thorin interrupted, "but standing on the side of right often is dangerous. I am with Stefan on this. We have to do something to get our nation back on the right track. Anyone of a different mind than this? We act together, or not at all. Who will join together to oppose this injustice?"

Stefan looked around the room as he saw conflict in the faces of those assembled. It was a lot to risk. But the cause was just and these were among the bravest people he had ever known. One by one, each head nodded giving him the answer he hoped for.

"Very well," Thorin spoke. "We will marshal our resources to be ready. Stefan, find a way to get me information. We will need all the advantages we can get."

"This isn't much," Stefan replied, "but I scanned all the lily information and planning information I was given access to. I apologize if the image quality if not great but I had to do it this way so there was not Oversite record of me taking it. Use it wisely or it will come back on me."

Stefan said his goodbyes and exited out of the building. Getting back to his vehicle, he removed the frequency override and continued the boring and uneventful routine the tracking drone had become accustomed to seeing.

∞ ∞ ∞

"Where am I?" Aaliyah asked as she looked at the mysteriously masked person in front of her. The air was cool and the lighting was dim. It was not unlike the cave behind the waterfall in appearance but she knew she was somewhere different. She was still trying to adjust her mind to the trip she had apparently taken in the transport tube. After helping Sharna with all of her research in trying to figure out how it worked, she had actually used it!

"You are far from where you left," the concealed person answered. "It is not very often where someone from Preath ventures to this place. It has been many, many years since this has happened."

"What is the place?" Aaliyah asked again a different way, somewhat frustrated by the cryptic response.

"This is a place of learning where you can grow in your understanding of the Way of the Lily," the person answered. "I am called Teacher and I will help guide you on your journey. I apologize for the mask, but it is safer for everyone if we keep our identities hidden. I have a mask and a robe for you to use if you would be willing to wear it.

Aaliyah went to where Teacher had motioned and followed the directions to turn on a voice modulation and attired herself as she was instructed.

"I will call you Novice here," Teacher explained as they walked down some sort of cavern like corridor. "The time we have is short as I have been informed too long of an absence will raise uncomfortable questions."

"What will I be able to learn while here?" Aaliyah asked with curiosity. "Raelynn from my dreaming said that this would be very important to me reaching the next level in my dream abilities with the Lily."

"I hope to answer questions you have not been able to figure out on your own," Teacher replied. "We have more books of learning available for you here to study. Only by strengthening your foundation of belief can we enable you to reach your full ability and potential."

Aaliyah followed Teacher into a small room. It had stone-like walls crudely cut out of some sort of rock structure. Books were stacked on a small table in the corner of the dimly lit room. There was a bed and a chair to sit in. There was nothing to distract. There were only the books.

"Start with the volume on top," Teacher instructed. "I will check in on you later on to ask you some questions about what you have learned."

Aaliyah picked up the first book obediently, unsure about the proper way to comport herself here. Teacher wanted books read, so she would start reading. She wanted to grow in her knowledge of the Lily and one thing she did not have back in the lab was access to a library this big. It should have been a feeling of great excitement that overcame her, but instead it was a pensive anxiety. She couldn't explain why she felt this way, but she did. Something felt wrong in the world and she was worried she was not doing the right things to help oppose whatever it was that wanted to be perpetrated.

The learning proved grueling. Granted, she was gaining more understanding than she ever hoped. Teacher discussed the tenants of the Order and how her life fit in with that context. Surprisingly, nothing she read seemed unexpected. It was an extension of what she had already learned when she was secretively exploring the Lily. It was like she had an intuitive sense on this. She had been prepared well and as a result Teacher had told her she was making very fast progress.

"Can I interrupt you for a few minutes?" A voice spoke interrupting her focus. The voice belonged to an elderly lady who had a vibrant glow about her that was hard to explain. She also was not wearing a mask, the first person who Aaliyah observed without.

"Sure," Aaliyah answered, not really sure who this person was.

"You have a more important role than you will ever know," the lady stated.

"I am not sure I understand," Aaliyah answered with some level of uncertainty.

"No, I suppose you don't," she replied. "What I am referring to is your relationship and interaction with Sharna."

"She is the most brilliant person I have ever met," Aaliyah replied, not sure what else to say.

"What good is knowledge if you do not also possess the wisdom of using it in an upright and wise way?" the woman continued. "I have not observed evil intent in her, but her indifference to the implications of her discoveries cannot be overlooked. The surveillance system updates she implemented have been responsible for a sizable count of deaths and detentions. Did you know nearly forty children were recently executed due to this work?"

"No, I wasn't aware of this," Aaliyah answered sounding somewhat unsure of herself.

"And that was just an early trial of the system upgrades. Many more innocent people are going to lose their lives," she continued.

"I am sad that I have aided this outcome," Aaliyah said with disappointment sounding in her voice. "It feels like it goes against everything I have been studying on the Lily. I should try to get reassigned when I get back. I am not sure I can continue to be part of this any longer."

"I do not recommend that," the person cautioned. "Sharna is seeking right now. In your absence she has tried to enter the dream state many times on her own."

"She has failed badly, hasn't she?" Aaliyah asked with a smile forming on her lips.

"Yes, and she isn't the least bit happy about it either," the woman responded. "That a mere technician can do something she cannot is a concept very foreign to her. She has an abundance of pride and an absence of faith. Only when she can put her pride aside will she be able to see the world in its full power and potential. The knowledge of humankind pales in the presence of the Lily."

"So, what are you asking me to do then?" Aaliyah asked.

"When you crawled into the passage behind the waterfall," she continued, "were you able to see?"

"Not at all," Aaliyah replied. "It was darker than anything I have experienced. "There is no way I would have found the passage to get here if I hadn't brought a portable light source."

"Sharna, like many others, is in a passage not unlike you were," the woman continued. She is in the dark, feeling around for answers and trying to see. But she doesn't have a light source with her to help her find the way. All she has ever known is that dark, unlit passage. But you represent a light source to illuminate her way. You can see the way through the passage and if she can see the reflection of the light through you, she may be able to make her way to the right path."

"You are asking me to be the light for her to try to turn her to a better path?" Aaliyah asked beginning to understand what was being asked of her.

"I am," she answered. "I asked Gabriel to do the same thing, but his time and role was to just plant some seeds, to show what was possible. It is up to you to nurture those seeds and hope they are able to grow. The Way of the Lily is for all who seek it, even those who have caused great harm."

"I will do as you ask," Aaliyah answered. "You seem to be very well informed. Who are you to know all of these things, if I am allowed to ask that?"

"I am the High Seat of Kayden," came the reply. "But you can call me Isabella. I am someone the government would greatly like to get their hands on."

"I can imagine they would," Aaliyah replied. "Thank you for sharing what you have with me."

"You are very welcome," Isabella answered. "We have one more thing for you to do before you leave. Follow me and we will get it started before we get you on your way back home."

Aaliyah followed Isabella to an isolated and enclosed room. There was a table and a chair setup inside it. On the table was a container of very clear water and a cup. There was also some sort of circular disc and metal like tools present. Aaliyah was asked to surrender her possessions to Isabella except for the lily plant she had picked up in the transport tube. When Isabella left, the room grew very dark as time slowly passed.

"Who are you?" came a voice.

Somehow, she knew the proper response to answer.

"I am Novice," she replied.

CHAPTER 15

"**W**elcome back!" Tom greeted Gabriel. "I think Alaine is getting pretty tired of me. I am sure she will be glad to have you back."

"You aren't in my way that much," Alaine replied.

Gabriel smiled at their interaction. It was good to have most of the team back together. He was looking for an excuse to get William down from Northfalcon but so far, the opportunity hadn't presented itself.

"You learn anything useful?" Alaine asked from the lab that Gabriel had setup for her.

"I think I may have," Gabriel answered, "but I am still trying to understand all I learned. There is some sort of dream state I read about that won't let the transport tube work. I am hoping that means it uses a different frequency spectrum as opposed to it just not being a real dream state."

"Are you able to get yourself into this state?" Tom asked.

"Honestly, I haven't tried yet," Gabriel replied. "I figured that I would rather experiment with you guys nearby. Otherwise, it will be hard to know if I am actually doing it."

"I got a few things made up to test you," Alaine offered. "Give me a bit to get it all ready and you can try whatever you want to."

Gabriel watched Alaine as she arranged her equipment for him to try his dream experiment. He felt as ready as he was going to be and wasn't certain if he could replicate what he learned about. Beyond the reading content, he had listened in on original discussions by the author who discovered it. The key seemed to be the way the dream state was initially entered.

Getting the go-ahead from Alaine, Gabriel focused his mind similar to preparing to enter the dream state. This time, however, he kept his eyes open, taking in the surroundings around him. He carefully set his thoughts to target a state of equilibrium, feeling the peace needed for the dream state, but also keeping awareness of the word around him. Gabriel hovered in this state of mind, felling a strange pull balanced by an opposing force. He was somehow in the middle of this. The feeling was foreign but he did not feel any unease or anxiety.

Gabriel looked around, realizing that he was now experiencing a blur of sorts in his vision. It was like one eye was offset from another. One seeing in color and the other one in hues of gray. Gabriel tried closing one eye, seeing if he could resolve the color offset, but it remained. He was seeing in two domains at once.

An idea came to Gabriel and he tried to focus his vision on one of the images before him. Gabriel focused in on the black and white view, trying to filter out the color in his vision. Slowly, the color began to fade and he saw the dream state more clearly, with just a faint reminder the color was there and able to be restored if he needed it. Gabriel focused on a tool on Alaine's workbench she had setup and moved it to the other side off the room using a translocation method. It seemed to move. Then shifting his focus, he brought himself back into the color spectrum, as he watched Tom and Alaine observing him and some instrumentation carefully. The greys were still there faintly as Gabriel did his best to keep them at bay.

"Is anything happening that you can detect?" Gabriel asked, hoping he was in a state where his voice could be heard.

"We don't see nothing yet," Alaine answered. "We waiting for you to get started."

"Look on the other side of the room. I think I moved your tool," Gabriel suggested.

Tom walked to the other side of the room and picked up the tool that Gabriel had relocated.

"Is this the tool you are talking about?" Tom asked while holding it up and showing it to Alaine.

"You moved it, all right," Alaine stated. "I had it right beside me a minute ago. So interesting I didn't scan that at all. You still in that dream state?"

"I think so," Gabriel replied. "It is kind of like being awake and dreaming at the same time. I just shift back and forth between them somehow but am always still partially in both."

"Well, I not detecting anything like a normal dream state," Alaine stated. "I'm even scanning a broader spectrum and don't see anything unique coming up. If you can do dreaming like this, I don't think it can be detected with the government's scanner array."

"Now I need to see how I get out of this state," Gabriel answered with a chuckle. "Hopefully I don't get stuck like this forever!"

Gabriel was making jokes about getting out of this dual dream state but it was a real concern. Shifting his focus full color didn't seem to do the trick. Relaxing his focus just brought him back to a state of equilibrium. It was clear a different technique would be needed. The uncertainty began to cause some anxiety in Gabriel. He had no idea what staying in this state long term would mean and had been cautioned to be very careful with the learning he had seen in the restricted library. Worry began to overcome focus and he was surprised when he suddenly saw everything in full color.

"I think I am back," Gabriel finally said after trying to shift focus a couple times unsuccessfully. "I am sure there is a better way to get back, but I just had to worry about getting stuck there and it broke my focus. Similar to how I used to have trouble staying in the dream state if I started worrying about life too much."

"You need to figure it out as soon as you can." Tom stated. "You will want to start training others, you know."

Tom was right, Gabriel reflected. But Gabriel didn't feel qualified to teach others. He was so new and raw in his abilities. But if a storm was coming, all who had ability to help had a part to play. And he had a feeling his part would be more than he could currently envision and imagine.

∞ ∞ ∞

Isabella did some quick mental calculations. No, there was not sufficient time to mobilize in time. How had she missed this coming? This must have been kept very close and in the hands of very few people. People unfortunately, she was not keeping a close eye on. She couldn't execute the primary plan, but the fallback one would have to do. Isabella sent out the message beacons. There was no time to waste.

∞ ∞ ∞

Thorin looked across the field through the lens of his visor view screen as the sun was just beginning its ascent across the horizon. Thorin occupied the point position today for his team to support this pending action. It seemed like overkill to task teams to capture these seemingly harmless individuals. But Oversite had provided a list of those who most frequented the lily frequencies as they were now being called, and these were enemies of the state. Thorn's unit was one of many deployed all across Xenon, acting in a covert way to accomplish a coordinated action. Surprise was of the essence. There could be no forewarning or the mission would fail.

Thorin was conflicted on following this set of orders. If there was a way to let it fail in a way that would not cast suspicion on him, he would do it. He did not want to be part of this suppression and capture. But he was not yet ready to act against orders. More time was needed to bring those plans into place and if he was relieved of his post too soon, the overall plan would fail. No, he needed to act within orders here and hopefully do the least amount of damage possible to these innocent people he was going to be part of apprehending.

Thorin saw his target come into view and proceeded to tap his microphone transmit button three times, the signal to indicate he was in position. The target didn't seem to be doing anything suspicious, just sitting on a chair outside of his home. Thorin heard the go code signal back in his headset. He checked the cartridge in his weapon and took careful aim, allowing the automatic sighting to work. After stilling his body and adjusting his breathing, he slowly squeezed the trigger.

The person he fired at made a slight twitch like he had been bit by an insect. After a few moments he slumped in his seat. The drug was apparently working.

"Point to team leader," Thorin spoke into his headset.

"Go for team leader," he heard back.

"Target is down," Thorin replied. "Recommend sending the rest of the team forward for full extraction."

"Acknowledged," his team leader replied. "Good shooting. Team, advance forward now."

Thorin kept watch in case a new threat emerged, providing cover to his team. The drug administered from his shot should last several hours. That would allow plenty of time to equip the now prisoner with anti-escape mechanisms.

"Load up," Thorin heard on his headset. "We have three more stops to make today. Good work everyone. We have the most important of the targets detained. Let's go get the rest of them."

Thorin carefully got up from his crouched position and proceeded to head back to the transport vehicle, knowing he was well ahead of the rest of the team. This was the opportunity he was looking for. Thorin looked around and then turned on a jamming signal to disrupt any communications and surveillance that may be in play. Once secured, he opened a hidden compartment in the vehicle to pull out a bag packed with a cache of weapons and military supplies. Thorin looked around quickly before hefting the pack on his shoulder and quick-timed it to a hiding area he had scoped out earlier. Once he had stashed the bag, he noted the coordinates and then once clear, removed the jamming signal.

∞ ∞ ∞

Annabel Raelynn Farwell was busier the last few hours than she could ever remember. Something was afoot and Isabella had sent out the beacon that all dreamers needed to be evacuated as quickly as possible. A mass detention was underway, one that had not been picked up in advance. Gabriel's warning about the dream gift being able to be detected was real and the government seemed to be making quick work of using the information.

Her job was made much harder since most dreamers had vastly curtailed dreaming since word reached them that the government could detect them doing so, which made them inaccessible to her. Regardless, every one she could reach would be one more that could be moved to safety. If only the warning had come at night, then she could have penetrated through regular dreams similar to how she had reached Gabriel and numerous others. But the day was still young and there would be many hours till people began going to sleep. And if her warning was correct, it may be too late by then. Isabella likely had deployed physical messengers as well. It was a race, and one that they were not winning.

Annabel checked the time. She had stayed on the surface too long already. She hoped someone would translocate her to safety, but no one had come. She would instead need to walk to a hidden location where she was able to access a transport tube to escape. She was about twenty minutes away from it. Quickly grabbing what she wanted to bring with her, she exited out the back of her home. There was an unsettling feeling as she traversed the trail intuitively knowing something was wrong. It was quiet in an eerie way and it felt like there were eyes watching her, although when she looked around, she saw no evidence of it.

She was almost to the entrance of where the transport tube was waiting when she felt a slight sting in her neck. Her hand immediately moved to feel what had caused the pricking sensation. It felt like a dart or similar was slightly protruding from her neck. As she closed her grip to begin to remove it, her head became woozy and she slumped to the ground fighting to maintain consciousness.

"Afraid we were going to lose this one," a voice called out. "Wasn't expecting her to take off like that. Good shot getting her on the move like that."

"What is happening?" Annabel tried to say as she struggled to annunciate her words. Her vision continued to blur before her world went fully dark.

∞ ∞ ∞

The High Seat of Kayden looked on at her assembled council. Well, what was left of it who had not been captured.

"I call this session to order," Isabella said. "Since we are currently lacking the Reader, will the Guardian please provide the guiding text?"

"I will, High Seat," the Guardian replied with a grim expression on his face.

"Oh, why must I endure the pain of this loss? My people are in suffering, yet all I can do is watch. I want to go to them, console them, rescue them, but all paths seem blocked. Though I am in great distress, I do not fear evil. The Lily will comfort me. In the Lily is the path to salvation. But woe, the path is long and the journey hard. Grant me the strength to endure. *The Carn Prophesies*, Chapter 3, paragraph 2."

"Thank you, Guardian," the High Seat replied after the somber yet appropriate text was read. "It has been a painful couple of days. Our ranks have been thinned greatly, as is our ability to protect our people."

"You are correct," the Chief Protector interjected. "in that we have suffered great losses, but hope is not gone. We have over half of our dreamers that haven't been captured and those who have been taken are not dead. They are being drugged and collared. Getting them released will be hard, but we can overcome it with time, as long as they can stay alive."

"Thank you for your encouragement," Isabella answered. "You are right, we can rise above this. What are our best options?"

"We can still evacuate the population, but with the reduced dreamer capacity, it will take much longer than before," the Guardian offered. "But I don't think the people will go for that this time. I think they would rather fight and die than go through what they did before. They may send their children into hiding but there is strong sentiment that enough is enough."

"But how will we defend ourselves?" a council member asked. "We ruled out resisting last time because we didn't have weapons capability to match the government."

"That situation has changed recently," the Chief Protector offered. "I am getting reports of weapons caches showing up across Xenon. These are unkeyed weapons that are usable by anyone."

"Has anyone heard where they are coming from?" Isabella asked. "I haven't had time to watch for this level of activity recently."

"I put a dreamer on that to find out," the Chief Protector answered. "There seems to be some CET soldiers that are stashing them. Not sure what it is all about, but we have seen a few drop weapons shortly after capturing a dreamer. Doesn't make sense but it is happening."

"Perhaps we have more allies than we thought we did," the Guardian stated. "Do we have any other assets at our disposal? Anyone who enters the dream state will be detected nearly immediately. It will largely neutralize our abilities to use our strengths on the surface."

"We do have some progress on that front," Isabella answered. "Gabriel has discovered a way to dream in a way that can't be detected by the sensor array. I am not sure everyone can learn how to do it, but it will be a way to get an advantage back if even a fraction of our dreamers left can adapt."

"We have to try to teach them as soon as possible," the Guardian stated. "I am not sure how long those dreamers who have been captured will be allowed to live."

"I know that the Council has had prior reservations on how far to let Gabriel into the workings of Kayden. I think he has proven himself and I trust him, but I am a bit biased," Isabella stated.

"It is time," the Guardian stated. "We may even want his voice on the council at some point if we cannot rescue those who are lost."

"Maybe we need to elevate some temporary replacements until the day of their rescue," the High Seat offered. "Please get me some suggestions for the vacant slots. We need all the help we can get."

Isabella looked around at the Council. The burden of leadership weighed heavy today. If only she had seen this coming. Hindsight is always clearer but that did not diminish the load on her shoulders. She needed to find the strength to rally Kayden and rally the people. Times were about to get hard again and unlike last time, blood was likely to flow in abundance. If only there was a different way.

CHAPTER 16

$\mathcal{J}$oseph Lazerof stared at the growing mass of prisoners. At least he wasn't working on a stupid farm anymore, not that this seemed much better. As usual, the government took action without thinking out the consequences, and here he was to help them clean up their mess. If you conduct a surprise mass detention, you would think someone would have thought about the personnel needed to guard them. But they clearly hadn't. Oh, they determined that they needed guards, but only setup enough assuming they never got to sleep. That put them at about a third of what would minimally be needed to secure this facility. Well, facility was probably an incorrect word. It was mostly a camp like construction with very little shelter and a large fence surrounding it. At least they had quarters for the guards to sleep in.

"Why aren't you at your post?" Joseph's section leader came up on him suddenly.

"Larry is covering me for a minute," Joseph made up a hasty lie. "Needed to use the bathroom."

"Don't make me send you back to that general laborer farm work I rescued you from," he replied. "Just because I pulled some strings to get you restored to duty, doesn't mean I won't send you back in a heartbeat if you are not doing your job."

"Yeah, I am headed back now," Joseph replied with annoyance in his voice.

The pulled strings comment was a joke. And where was he when he had been unfairly booted from his guard position into the general laborer pool? No, Joseph didn't owe that jerk anything. It was his incompetence that had got Joseph fired the first time. Joseph was exceptional at his job and he had been discarded all while threatened with confinement and worse. Like he would ever collaborate with the prisoners he was about to execute to let them escape. And if his section leader had really pulled strings, he would have his old rank back instead of the low rank any green recruit gets out of the training program. No, he was going to get his old rank back and was going to make everyone pay who hadn't defended him last time.

Joseph walked by a huddled group of prisoners. It really wasn't that cold outside. They were probably up to no good.

"Break it up!" Joseph yelled while shoving a few of them to emphasize his point. One of them made a motion to stand up to him which Joseph was going have none of it.

"It is cold out here," the red-headed prisoner said. "Why can't we at least stay close together for warmth?"

"You should have thought of that before you did any of that stupid religious myth stuff that got you in here," Joseph answered while pulling out his handheld to identify the prisoner who was speaking to him. "I didn't ask what you thought. I told you to do something and I expect you to obey."

Joseph pushed a button on his handheld with masked glee as the prisoner fell down on her knees with the pain that was being applied through the collar around her neck. "I said break it up. That was only a warning level of pain. I can do a lot stronger and don't you forget it."

With a new found jump in his step, Joseph walked back to his post. Maybe this wouldn't be such a bad day after all. He wasn't supposed to kill them yet, but no one said anything about hurting them a bit.

∞ ∞ ∞

Annabel Raelynn grimaced as she tried to recover from the shock the collar sent through her body. She needed to grow stronger to allow the pain to be absorbed but not debilitate her. It was hard to achieve the level of mental agility required without going into the dream state. Some sort of sensor was installed that if the dream state was triggered, it would send an immediate shock through the dreamer's body and that of several other prisoners around them. And if someone disappeared, it would cause the immediate death of several others automatically though the collar mechanism or at least that was what they were told. The government didn't understand how they disappeared but had set precautions in place that made those detained very unwilling to attempt escape. It also pretty much stopped all hope of entering the dream state.

Annabel was pretty sure if she could build up enough of a tolerance to the shock, she could manage fast dream state interactions where she could get communication out. Time didn't always work the same in the dream state and a few seconds could be enough to communicate with those outside the prison area. But would there be anyone in the dream state when she got there to await her call? She didn't have the gift of traversing other people's timelines, so the only way she could find out what was going on was to meet up with someone in the dream state who knew. Plus, if she started of habit of going into the dream state what would happen? Would she be executed or would the shock intensity begin to be ramped up. No, she probably didn't have very many times she could choose to dream without that avenue being closed out. Isabella would be able to find out where everyone was taken to. At least she was safely hidden and could look out for them. The question was how many were left to help Isabella? And would that be enough to mount any sort of successful rescue attempt? In the meantime, this monstrosity of a camp was home, wherever that was.

∞ ∞ ∞

Ara's rage was beginning to boil over. His grandfather was missing, and he was pretty sure he hadn't just gone for a walk. Rumors of people disappearing were all over Xenon. Soldiers wearing black had been observed swarming various residences and leaving carrying limp bodies who were either dead or knocked out by some sort of drug. Normally, there were clues given when people disappeared, but this was some sort of mass event, and one where nothing was communicated. People just went missing. Two days had passed since his grandfather had disappeared. While his grandfather was highly respected in his town, he was not outspoken and did not ever appear to do anything that would attract the attention of the authorities. That is what made Ara the most upset. Why would he be targeted?

Today he was going to try to discover what he could about his grandfather. He probably should have tried to look when the trail was fresh, but his father had forbidden him from taking any action in case he got detained. That risk seemed to have passed and he was finally able to look for clues to what happened around his grandfather's house. Ara was seventeen and very close to finishing his schooling. He saw first-hand a couple years earlier the extremes the government would take to get its way and still retained vivid memories and resentment from that. People his parent's age and older seemed to be so passive and accepting of the tyrannical actions the government seemed to do regularly. Why didn't they fight against it? But instead they were so careful, trying to not be noticed, hoping that they didn't get arrested. But they didn't stand up for anyone who did get detained. They just quietly murmured and complained but wouldn't do anything about it.

"You ready to go over there?" Ara asked his cousin Dom. Dom was about his age and was also curious about what had happened to their grandfather.

"Yeah, let's see what we can find out," Dom replied after looking around to make sure they wouldn't be noticed leaving. They didn't exactly have permission to go over there, but they hadn't been told they couldn't go – today.

Ara and Dom made a quiet exit from the farm. His grandfather's house was about an hour away by foot. Once they were clear of the farm, they both relaxed considerably.

"I was worried your dad would catch us leaving," Dom stated.

"Nah, he is working on the other side of the farm today," Ara answered. He was still internally concerned he would get caught but this was his idea and wanted to put on a confident face to things. "Let's take the back way over there. Should avoid seeing anyone we know."

"Good idea," Dom replied as he changed direction based on Ara's suggestion.

"If they took Grandpa, someone is going to pay," Ara said with passion in his voice. "We need to get him back."

"We aren't the only ones who feel that way," Dom said in response. "Most of my friends at school feel the same way. I bet if we could get some weapons, we could do a lot of damage to those government soldiers causing all these problems."

"You got that right," Ara replied. "But all we got right now is a bunch of nothing to fight them with. Maybe we could sneak into where they keep the weapons and take what we need?"

"That is a great idea!" Dom answered. "We just need to find out where they are keeping them. I bet we can."

Both boys walked quietly the rest of the journey looking for anything out of the ordinary and being extra quiet as they got closer to their destination. Ara had some rudimentary tracking skills. His grandfather had once been a hunter of animals and taught basic tracking to his grandchildren, even though hunting was not allowed anymore.

"You think we will find anything?" Dom asked in a quiet voice.

"Hard to know," Ara replied with a whisper. "The trail is a couple days old. At least there hasn't been any rain or weather to wash away the clues."

Ara and Dom arrived on their grandfather's land and did a careful and deliberate sweep as they had been taught.

"Looks like a vehicle parked here," Dom observed based on the indentation in the ground that still remained. "Someone probably took him."

"These cluster of tracks seem to head toward his house," Ara stated with a look of concentration on his face. "But there is what looks like a single set of tracks off this way. Based on how deep the tracks are, this person must have weighed a ton!"

"Or was carrying something heavy," Dom suggested. "Let's follow this one. I think the other one will last longer since it is more people."

The boys followed the tracks carefully, almost losing them a couple times when the ground became firmer.

"Looks like he turned around here but the tracks are much lighter," Ara offered. "Maybe he got rid of what he was carrying."

It was hard to see what he could have unloaded. There didn't seem to be any evidence of anything. Ara and Dom started feeling around blindly in the area around this, trying to find any possible hiding places when Dom's hand pushed through an obstructed opening.

"I think I may have found something," Dom whispered excitedly while removing the brush covering to reveal an opening. Inside was a large bag, big enough to hold a body.

"I hope this isn't what I think it could be," Ara said with some fear in his voice. "They wouldn't just dump grandpa out in woods like this would they?"

"Hard to know what those horrible people will do," Dom said with rising bitterness in his voice. "I guess we have to find out."

Ara and Dom carefully found the zipper on the bag to open it. Both let out a sigh of relief when it was quickly apparent it did not contain a body, but instead something else.

"What is in this bag?" Ara asked excitedly, thinking he now had an idea what it contained.

"It looks like weapons of some sort," Dom replied back. "Why would someone hide them out here like that, especially after taking grandpa?"

"I don't know, but we said we needed weapons," Ara stated with bravado growing in his voice. "These may not be meant for us, but with them we could maybe rescue him, if we could find out where they took him."

"Let's move them to a new place in case whoever left them comes back looking for them," Dom suggested. "You remember that spot we used to hide in when we were younger? Let's put them there."

"I remember," Ara replied with a smile recalling how his sister could never find him. Grandpa's place had all kinds of fun secrets in it like that.

The bag was extremely heavy and it was all they could do to hoist it between them as they began to make their way to the spot they agreed to take it to.

"Going somewhere?" came a voice behind them that they didn't recognize.

The boys turned around quickly to see a monstrous man looking down at them with an intensity in his stare that would make the strongest person whimper. The man had some sort of ministry emblem on his clothing and was holding a weapon that was pointed at them. The boys set down the bag quickly and started to make a motion like they were ready to run.

"I wouldn't be going anywhere if I were you," the man said with a stern but frightening tone. "Where do you think you are going with my bag?"

"We just found it," Ara finally was able to get out with a slight stutter in his voice. "If we knew it was yours, we would have left it alone."

"Did you look inside of it?"

"Just quickly," Ara admitted not seeing any reason to lie.

"And what would you want with a bag full of weaponry?" he asked.

Dom looked up defiantly. "They took our grandpa and we mean to get him back!"

"You do now do you?" the man said with a menacing smile growing on his face. "And how do you plan to do that? Have you even ever used one of these weapons before?"

"No, but we are not afraid of figuring it out." Ara stated starting to get his confidence back.

"Don't think you will survive very long to find out. You do know most weapons are keyed and if the wrong person uses them, it will not go well for the person to tries to use it?" the man questioned.

"No, I didn't know that," Ara answered, slowly losing the confidence he had just built up.

"And did you also know that there are sensors everywhere that even if you managed to not kill yourself figuring these out, you would be detected mere moments after firing one?" he asked.

"No, I didn't know that," Ara answered again, all of a sudden feeling dejected fully.

"Are you going to arrest us or kill us?" Dom asked with a glowering look still burning in his eyes. "That is what you ministry people do isn't it?"

"Some do, that is true," the man replied evenly. "But is your lucky day I am not one of them."

But if you put the weapons here, you helped arrest my grandfather," Ara challenged. "We saw the tracks to the weapons."

"In battle sometimes you need to give up ground before you can take it back," the man answered.

"Then what are you going to do with us?" Dom asked not fully understanding the reply.

"I am going to train you," came an unexpected reply. "I can't let that passion go to waste when I need help gaining Xenon's independence.

Dom and Ara looked at each other with a very confused expression. "I don't understand," Ara finally replied.

"No, I suppose you don't. There are some of us who believe the government has massively overstepped lately. I lost a friend in Preath who gave his life with thirty-nine other children who died because they would not renounce their beliefs. We need a safe place where people who believe in freedom can come. I and others who share my beliefs want to make that place here in Xenon."

"This is a trick," Ara said suddenly. "You are just trying to get us to admit to rebellion so you can harm us more."

"No, we already admitted that," Dom said thoughtfully. "Assume we believe you, then what happens next?"

"We recruit others who feel as you do then we train them. And when we are ready, we will strike back and not only free your grandfather and others who were taken, but will free Xenon from the tyranny that has gone too far one too many times."

Dom and Ara looked at each other carefully, reaching an unspoken agreement. "I know a place you can hide," Ara offered. "I will bring others who will want to help. I am Ara and this is my cousin Dom."

"Call me Thorin," the large man replied. "We have a lot of work to do and very little time to complete it."

CHAPTER 17

$\mathcal{G}$abriel was normally a confident person, but in this setting, he felt out of his element as he looked at the more seasoned dreamers in front of him. He was growing reacquainted with the slight chill through his body, as was typical when being underground. Each dreamer had so much experience that he could learn from, yet here he was in the center of the room preparing to show them how to enter the dream state in a new way. There was notable skepticism on some of their faces, probably wondering what this new dreamer of suspect origins would have to offer. But he also saw some who he knew from before, who knew his actions in the Great Evacuation. Here he saw genuine interest and positive feedback and a willingness to give his words a fair hearing.

"Alaine assures me that this room is undetectable by the Oversite scanner array," Gabriel began as he looked around the underground room to see the copper mesh he had become familiar with. "So, anyone is able to dream safely in here without jeopardizing our position, even if you dream the way you are accustomed to."

Gabriel heard some grumbling from the crowd about how it was unfair that they had to hide even more than they had been. They were not frustrated at him, but more the situation where many of their friends and loved ones were languishing in internment camps while they were stuck hiding deep below the surface in a copper lined cage.

"Isabella asked me to try to conduct a lesson in an alternate way I recently discovered to enter the dream state. This way is not detectable by the Oversite scanner array, and while interacting in it feels different, there isn't anything I could do before that I cannot do this new way."

"Is the ability to do this a gift or is it something everyone can do?" one of the audience members asked.

"I don't know," Gabriel answered. "So far, I am the only one who has successfully done it. I don't view myself as an expert at this in any way but I will gladly tell and show each of you everything I have put together so far. So, to start with, I need a volunteer."

"I'm game," a volunteer offered. "I am Carson."

"Thanks Carson," Gabriel stated while holding up his sensor used to detect active dream state activities. "This device will detect the dream state and uses the same technology the government has deployed to detect us. I asked three of you to enter the dream state earlier. Please do so now. Carson, point the scanner around the room and see if you can identify who the culprits are."

Carson waited a few moments then proceeded to walk around the room and quickly identified all three volunteers Gabriel had picked. Some murmuring echoed around the room.

"Pretty bad, right?" Gabriel asked. "These sensors are everywhere. They can penetrate our basements and anywhere we typically use transport tubes. Nowhere is safe unless we are far under the ground or in a copper cage like we are now. The government didn't act right away because they were tracking us, building a database when they were ready to strike."

"So, we aren't safe even if we return and don't dream anymore?" Carson asked with resignation.

"Correct," Gabriel replied, "but we can use facial recognition disruption tech and dream in different ways to make short trips to the surface. This is why learning this is important. Because, if we are going to be able to make a difference to rescue those who are in the camps, we will need people who can move without being detected on the surface."

"Ok, you sold me," Carson offered while Gabriel noticed other heads nodding around the room. "How do you do it?"

Gabriel proceeded to walk them all through the steps he took to enter the modified dream state. Teacher had allowed him to scan and make copies of the text passages that had been helpful to him and Gabriel walked through the observations he had made in his research.

"Ok, put the scanner on me," Gabriel requested. "I am going to do some translocation. See if it can pick me up."

Gabriel centered himself and split his focus as he had before. His vision once again attained a dual focus, half in color with an image offset in black and white. He shifted his perspective to focus in on the greys and then seeing Carson through this lens, took in his features and imagined him on the other side of where Gabriel was standing. Once he was there, Gabriel shifted his focus back to the full color view with just a shadow of the other still present.

"Did you detect anything?" Gabriel asked with a smile on his face as he saw the amazement on Carson's as well as the assembled audience.

"Wasn't expecting you to move me!" Carson said with a laugh. "But no, there is nothing showing."

"Good, now each of you needs to try to practice. I'll have Alaine monitor the scanner to let us know if anyone goes into the regular dream state by mistake."

After a couple of hours of instruction, Gabriel made his excuses to leave, walking to the area he had claimed as his sleeping quarters. Three people had succeeded. This was more than he had before his lesson, but was woefully inadequate for what was needed to mount a successful rescue or similar action.

"How did it go?" Isabella asked, interrupting his internal thoughts.

"Not well enough," Gabriel said with a hint of dejection in his voice. "Three succeeded. Only three."

"Others will learn in time," Isabella answered while putting her arm around Gabriel to give him a small hug of reassurance. "It took you a long time to learn how to dream the first time. It is a lot like this for those you are teaching."

"I suppose you are right," Gabriel answered. "But we will need a lot more help than that if we are going to get the others back."

"You are worried about her, aren't you?" Isabella asked.

"Yeah, I sure am," Gabriel replied with a faraway look in his eyes. "I miss being able to talk to her. They have done something to those they captured to keep them from dreaming."

"Why don't you visit the camp she is in tonight," Isabella suggested. "Not in person of course, but dream your way there to see how she is doing."

Gabriel nodded. It wouldn't be the same, but it was something he could do. She just needed to stay alive long enough for a rescue to be staged. That is, if they didn't just execute her and the others first.

Gabriel watched as his grandmother exited the room. He quickly shifted his focus and traversed his view to the camp where she was being held. He found her quickly enough. She was lying in an open area by herself in the compound. It looked like she had lost some weight. In fact, everyone there looked like they had lost some weight. Food must not have been provided in sufficient quantity. At least she was sleeping but seemed to be shivering through her tattered clothing. He took some time to investigate the compound she was in. Was there a way out, some sort of vulnerability? Gabriel looked inside the only real building structure. It seemed a lot warmer based on how the guards were acting inside. They seemed to have plenty to eat. Gabriel nearly lost the dream state with his anger due to the disparity of conditions.

But he fought that back and kept looking around. He found a room that looked like a doctor's clinic but it was anything but that in a traditional sense. Inside appeared to be two prisoners strapped to a bed having who knows what being done to them. Gabriel looked closer feeling shamefully thankful he didn't know them. The electronic chart above their beds indicated they were subject to some sort of experiment. Someone was trying to figure out what gave them the powers they had and were being very invasive into their bodies to try to find out.

Gabriel developed a sickening feeling in his stomach. Would Raelynn be next? This was not right what was being done and they were probably using science to justify this outrage. Gabriel fought back tears as he brought his focus to the locked food storage area. He was a long way away and had never tried to translocate from this distance before. It was a risk, but Gabriel focused in on some food rations. With some effort, he translocated them to where Raelynn was sleeping, doing his best to hide them under her body. Suddenly feeling tired, he exited the dream state and collapsed into a deep and now troubled sleep.

∞ ∞ ∞

"Do you need anything more tonight?" Aaliyah asked Sharna.

Sharna looked up absently, barely registering the question. Aaliyah had been asking that daily, Sharna considered, a change since she had returned from her leave. At least she improved in her time to get into lily meditation state. It was sort of like Aaliyah was expecting her to ask for advice on the lily, not that she would have a lot to show her. After all, she was just a technician versus the accomplished researcher Sharna was.

"Unless you have recovered enough for another experiment, I do not have need for you further tonight," Sharna replied with the sound of indifference in her voice.

"Good night then," Aaliyah answered. "If I can help you on anything, please let me know. Even your lily meditation."

Sharna sighed internally, so this is what is was about. She wanted to be asked. Sharna hated it when people wanted to be validated. People should be confident in themselves and not need others to pat them on the head and say they are worth something.

"Do you know why you got better at the meditation since you went on the vacation?" Sharna asked finally, figuring that would be the fastest way to get back to work.

"There are probably several reasons working together," Aaliyah answered, brightening up some to be asked a question. "I think having time to be away from all the distractions did more than anything. When all you have is yourself to keep you company, it really makes you take time to look within and work some things out."

Sharna stared into the distance contemplating what Aaliyah had said. Could it be as simple as that? Being able to tune out all the distractions? There were so many open projects, ideas and things to do. But this lily meditation was central to her research and while you can learn a lot measuring and testing others, being able to experience it on your own would be the most enlightening form of research that could be done on this topic.

"I am going to be away for a while," Sharna said. I will leave you instructions on some testing I want run on you in the lily mediation state. In the rest of the time, see if you can continue improving."

Aaliyah looked surprised by the comment but did not question it. "I will do as you instruct," she finally answered before making her way out the door, as it was clear she was dismissed.

Sharna pulled up the travel log Aaliyah had submitted prior to her vacation. It looked like some sort of tourist nature preserve. Sharna quickly queried what she would need to bring with her to visit one of these sites. After gathering what was recommended, she used her Oversite access to secure the necessary travel approvals and logged that she was going to be in the field researching for the foreseeable future. Then with a slight smirk on her face, ran a filter in Oversite that would mask her presence and location on the surveillance grid. No mid-level bureaucrat was going to interrupt her research. It would take a full minister level access to unlock it, something she was pretty sure Xavier would only do if it was absolutely necessary.

Sharna looked around her lab one last time, taking in her kingdom. She wondered how long it would be until she was able to return. Sharna decided to pack lightly, leaving most of her electronic capabilities behind. She did pick up some literature on the lily religion and one of the lily plants Aaliyah was using. Sharna made the short walk to the nearest travel hub while contemplating how well the patch in Oversite was keeping her location hidden.

∞ ∞ ∞

Thorin read through the latest intelligence Stefan had managed to smuggle to the CET rebel group. Those participating in the rebel action did not seem to be identified so far. No one was absent without leave – yet. His superior thought it odd that he asked for some leave in Xenon of all places, but since the planned extractions had occurred and things had been quiet for some time, there was no reason to deny his request. Others had acted similarly and had spread themselves around the sector of Xenon. Thorin wondered if he would gain any sympathy from the rest of the CET community. Chances are some would follow and some would maintain their loyalty to the capitol. He really didn't want to take on his own soldiers, but the cause of freedom was something that weighted heavily on him and others who had joined him.

Thorin glanced out at the assembled group of youngsters who now counted themselves for this rebellion. They had passion all right, but were so undisciplined. What they needed were more arms and munitions. Thorin smuggled enough to be a seed for some units, but more would have to be gathered. The best way to do that was to capture some armories and build out from there. Stefan provided him some possible targets, he just needed to choose the one he wanted to raid. Easy to say, but with this group of untrained misfits, success was far from guaranteed.

"All right recruits," Thorin finally said to those assembled in front of him. "I have some information that we may choose to keep busy with tonight."

The group of about twelve in front of him let out an unprompted cheer.

"Don't get too excited," Thorin cautioned. "In battle, sometimes people die, and when it happens the first time, it will change you forever. Now, we are going to be careful on this so we can avoid that happening, but I need you all to follow my orders exactly."

Their countenances got more serious but they didn't really understand yet. It felt wrong to risk these excitable kids, but it was their freedom that they were fighting for also. It could be them next standing on a pond, waiting to freeze to death. They at least saw the world for what it was and were willing to do something to change the path it was on. Their parents were much more cautious. They had watched so many people be taken and lacked an effective means to fight back. But would they join or would they again run and hide? That was the question he really wanted to know.

First, he needed to get some wins that would grow confidence in this uprising and hopefully swell the growing ranks. If there was hope, then maybe more would join. In a world of despair, an arm reaching down to rescue is often ignored, even at the cost of one's life. This narrative needed to change and hope was calling.

Thorin assembled his team and distributed weapons to those he had sufficiently trained.

"Put these on," Thorin instructed handing each recruit a face recognition disruptor before reminding them how to enable it. "You know the plan. Those without weapons are our lookouts and are supposed to distract if needed. Let's go."

The team moved with stealth through some farms to approach their target destination by infrequently traveled roads. At this time of night, there should be next to no one at the district office for the Ministry of Scientific Compliance enforcement. There should be a weapons locker if Stefan's information was correct. It likely wouldn't have a large cache available but a few more weapons would make a big difference to fully arming his growing team.

Thorin nodded to his point person who took out a rock and hurled it at the door, trying to make as loud of a noise as possible. There was no response.   Thorin's scanner picked up a person inside, but he was probably sleeping, instead of being alert on watch like was his duty. He nodded again, and another rock was thrown, this one seeming to get a reaction from the lifeform on his scanner. Thorin readied his weapon in backup should his trained shooter miss. He could do this mission by himself with one arm tied behind his back, but that wouldn't develop the team.

The guard came to the door, turned on the light and looked around. Another rock hit the door per plan.

"Who is there?" he called out. "You better hope I don't catch you after you woke me up like that!"

Thorin shook his head at the absurdity of admitting he had been sleeping. Didn't he know he was likely being recorded and it would be reviewed if there was a loss of weaponry. The door opened and a burly man stepped out, shining a portable light source to see what had happened. Suddenly he slumped down to the ground. Looked like the kid had delivered his shot successfully.

Thorin advanced to meet up with the team. Stefan was right, there was a weapons cache here. Thorn made quick work of the locking mechanisms and had the recruits help put the newly captured weapons in carrying bags. Thorin would decode them later. It was only twelve pieces, but that was twelve more than they had before. Motioning the group to leave, they quickly left the building and walked past the guard lying on the ground. With the amount of drug that was given him, he should be like that until his relief came in the morning.

Once they returned to their hidden alcove, Thorin spoke, "Outstanding work everyone! No one got hurt and we completed our mission. And we are better armed than before. We have more work to do before we are ready to stage a rescue mission but we are one step closer. I think you have earned a name. How does Nightstalker One sound?

"Oh yeah!" Ara exclaimed. "Let's hear it for Nightstalker One!"

CHAPTER 18

Stefan watched Quintin stroll into the room like he owned it. Ever since the raid where the lily adherents were captured, accolades had not stopped flowing in. While Xavier received much of the acclaim as overall Minister, Quintin was over the Xenon sector and got a lot of positive publicity as well. His career was on a skyrocketing trajectory, provided he could take this mission to the finish line. Stefan thought this fast-developing arrogance was making Quintin careless, something he hoped to exploit.

"What is the good news today?" Quintin said excitedly, hoping for more wins to report up the chain.

"I am not sure we have a lot of that today," Ursula said carefully, "although this may be the pretext we have been looking for."

"I haven't read the daily brief yet," Quintin answered. "Explain what you are talking about."

"There have been some isolated raids on local Scientific Compliance enforcement offices in the past few hours," Ursula answered. "No one has been killed, but it appears that the local armaments stored on site were captured in each event."

"How many is some and how many weapons are believed compromised?" Quintin asked more briskly now.

"I have been reviewing the reports, sir, and so far, we have reports of eight raids and between fifty and a hundred weapons are missing," Stefan answered. "There may be more than this. We have been getting steady reports coming in the last few hours."

"Who is responsible?" Quintin asked, agitation increasing in his demeanor.

"We don't know," Ursula interrupted Stefan before he could answer. "They were somehow blocking their identify to Oversite. But the surveillance we do have shows they used approaches our troops would use if they were to do something like this. They also used top flight weapons and based on what I saw, they had some idea how to use them."

"Do you agree, Stefan?" Quintin asked.

"Yes, they didn't move with the precision of a CET grouping, but did appear to have some rudimentary training." Stefan answered, hoping he had said enough to throw off the focus on the CET members who had helped with the raids.

"Well, this clearly requires a strong response," Quintin said after a brief consideration of the information that had been presented. "We have been looking for a reason to take a strong action, maybe this will be what we need."

"Are you going to mobilize the CET community again?" Stefan asked.

"No, I don't think that is the best tool for this," Quintin answered thoughtfully. "They did not get embarrassed with these raids. No, we will mobilize some groupings of Scientific Enforcement officers and give them the duty. When we actually figure out who is responsible for the raids, that is when we will task the CET to neutralize them."

"What we need is someone who is skilled in Oversite enhancements to help track and identify who is responsible for this," Ursula offered. "I am pretty good at using it, and so far, there is nothing coming up."

"Who do we need?" Quintin asked impatiently.

"Everything I have seen, says the best person for this is Sharna Malloy," Ursula replied.

"Her again," Quintin said with frustration. "If I go to Xavier, I will be told no for her help based on she is working on, but if we ask her directly we could maybe get her to aid us."

"Good luck with that," Stefan said with a straight face, trying hard to not reveal the smirk he was feeling.

"All government employees of her rank are tracked on Oversite at all times," Quintin said dismissively. "I have access to the location services as do each of you."

"Try to find her then," Stefan said. "She doesn't show up for Ursula or me."

"Why do I have to do everything?" Quintin said while muttering under his breath. After quickly authenticating to Oversite, he put in this search query to be rewarded with subject not found. "That is odd. If it was on a need to know basis, I would expect to get a message saying needed authorization. This says she just isn't there."

"I can investigate her lab if you want," Stefan answered. "May be some clues to where she is at."

"Fine, do that," Quintin answered. "Ursula and I have a lot of planning to do anyway on our response to these raids. Hurry back. We will need your military expertise before we deploy."

Stefan really didn't expect to gather any clues to Sharna's disappearance. But visiting her lab was the next logical step in finding her. And what he knew about Sharna, she wouldn't help someone who came to bother her unannounced no matter who they were unless she wanted to help. But Quintin thought he was so important his mere request would summon the stars. No, this was going to be a futile trip, but at least he could get some word out to Thorin on the fury that was about to be unleashed on a largely innocent population.

∞ ∞ ∞

Sharna surveyed her surroundings, beginning to have doubts about her course of action. Why was she going to the middle of nowhere again? Nature studies were never a passion of hers. She likely knew more about nature than most of the population did, but it had never been interesting.   Computers, electronics, and technology, those were interesting. Biology and nature, not so much. But you couldn't always choose what path the research would take if you wanted to get to the answer.

Good experiments and research needed controlled conditions, and for sure didn't need any annoying tourists messing up her work. Some quick work in Oversite had revoked all passes for anyone who wanted to come here. Beyond the people distractions, she wasn't fully sure what to expect. Her research determined that some people ventured off of the protected path and put themselves at undue risk from wildlife. It was somehow a thrill to do that? That didn't make any sense to Sharna. She planned to stay in the path which had the protective field. In hindsight she should have got more information from what Aaliyah did on her trip but it probably wasn't that important of information anyway. You didn't want assistants to think they knew more than they actually did or they start making their own decisions on experiments. That could be catastrophic.

The entrance to the preserve was monitored only by an electronic gate. Sharna allowed herself to be scanned, which confirmed her authorization to enter. Once passing through the gate, Sharna looked at the layout of the protected nature preserve. It was bigger than she had envisioned and would require a lot of walking. The location at the far end of the expanse appeared to be the most isolated, so that seemed to be as good of place as any to walk to. If she saw something better along the way, she could always stop prior to arriving there.

The journey on the trail was quiet. Sharna mostly heard just her breathing and the sound of her feet walking. Plus, if she tried hard enough, she could hear the faint humming sound of the protection field. These fields were setup to act as a natural repellant for wildlife. Great care was taken to ensure these valuable animals were provided a natural habitat, not interfered with by the toxic expansion of civilization. It wasn't practical for animals to run wild in populated areas, protected against harm. In response, the government had worked to reduce population zones for people, trying to reserve more and more land areas for nature in its natural state. These forcefield type zones helped maintain the segregation in order to better protect the ecosystem of the planet, pursuing a defense against manmade climate change.

Every so often Sharna encountered a bridge that would create places where wildlife could pass through the observation zones. Wildlife were given every advantage here with only small zone of refuge for the human observer.

The sun was nearly down as Sharna finally reached her intended destination. Sharna even had to admit the scenery here was appealing. In the distance she saw a waterfall and if she stood very still and held her breath, she could swear she heard the water traversing it. This was a place of calm, one where she hoped to gain clarity on the problems that were challenging her.

Sharna took off her carrying bag and sat down in the designated resting area. In her role in the lab, she very rarely had an opportunity to view the world around her and take in its beauty. She fought an internal urge to do a work-related activity, and instead took in the view in front of her and watched as the sun slowly set across the horizon.

"It's beautiful, isn't it?" a voice behind her spoke out causing her to jump slightly.

Sharna turned around with an annoyed expression showing on her face. This area was supposed to be locked down to only have her in it for her research, yet someone was still interrupting her. This girl was likely still in the school system based on her perceived age.

"You aren't supposed to be here," Sharna said in response trying to figure out a way to make the girl leave.

"But yet I am here," the girl said with a mischievous smile on her face. "I'll bet you are used to getting your way, aren't you?"

"That is not material to you being here," Sharna snapped. "I should report you for intruding right now."

"You could," the girl answered looking at the lily plant by Sharna, "but then you would never learn how to complete the lily meditation you clearly came here to try to figure out. Plus, then people would know you were here."

"What do you know about that?" Sharna said suddenly and with suspicion. "I didn't tell anyone I was coming here to research that."

"Does that make me wrong?" the girl said with a cheerful but antagonizing smile.

Sharna was getting increasingly frustrated and just wanted to be left alone. But here was some annoying kid interrupting her plans and somehow knew too much about what she was up to that shouldn't. "What do you know about lily meditation that could help me?" she finally asked.

"If you could get rid of your prideful attitude and be willing to truly learn from some dumb kid, you may find out that I know enough to help you accomplish your goal."

Sharna tried her best to suppress a smile. Despite her annoyance, she had to admit she liked the attitude and confidence that was being projected. She was used to having her way and cowing those around her. But this girl was willing to speak to her like she knew more than her. And possibly she did. "Ok, I'll give you a few minutes to convince me you know what you are talking about before I get you forcibly removed. The clock is ticking."

The girl simply smiled and sat down saying nothing while staring at Sharna with a look that dared her to follow through on her threat. After several minutes of silence, Sharna was again getting frustrated.

"Well, don't you have anything to say?" Sharna finally interrupted the silence.

"I have a lot to say, but you haven't asked me any questions," the girl replied while keeping her gaze intense on Sharna, unbothered by the threat hanging over her.

"What do you know about the lily meditation?" Sharna asked in an exasperated tone.

"I know that you will never achieve it unless you can get past your self-importance and humble yourself," the girl replied. "You need to approach in faith, not in intellect. You can succeed if you have intellect but you must rely first on faith, to believe it, to bring control over the competing urges and impulses inside of yourself to center yourself. Only when you do that, can you hope to enter this state."

More of this faith talk, Sharna thought. Why did it keep coming back to this? Gabriel had hinted at this, as had Aaliyah. How could she suspend her disbelief enough to jump through this hoop? "I am sorry, but I have a very hard time suspending logical thought for some hope of an outcome. You may be wired that way, but I am certainly not."

"Aren't you some sort of hotshot engineer researcher?" the girl asked. "If you don't like how something is wired, you change it, you don't just give up and accept it do you?"

"That is different and you know it!" Sharna said sharply.

"Is it really that different?" the girl replied. "Sometimes we need to be remade to become the design we were meant to be. The Way of the Lily can help with that, but you first have to take a step in faith. And when you have taken that step, only then will you fully understand."

Sharna let the girl's words absorb and gave them some serious thought. Could she really redesign herself? And if she could, did she want to? After some time considering this thought she looked up ready to respond to the challenge. The girl was nowhere to be seen. Well, at least she was gone now. But the girl's words would not leave Sharna. As much as she tried to sleep, her mind kept racing to process the words that were spoken. Was she really willing to change her design, to allow herself to be remade in a new way? At last, a troubled sleep overtook her.

Sharna felt something was off. It was like a fog was enveloping her and her view absent of normal colors. The fog cleared slightly and she saw a closeup view of the waterfall she had previously seen in the distance. The sound of the rushing water was louder than she had remembered before. Even without color, it was breathtaking.

"It really is something to see up close, isn't it?" a voice behind her suddenly said.

Sharna turned to see someone she had seen before, standing there with a mischievous smile on her face. "Who are you?" she finally asked.

"I am Trisha, thanks for asking," came the reply. "I am a Seeker and with a bit of prompting, you have entered the dream state."

"What does that mean?" Sharna asked with a combination of confusion and curiosity.

"It means your fancy little detector is probably going crazy that you are doing the lily meditation right now," Trisha answered.

"But I just went to sleep," Sharna replied. "I wasn't even staring at the lily. This is just a dream and I am imagining all this."

"That is something you will need to decide in the morning," Trisha answered. "For now, follow me for a bit. I have something to show you."

Sharna looked around sullenly, not sure what to do or what to believe. Lacking a better option at her disposal, she walked to catch up with Trisha.

"Where are we going?" Sharna asked while trying to hold back a helpless frustration.

"You will see," Trisha answered while continuing her brisk walk toward the waterfall.

Trisha walked on some sort of stone stairway and disappeared behind the water. Sharna moved quickly to keep up with her until she saw she was stopped in front of an opening behind the waterfall.

"When you can muster some faith, come to this location when you are awake and I will meet you here," Trisha spoke. "Many answers await you."

As soon as Trisha stated these words, the fog Sharna experienced at the beginning began again to consume her, erasing her presence in this place. All that remained was a vivid memory primed to haunt her when she at last awoke.

Sharna stirred from her slumber as the light began to form on the skyline. She was troubled as she reflected on her dreams. Something didn't seem right and she had this strong urging to visit the waterfall, beyond the protected forcefield. But how could a suggestion in her dream have anything but an illogical hope associated with it?

Sharna pulled out the scanner she had developed to sense lily meditation state activity. It had detected some activity in the proximity in the last few hours. That didn't mean it was her though. It could have been that girl who claimed to know so much about it. Sharna had trouble explaining it, but inside her she knew she needed to go on. This acted against all logic and sense but with an unexplainable pull, she carefully scanned the countryside for evidence of predatory animals, she then began a brisk walk toward the waterfall. Either she was making an utter fool of herself, or she was about to have the breakthrough she had been looking for.

CHAPTER 19

Thorin minimized his motion to stay unnoticed so he could get a better view of the Merrifield town square. Dom and Ara knew this area well and had suggested several hiding places where Nightstalker One could monitor and if necessary, protect the town without being easily observed. If Stefan's warning was right, something was going to go down here today, and not something that would bode well for those who occupied the town.

The morning passed slowly with nothing of significance occurring. There were town locals mulling around, doing normal activities. Dom and Ara signaled nothing was amiss, pointing out anyone who may not be a local to Thorin's watchful eyes. Thorin was worried Stefan had been misled on the intended target, but it was unrealistic to expect the government to be on time. Regardless, he stayed patient and hoped his lightly trained team could follow his example and do the same.

He heard it before he saw it. There was a lot of yelling and barking of orders from all sides as a group of about thirty Scientific Compliance enforcement officers converged on the town center, directing a group of confused residents including Dom and Ara ahead of them. It was likely they had been doing a cursory sweep for locals house by house moving toward the main square. Contained in the masses were a cross section of people ranging from small children to elderly and those in between. If they hadn't rounded up every resident of the town and surrounding area, they had accomplished something close to it. Thorin recognized one of the most vocal officers as the person who had been drugged during the weapons raid. He was clearly furious and out for revenge for the embarrassment that had been perpetrated on him. And those with him demonstrated a very similar level of enthusiasm. People would do a lot to defend their pride or loss of face. This gave Thorin great concern. Their entire group had been shamed and they were on a mission to restore their view of their own honor. Maybe honor was the wrong word, Thorin reflected. The intensity on the faces gave the feeling of evil that he could not quite explain. Something bad was going to happen.

"I am officer Damien," the burly officer that had been disgraced yelled out. "Bring me the first witness."

Thorin watched as an elderly woman was forcibly pulled forward then shoved hard to stand in front of Damien.

"Who is responsible for attacking my post?" Damien yelled at the woman.

"I don't know, officer Damien," the feeble woman replied. "I heard about it in the morning just like everyone else did."

"Liar!" Damien screamed and drew his arm back and unloaded a forceful strike across the head of the lady causing her to fall to the ground as blood began to flow from where she was hit. She appeared to be disoriented and when she tried to stand, she seemed unable to. "I will not ask you again, who attacked my post?"

The lady looked up with bewilderment and sadness through the blood dripping over her eyes as the crowd began to murmur in distaste and agitation. "Why are you striking me? I said I don't know!"

Damien pulled out his weapon with a slow evil grin and pointed it at her head, slowly and deliberately pulling the trigger. The sound of the shot echoed across the stunned silence of the townspeople watching as the woman collapsed dead.

"You just murdered an innocent woman!" Ara called out breaking the silence as those with him began to clamor with outrage.

"No one is innocent!" Damien answered with rage still unsatiated. "I will kill each and every one of you if I have to until I get my answer!"

"No, I don't think you will!" Ara cried out, pulling out his concealed weapon and firing it at the open target of Damien.

Damien jolted like he had been stung, his hand reflexively moving to his shoulder where the shot had penetrated. The remaining officers quickly brandished their weapons, preparing to open fire into the massed group of town residents.

Chaos broke out as the assembled people began to run and screams of panic echoed throughout the town center. Thorin leveled his weapon at the first officer who started to reach for his weapon, hitting him between the eyes. He had no interest in giving mercy to a rabble of miscreants set on committing genocide. One by one, Thorin put down each new threat he saw. Others also fell, as the rest of Nightstalker One joined in and some of the townspeople took what tools and implements they had to charge the Scientific Compliance officers. Thorin watched as Ara and Dom bravely evacuated many town residents to places of safety. The action was fast and the devastation overwhelming. Most officers fell in the first round of action, but some had the sense to try to flee, not that it created a different result as sharpshooters picked them off one by one. It did not appear that any of the instigators survived.

An eerie silence descended on the town soon replaced by wailing of those who had lost loved ones in the fighting. The collateral damage was tragic. Thorin would have preferred to take the officers out before they rounded up the people, but until they killed the woman, they hadn't done anything to justify that level of response. The defense was righteous but innocent people had perished.

Thorin surveyed the damage and commanded most of his team to aid the wounded while he asked the rest to gather the weapons the attackers had been carrying to be later decrypted and reissued. The town got off easier than they would have, with five dead and a score more wounded. But beyond the casualties, the town now had their allegiance decided. They could no longer stand back in neutral passiveness but instead had stood up to tyranny and would not accept anything less than their freedom. This was no longer a pastime of the young, all were now united in the opposition of injustice.

Ara come up to Thorin with a makeshift bandage on his arm and a pained expression on his face. "Why did they have to kill her?" he asked. "She didn't do anything wrong."

"No, she didn't," Thorin reflected. "She simply spoke the truth, and there is no place for truth when someone is on a quest for vengeance."

"How do you handle it?" Ara asked. "I mean, taking the life of someone."

"You do what you must," Thorin replied. "Just never come to love it or you will be no better than that beast Damien was."

Ara nodded as he slowly walked away. The passion and excitement Ara had originally began with appeared to be replaced with something new. Oh, the resolute focus remained, but the boyish passion was now replaced with a serious countenance –seemingly robbed of its innocence. And Thorin did not think Ara would be the last person he would witness this transformation in.

∞ ∞ ∞

"Gabriel," Isabella implored, "you really need to slow down. If you keep this pace up it could be very dangerous for you."

"Everyone tells me that I have a lot of strength in the dream gifts," Gabriel answered. "How can I take it slowly when so many people are suffering, and a full-scale rebellion is happening? Besides, as I push myself harder, I feel like my gifts are getting stronger as well."

Gabriel saw the concern in his grandmother's face. She didn't give bad advice on this, but he really needed to keep pushing. With so many dreamers in captivity, every little bit by the remaining people with the gift helped, not to mention those who could do so outside of the surveillance grid.

"It just makes me afraid for you," Isabella answered. "You are doing so well but what if you make a mistake and can't get yourself out of something? I am not sure I could bear losing you after having lost you once before."

"I will try to be careful, grandmother," Gabriel answered in a slightly distracted way. "I know you are trying to look out for me."

"I heard that we have several more dreamers trained to the new way," Isabella offered. "One of them we sent to try to influence Sharna. She is really seeking I think."

"Be careful with that one," Gabriel cautioned. "She doesn't mean badly but her values are very out of sync with those in Kayden. She cares purely about her research from what I gleaned in my time with her."

"Everyone deserves a chance to recalibrate their compass," Isabella said with a smile. "I think she will have her hands full with Trisha. I have been watching her some and it has been very entertaining so far."

"She learns quickly and isn't afraid to speak up," Gabriel offered. "It makes me sort of sad that she is filling in for Raelynn, but I am sure she will do a good job."

"I am glad you are taking that so well," Isabella replied. "I don't know what you have in mind for tonight, but please be careful."

Gabriel returned his grandmother's embrace as she left him alone to his thoughts. The rebellion was truly happening. People without dreamer assistance were rising up in Xenon to fight for their freedom. But that would only increase the risk for those who were in detainment. Would they be killed in retribution or would they be moved to a more secure location if the resistance closed in on their location? Gabriel didn't know the answer, and in the time he had spent watching the decisionmakers he didn't even think that they had got that far in their thinking yet.

Gabriel checked the time realizing he was overdue and quickly scurried to the transport hub.

"Sorry, I am a bit late," Gabriel said apologetically. "I hope you haven't been waiting very long?"

"A bit," Tom answered, "but we will cut you some slack. I know you have been pretty busy."

"So, do you have it prepped?" Gabriel asked, looking in Alaine's direction.

"Pretty sure it ready," Alaine replied with confidence in her work.

"Reconnaissance only this trip, right?" William asked who had recently found a way to join back up with Gabriel and the team.

Gabriel nodded. He wanted to confirm that they could travel undetected plus get a better feel for the compound that Raelynn was being held in.

"Shall we load up?" William asked while checking his gear to ensure he had weaponry and other supplies needed for this mission.

"Yes, let's get going," Gabriel answered. "Alaine can you remind me what I need to do to operate the transport tube after your modifications?"

"It is pretty much the same as before," Alaine answered. "Except get in the dream state first before you press the button. Pretty sure it will work. I bypassed the gate signal that makes sure you are in the dream state before it engages since you are dreaming at a different brainwave pattern. Tom, if something happens to Gabriel and you need to get us back, flip this switch right der here before you use it and it will work the old way."

"Probably safer with detection coming back. They may know we were there but won't be able to be caught," Tom suggested to an agreeing Alaine.

"I wish we were back together under better circumstances," Gabriel offered, "but it is good to see everyone. Let's be safe."

Gabriel shifted himself into the new form of dreaming, seeing the double-vision suddenly. He wasn't sure what point he should press the go button but first shifted his focus to be mostly in the dream view, in case that had some bearing on how this would work. Once he had steadied his focus, he reached forward and engaged the two buttons and felt the familiar jolt that followed a translocation in a transport tube.

"I think it worked!" Tom said in an excited whisper. "I was honestly a little bit worried something would go wrong."

"I did it right," Alaine said with a smile. "You just need to have more belief."

Gabriel nodded curtly, acknowledging the work to get there but clearly focused for the business at hand. "Spread out together with a partner just like we discussed," Gabriel instructed. "Tom and William, why don't you secure the perimeter, Alaine and I will try to get closer to the compound."

"Wouldn't you rather partner with one of us? We have the weaponry in case something goes wrong," William asked.

"I can get us out in a hurry if we have trouble. I really need you to keep the transport tube safe and keep watch. I think your weaponry is much more valuable for that," Gabriel replied.

William didn't look convinced at Gabriel's explanation, but he moved to follow Gabriel's instructions, motioning for Tom to follow.

"The watch is usually the least vigilant this time of night," Gabriel whispered to Alaine. "I can get you into the control room, but you won't have much time. We will have to time it when the guard on duty gets up to use the bathroom."

"Whenever you are ready, I am," Alaine replied. "But shouldn't we get closer to the compound? This is pretty far away to translocate from."

"It is not so far anymore," Gabriel answered back quietly. "I have been practicing at much further distances than this recently."

Gabriel shifted his focus to the full dream state, shifting his gaze to monitor the actions of the guard on the main control room console. The past few nights, he had left in about a thirty-minute window. It would hopefully not be much longer now. Gabriel quickly shifted his view to the courtyard. The food he had been stealthily translocating seemed to have provided some strength to the prisoners. Raelynn shared nearly all she was given. He really wished she had consumed more for herself but that was the kind of person she was. Even with that help, they all looked weak. Gabriel found Raelynn resting in her usual place, showing new bruises on her body, evidence she had again been mistreated.

Gabriel shifted his focus again back to the control room and saw the guard was just standing up to leave.

"Are you ready?" Gabriel suddenly asked Alaine.

"Yes."

"I'll bring you out right before he comes back," Gabriel explained. "Be careful."

Gabriel quickly took in Alaine's features and reimagined her in the control room. She appeared there suddenly and went to work determining the level of security present and what systems would need to be bypassed in order to get the prisoners out safely. Gabriel wanted to check on Raelynn some more but instead kept his focus on the security guard who had left as well as the entrance to the control room. Every second mattered and the more Alaine could learn, the better chances they could develop a workable rescue plan. Not much more than five minutes passed and the guard began to head back to the control room. Gabriel quickly focused in on Alaine and brought her back to where he was, just before the guard came back into the room.

"Were you able to learn anything?" Gabriel asked urgently.

"I wish had more time," Alaine replied, "but I found a few things that can help us. We need bring some gear with us, but I think we can jam them things long enough to get the kill collars off everyone without them going bang. But we will still need to keep the attention of them guards somewhere else."

"Good," Gabriel replied excitedly. "I was hoping you would say that. Call back the others, I should return in a few minutes. If I am gone longer than thirty, have Tom take all of you back. I can transport myself back if I need to."

"We didn't talk about do'n this," Alaine said. "Tom won't be happy."

"It will be fine," Gabriel answered. "See you shortly."

Gabriel laid his body in a prone sleep like position then dream shifted himself next to where Raelynn was lying on the ground. He translocated some additional food rations under her threadbare clothing to conceal them.

"Raelynn, it's Gabriel," he whispered while gently nudging her.

"Am I dreaming?" she answered as her eyes slowly opened. "It isn't safe for you here, Gabriel."

"We are going to rescue you soon," Gabriel promised. "Hold strong a little longer."

"You can't just rescue me," Raelynn replied with force of conviction. If I leave, it will kill several others. They have us tied together somehow."

"I know," Gabriel replied gently. "We will rescue you all. Help is coming. Keep up your strength just a little bit longer.

"What a nice dream," Raelynn muttered as she drifted back to sleep.

Gabriel looked at her sadly for a bit longer. She would not last much longer. Her strength was clearly waning and her body was badly beaten. He could not wait much longer. Gabriel shifted himself back to where the rest of the team was assembled.

"Let's head back," Gabriel announced. "There isn't much time and we have much to do."

CHAPTER 20

"You know what to do," Thorin calmly pronounced to his Nightstalker One advance team. "Be careful out there. The rest of us have your back if you need to pull back."

"We got it," Dom echoed back as he took two teammates with him in the advance scout position. Making a few hand signals Dom slowly moved toward the rail hub right on the border with the Villron sector.

This was a desolate looking place, but a strategic one. Nearly all rail traffic into Xenon came through this hub. There was technically one other, but it was rarely used and far out of the way. Thorin shook his head at the absurdity that in a time of active guerilla activity, that this was left unguarded. Granted there was no weaponry stored here, but the tactical importance of this place if the capitol wanted to bring a lot of troops or equipment in quickly was vast.

Most government installations like this had a designated fast response team assigned to respond to suspicious activity, usually within thirty minutes or less. But Thorin was pretty sure the planned action would be done well before that response arrived.

Thorin looked through his closed-circuit drone feed. It was nice having some technology again. It was a bit rudimentary, but it gave him live images of what was happening with Dom and was not tied into Oversite. As the resistance had grown, so did the addition of some new skill sets as evidenced by the drone he could now use. And with all the technological advantages the capitol could bring to bear, every little bit helped.

Dom carefully laid down explosive charges to hit multiple rail lines. It would be repairable, but would take considerable time to bring back online. Meanwhile, teams such as Thorin's would be able to harry anyone sent to repair the lines. It wasn't perfect, but it would definitely disrupt the flow of additional troops to immediately reinforce Xenon following the many recent disturbances. If the capitol wanted to bring soldiers in, they would have to now march them in on foot which would take days to get into position. There were still aerial options to fly troops in, but due to the required energy outlays, Thorin was pretty sure that would only be done in moderation.

"Ready to blow the charges, sir," Dom reported.

Thorin smiled how well Dom had snuck up on him. He really had a talent for moving with stealth. If Thorin wasn't tracking him on the drone feed, he wasn't sure he would have been warned of his arrival before it was announced.

"Let's show them some fireworks!" Thorin said with a grin. "Ara, why don't you push the button today. If that doesn't put a smile on your face, I don't know what will."

Ara walked up to the detonator trying hard to not show too much excitement. Getting an affirmative motion from Thorin, Ara triggered the detonator, unleashing a huge fireball of explosions. The ground shook from the concussive blast and loud sounds of metal being destructively remade shook the countryside. Thorin experienced ringing in his ears which he was pretty sure would wear off in a few hours.

"Let's move out, Nightstalker One," Thorin called out. "Let's make sure we have another successful mission where everyone who left together, returned together. I think some company will be here very soon, and I would rather not be here to greet them until we are ready to."

Thorin glanced back at the troops assembled behind him as they made a fast exit from the rail hub. This unit was still pretty green but what they lacked in experience they made up for in enthusiasm, not to mention some open country skills that was not common to have in raw recruits. If things went right, the other rail hub to Xenon should have been hit about the same time they took out this one. Xenon should be temporarily isolated, an advantage that Thorin did not plan to waste.

∞ ∞ ∞

Sharna moved deliberately toward the waterfall. The low-level buzzing sound that protected the secured path was gone and she no longer heard any sounds of wildlife. All she heard was an eerie and foreboding silence. Sharna shifted her gaze with a sense that someone or something was watching her. Suddenly, she stopped when she saw what it was that was there. There was no question about it, it was a large wolf, staring back at her. Canis Lupus was the scientific name she recalled from her early school studies. And where there was one wolf, there were usually more.

Sharna was far away from the protected walking path and not near enough to the waterfall. She was stuck in the open, without even having a portable forcefield present or any sort of weapon to fend off the animal, not that it was allowed anyway under current law. All animals were protected in a nature reserve, and there was no mercy given to those who harmed an animal even in self-defense. This was the pure wild where predators had no fear of humans. No, if this wolf was hungry, there was little she could do in order to fend it off.

Ridiculous, Sharna thought to herself. Brilliant scientist gets killed following a dumb idea she got while dreaming. She didn't even want to think about how that would be received. Why had she left the protected area? Now she was going to be eaten alive in the middle of nowhere by a hungry wolf. What was the sense in that?

Sharna looked back at the wolf, hearing the low-level growling coming from it and also hearing another similar sound coming from the left of the wolf she saw. How could it be she didn't know the recommended reaction to scare a wolf off? Should she run or stand tall? Wolves usually chased their prey so running would probably encourage them and she didn't think she could get to safety in time. Instead she stood tall and feigned confidence as she looked at the wolf straight in the eyes. She imagined she was staring down an annoying government bureaucrat and tried to convey the same level of disdain she had done so many times to others.

Sharna saw the wolf did not advance and continued staring at her. But her heart fell as she now heard a growling sound behind her progressively getting closer. Turning her gaze quickly she saw a different wolf advancing on her and braced her body as it leaped upwards toward her with its mouth open ready to tear into her body.

Instead of feeling pain, she suddenly felt wet as she sloshed around in a pool of water, trying her best not to ingest it.

"Well, that wasn't how I envisioned you getting this far," Trisha said trying her best not to laugh but failing miserably at it.

Sharna looked up with a confused expression on her face, which quickly transformed to that of fury. "What is the meaning of this?" she snapped. "Did I die or something? I swear I was about to get eaten by a pack of wolves."

"Sorry," Trisha said still holding back laughter. "I haven't been qualified to translocate a person yet. I didn't mean to drop you in the water. But I was hurrying so you didn't get eaten. You should see your face though! Sorry, I am not very good at it. I am just glad you didn't get rematerialized into the void and you still have all your parts. That would have been bad for you, although it was probably good I took the chance so you didn't get eaten."

Sharna's eyes could have bored holes into Trisha, so intense was her gaze. "I don't know how I got here or what you did, but I am going to get out of this water now. Are you capable of helping me out or are you going to just keep jabbering nonsense for a while longer?"

"I am not supposed to help you yet," Trisha replied. "But I guess my directions didn't account for this happening."

Trisha offered her hand and pulled the soaked Sharna up out of the water to the bank. Sharna did her best to shake the water off of herself, quickly realizing it was hopeless. She checked in her carrying bag only to find that its contents were soaked also. There was not much to do that would enable her to dry off other than wait to air out on her own.

"Sorry, I don't have my bag with me, or I would give you a change of clothes to wear," Trisha said apologetically, no longer fighting to hold back laughter. "So, where are you headed to now?"

"Well, I can't easily go back the way I came, can I?" Sharna said resignedly. "Somehow I had the idea of going behind that waterfall. I suppose you know something about that?"

"It is possible," Trisha answered. "But you need to decide your destination on your own."

"Very well," Sharna muttered while examining her dripping clothes. "I guess I have come this far, I might as well finish this insanity."

Sharna looked toward the waterfall and began the walk she remembered from her dream. As she traversed the path, she reflected on the near rescue from the wolves. That shouldn't have been possible. She was about to die and then she didn't. Was she happy with her life so far? When one looks death in the face you make an account of your life. Was her life something she could be proud of, or was there something missing? She was living her dream, being given cart blanche to innovate and had autonomy to mostly do what she wanted. But was she happy? Consumed, yes. But happy and fulfilled? She was not so sure. And now all this business with the lily and whatever happened to rescue her. Maybe she didn't know everything she thought she did.

"You seem to act like you know a lot about this lily religion," Sharna asked suddenly to Trisha who was quietly trailing behind. "What does your lily philosophy say about knowledge?"

"It says a lot," Trisha answered after pausing to consider Sharna's question. "I think my favorite passage on this says something like, 'Humility is the beginning of knowledge, but the prideful finds only frustration and folly.'"

"I didn't read that in any of the books we have captured," Sharna answered. "I guess if you already think you know everything, you can't learn anything new, can you?"

"Makes it hard," Trisha answered.

Sharna continued to walk and approached the rock pathway leading up to the waterfall, carefully balancing herself so she didn't get reacquainted with the water.

"What is so important that I have to choose to go here on my own?" Sharna asked after a long period of silence.

Trisha followed without answering as Sharna slid her body behind the waterfall and ultimately finding the passage she had seen in her dream.

"It is here, just like my dream said it would be," Sharna said with a perplexed expression. "How would I know this is here?"

Sharna looked back at Trisha, hoping for some clue of what to do next. "I guess it can't be worse than being attacked by wolves," Sharna said dryly before pulling out her light source. She shined it in the opening enough to find a foothold to safely slide her body inside. The light made traversing the passage easier, but she could hardly do more that crawl through the opening. She thought she heard Trisha follow her inside, but it was hard to tell. There was no room to turn around; it was either go forward or try to back herself out. She crawled for several minutes before finally reaching an open cavern space that was large enough to stand up in. She came to her feet and began looking around. A couple minutes later she was joined by Trisha.

"I am here," Sharna answered. "Now what?"

"Now we go on a ride," Trisha answered with a smile. "Congratulations! You just demonstrated faith."

"Yes, that meets the definition," Sharna said with frustration still soaked in her clothing. "But it doesn't mean I liked doing it."

"Follow me," Trisha directed while doing something to the wall to reveal a hidden passage. Inside was a transport tube that Sharna had become so familiar with. "You know the theory of these, come experience the reality."

"Where are we going?" Sharna asked while getting into an open seat.

"We are going to a place where you will get a chance to gain a lot more knowledge," Trisha said with a mysterious smile.

"I can't wait," Sharna said with an unconvincing response. But inside she was excited. Today was nothing like she expected it to be. She couldn't wait to uncover new learning, yet she was still struggling to process all she had seen. The world did not exist how she thought it did. That revelation was at the same time both frightening and exhilarating.

Trisha focused herself while putting her hands on two buttons on the console. After a few short moments, Sharna felt a flash of light and when she refocused her vision, she was clearly somewhere else. Outside of the transport tube were two robes and some strange sort of masks. At least she could get out of her wet clothes.

∞ ∞ ∞

Stefan watched as Quintin stormed into the room. He did not look happy about the latest escalation from Xenon.

"Why weren't the rail hubs guarded?" Quintin asked with an angry sounding raised voice. "Everyone is telling me we can no longer get troops in fast enough to quell this growing rebellion short of air-flighting them in. I need options!"

Stefan almost choked when he heard the question. He had already reported that the rail hubs were a critical venerability in a prior report. Quintin had dismissed his concern at the time which made Stefan more confident recommending it as a target for the resistance. No, Stefan was covered on that miss and Quintin would take the brunt of any blowback.

"Why am I always cleaning up your messes?" Xavier asked as he briskly entered the room unannounced. Those in the room quickly stood to recognize the Minister's arrival.

"I wasn't expecting you, sir," Quintin offered. "We were just discussing our options for the response in Xenon after the recent destruction of the two primary rail hubs going into the sector."

"Why wasn't this nipped in the bud when it was just starting?" Xavier asked coldly.

"We thought by taking all those we identified to be practicing the lily religion there would be no one left to organize resistance," Quintin offered.

"And how is that working?" Xavier asked sarcastically. "You rounded up a bunch of non-violence adherents and wonder why the resistance has now turned more violent with who is left?"

"What I don't understand," Ursula interjected, "is how they became armed so well. I thought we had gotten rid of most of the weapons the common people had access to years ago."

"We did," Stefan answered. "However, what I have seen from surveillance footage, the arms used to conduct this resistance campaign consist of a lot of latest generation weaponry, that is, besides what they have captured in raiding the local field offices."

"I saw that same report," Xavier interjected. "And the only place that weaponry is issued to is the CET units. I also have information that states several of their experienced soldiers haven't returned from leave they were granted in the Xenon sector, not to mention the weapons shortages that have arisen in the latest inventory. Oh yes, I have my sources also, Quintin."

"But I have just sent orders to send the CET units out on roving patrols to seek out the people who are causing all the trouble," Quintin said nervously. "That doesn't seem like such a good idea anymore."

Stefan became moderately concerned guilt by association would come back on him. If the entire CET community was suspect, then that would put him at risk also.

"Recall the order," Xavier commanded. "We can't enable that risk in the field. Contain the CET groups to a designated compound in the Xenon sector until we can determine everyone's loyalty. I'll get some researchers combing Oversite's archives to determine if all can be trusted. And Stefan, I am sorry that includes you right now also until we know more."

Xavier made a motion and a couple of uniformed escorts came into the room and pulled Stefan out of the conference room, handling him roughly once they were out of sight of Xavier.

"Where are you taking me?" Stefan asked.

"You CET people are all alike," one of his escorts bitterly stated after they had left the room. "You act like you own the world. Well you are nothing right now. The minister said to contain you. He didn't say how, and I am not of a mind to make it comfortable."

Stefan looked at them evenly with a cool expression on his face, his training asserting himself. So, this was how it was going to be. Suspect everyone and give no one the benefit of due process. The irony was he deserved to be restrained. He had broken the law in aiding the resistance. But he was not going to be of use to anyone locked in a cage. He just needed the right opportunity to make his move. These guards were not very bright he considered. They hadn't even restrained him, thinking that the weapon they were blatantly aiming at him would be enough to ensure his compliance.

"I am thinking the general lockup for miscreants down the street?" one of the guards asked the other.

"Seems as good of a place as any," the other agreed as they cleared security to exit the ministry building.

About halfway to the proposed lockup location, Stefan looked around, realizing that there were not many people about. Approaching an alley, he decided to make his move. Stefan came to a stop suddenly, just standing still. One of the guards responded with a big smile forming on his face.

"Oh, thank you for showing resistance," he replied gleefully as he pulled back his arm to swing at Stefan to strike him.

The guards arm came flying in Stefan's direction. Stefan stayed still at first then moved at the very last moment such that the hit only grazed him instead of making solid contact. This caused the guard to be slightly off balance, which Stefan took quick advantage of. Stefan grabbed the guards outstretched arm and threw him in the direction of his partner who panicked and fired his weapon on his partner by accident. Stefan then threw out a kick toward the shooter's feet causing him to collapse to the ground. Stefan threw an elbow to the fallen guard's head which caused an immediate woozy effect that stopped all resistance.

"Incompetent," Stefan muttered to himself as he dusted himself off and removed the weapon from the limp hand of the fallen guard. Stefan took the weapon and smashed it on the pavement to render it inoperable, knowing that it would not work for him if he tried to operate it and probably had a tracking beacon in it which would aid tracking. Looking both ways, he calmly exited the alley and made his way in an inconspicuous manner down the street. Hopefully, he had not been labeled a fugitive in Oversite yet which would prompt an automatic system response. Stefan needed to make it safely to the CET hub. They deserved to be warned what response was coming.

CHAPTER 21

*T*horin looked around, assessing the terrain and the risks around him. With the tracking technology that permeated everywhere, you could never be truly safe. Each day more people from Xenon were joining the active resistance, seeking a way to help and to push back the outside invaders. There had been great small victories but that was mainly because the capitol had been taken by surprise. If they brought all their available resources to bear, there would be some trying times ahead. Thorin just hoped there was enough grit in these people from the north to weather what was going to come.

"Status?" Thorin asked Dom who was approaching.

"Perimeter is still secure," Dom replied. "All positions have been checked and accounted for within the last ten minutes."

"Good to hear," Thorin answered approvingly. "Continue rotating audits until you are relieved. We need to be ready to move in an instant."

"Yes, sir," Dom replied as he saluted and went to check on the next point.

This would have been so much easier if they had a secure communications channel, but electronics were hard to come by, especially the kind tracked by Oversite. That left manual checks and a lot of movement just to keep confirmation that your camp was secured. At least discipline was good on this team. Thorin looked at the remainder of his team who was resting. Rotating watches created intermittent sleep patterns. He knew he should try to get some shut-eye himself, but the role of a leader is often the one most devoid of rest.

Just as he was considering taking a break, Thorin saw something in the side of his vision that did not belong. Thorin reflexively reached for his weapon preparing to confront this disturbance.

"Do not move!" Thorin said forcefully while pointing his weapon at the intruder. The trespasser did not appear to be armed and had a strange expression on his face like he was completely focused but at the same time distracted. Thorin's loud warning stirred those who were sleeping and they quickly added to the weapons leveled at the mysterious stranger. Whoever was here better hope he had backup or it would not go well for him.

"Greetings Thorin, you have done well," the intruder answered. "I am unarmed and mean you no harm," he continued as he raised his arms above his head to indicate he did not mean to resist.

"If you harmed one of my sentries you will not live to celebrate it," Thorin said with a menacing tone. "How did you get in here?"

"Emily always talked about the great Thorin and how she hoped she would have a chance to serve with him," he continued. "If she was still alive, I think she would be jealous of me. And no, I did not harm any of your sentries. They are still vigilantly watching for security threats unharmed."

Thorin was slightly taken back but did not stay alive this long by letting his guard down. This person was dressed like someone from Xenon but had the marked accent of someone from the capital.

"Who are you and what are you doing here?" Thorin finally asked before motioning one of his soldiers to check on the status of the sentries.

"My name is Gabriel Carasa and I am part of a group called Kayden who shares similar goals to what I believe yours are."

"And what are my goals?" Thorin asked, trying to stall time to make sure his soldiers on watch were unharmed.

"To secure the independence of Xenon," Gabriel answered with no uncertainty in his voice. "That was pretty clear when you discussed it with Stefan and other CET members. Your reasons for wanting independence are a bit different than ours, but ultimately we want the same thing."

Thorin was not sure what to think. The circle of people who knew about that meeting was extremely small and he was certain each one there would give their life before compromising the secret to others.

"The way of man fails, but the Way of the Lily brings hope," Gabriel added with a slight smile now showing on his face. "I know you know something about the Lily. Aglas died because of it. I know you have talked about it."

"You are speaking some things you shouldn't know about," Thorin stated with some level of concern. "Say, you are from Kayden, what do you want with me?"

"I need your help," Gabriel answered simply. "And I think you know for what."

Thorin thought a moment on the last comment. In order to provide cover for smuggling in weapons, he had helped capture many people associated with the lily religion. As far as he knew, they hadn't been killed but had been shipped off somewhere to be detained.

"This have something to do with the lily people that were captured by the CET groups?" Thorin asked.

"Yes, they are being detained in a way that many won't survive if they are not rescued soon," Gabriel answered. "If we are going to achieve freedom for Xenon, we will need the help of those who have been captured."

"We already plan to do something in the future to free them," Thorin stated carefully, not wanting to give away anything that could compromise them later.

"But if you just charge in there, they will all die," Gabriel answered. "They have detonation collars tied to each other. If one escapes, then all attached will be killed. I have a technician who thinks she can create a window where the collars can be removed but we need the guards who patrol distracted during this time so a full rescue can be mounted."

"My grandfather is probably there!" Ara said suddenly before realizing that he should not have interrupted.

"I want them rescued as much as the next guy," Thorin answered, "but first I am not sure where these places are currently at and second, a rescue would require a lot more intelligence then we currently have. Our team is improving but that is an operation that would scare most fully trained CET units."

"You do not fully understand the kind of help I am able to provide," Gabriel said confidently. "I can get you intelligence. I know where the camps are all at. And I can provide you some advantages you did not think possible. All you need is a bit of faith."

"You are just one man," Thorin said skeptically. "What can you do for us?"

"I know that there is no threat within fifty kilometers of your position," Gabriel answered. "I know that all active CET units are going to be detained before the day is done due to suspicion of disloyalty. And if you would like, I can summon each of your sentries right now."

"They will not move from their position unless we are threatened or I order them to," Thorin replied while internally wondering about the CET comment. "I think you overstate your position."

Gabriel smiled then showed a slightly glazed over expression in his eyes. One by one each sentry appeared standing initially in a watchful position before becoming quickly disoriented wondering why there were no longer where they were moments before. The group quickly showed disbelief followed quickly by an awe mixed with fear.

"You just did something with the lily meditation didn't you?" Thorin asked. "That probably set off every sensor in this area. Team, we need to be ready to move."

"I am one of a few who can operate outside of the sensor grid. It cannot detect me," Gabriel answered. "But if you want to move to be sure, I will not stop you. In fact, I would like to accompany you if you will allow it for a little while."

Thorin gave him a quick assessment before answering. There were some things going on that he didn't understand, but what he did understand was someone who could move his troops around at will would be an extremely large advantage in the field, provided he was truly undetectable and could be trusted. Maybe he could do some other useful things also.

"I don't trust you yet," Thorin answered. "Ara, he is your responsibility. Make sure he doesn't compromise us."

"Thank you," Gabriel replied. "You won't regret this."

"No, I am pretty sure I will," Thorin said. "But for some reason I am willing to give you a chance. I have heard a lot about this Kayden and would like to learn about your story once we get safely relocated. Until then, no more lily meditation in case you are wrong about detection."

∞ ∞ ∞

"Now what?" Sharna asked in Trisha's direction after she had donned a robe and programmed the voice modulator in the mask.

"We go see Teacher, at least once we get scanned for tracking," Trisha replied. "I know you have some electronics with you. You will need to leave them here and then we will get scanned to make sure we are not providing a way to be spied on."

Sharna looked around the room she was in, noticing the wire mesh design used to block wireless communications. "Are all your rooms lined with this material?" she asked through the voice modulator.

"Not that I am aware of," Trisha answered. "I think we just use it in places where we want to make sure someone doesn't have tracking beacons on them. I don't know how it all works. I am just told to follow a specific procedure."

Sharna looked at the design, internally approving of the methodology used to circumvent detection from Oversite. Now even a minister would not be able to determine where she was. Maybe she could line her lab the same way.

Some sort of scanner was used on them before a door opened and she was able to follow Trisha through some sort of maze. She never had got around to working on technology that could enhance underground detection. It was clear these people were exploiting that gap in surveillance. It would be interesting to try to solve that problem as some ideas began to form in her head on some innovation that could be applied to this space.

"Welcome," another masked person wearing a robe of a slightly more complex design greeted her. "I am glad you made it safely here. I am told you had a near event with a pack of wolves in route?"

"I recall something of that but I am still unclear how I escaped them," Sharna answered. "Why am I here?"

"Do you want to be able to meditate on the Lily or not?" the person asked her. "I know you have been failing miserably and it has not been for lack of trying."

"It is something I wish to understand better," Sharna answered in a guarded manner. "But that still doesn't answer why I am here."

"I am called Teacher," the person replied. "Normally we would call someone coming here for the first time Initiate, but I do not think that will apply for you. I think I shall call you Inquisitive, since you have not yet decided your path."

"Whatever makes you happy," Sharna said dismissively. "What happens next?"

"We let you learn," Teacher said. "And when you have your questions all answered, you can leave."

"And what can you teach me?" Sharna asked skeptically. "There are not many people who have been able to do that in my life."

Sharna heard a light laugh though the mask of Teacher. "You will teach yourself, Inquisitive," he answered. "That is, with the aid of our extensive library and Trisha here to keep you company. If you want to ask me questions, I will be glad to answer them once per day. Otherwise, you are on your own. Just let us know when you are ready to leave."

"That's it?" she said with incredulity.

"The path to the Lily is open for all," Teacher replied. "But you have to approach it on your own accord. I cannot make you accept it but I can show you how to reach it. The rest is up to you."

"I'll show you to your room," Trisha offered. "And more importantly I will show you where the library is."

Sharna followed Trisha silently through the underground abyss until she stopped at an opening. Inside was a spartan sleeping area and a small shelf full of books.

"These books are recommended for you to look at first," Trisha offered. "But I will show you were to find more, should these not meet your interest sufficiently."

Sharna nodded dismissively, glancing at the titles then followed Trisha a way further, doing her best to note the route being taken. Going down a new passage, she stopped in front of a new opening. Inside was a sight that Sharna could hardly imagine. As far as she could see, there were shelves and shelves of books. The amount of knowledge contained in this room was hard to fathom.

"Why keep all these paper books?" Sharna asked. "Aren't these all available in the Oversite library portal?"

"These are all banned," Trisha answered sadly. "They have references to forbidden topics and have been suppressed."

"These are all religious books?" Sharna asked.

"Some are," Trisha answered, "but many are just texts that do not match government positions. There are even a lot of science research texts here that present different conclusions than are in current capitol favor."

"Show me where those books are kept," Sharna said with interest.

Trisha took Sharna to the section of the library where the science related books were located. There were many shelves worth of them.

"If you see any you are interested in, take them down," Trisha offered. "I can get you a cart if it is more than you can carry."

"Yes, to a cart," Sharna said as she started rapidly pulling volumes down off of the shelf and started piling them into the cart as soon as Trisha came back with it. There were prominent scientific names on these books. How was their research banned? When the cart was full, Sharna briefly considered asking for a second cart but instead decided she would come back if needed more. "I will go to my room now."

Trisha directed her back to where her sleeping and study area was located. Sharna thought she heard something out of Trisha's mouth but was so distracted by the books in front of her, she didn't acknowledge it. She had more pressing matters on her mind.

Sharna spent unaccounted for time combing through the many volumes she had gathered. What was wrong with these works she wondered? These were brilliant minds conducting scientific research, some of which would have been very helpful to some of her prior projects. Was it the topics or the person itself that had violated the prohibitions she wondered? Ultimately, it didn't really matter. This was true scientific pursuit, suppressed by a government who professed to follow science above all else. Sharna finally looked up after she had finished reading through the last of the books she had selected.

"Thought you may be getting hungry," Trisha offered, bringing something to nourish her.

Sharna absently took the prepared meal shake from Trisha and quickly consumed it. "Take me back to the library. I am done with these books and will get more now."

Trisha carefully stacked the books Sharna had finished looking at and headed out of Sharna's room. "Did you find your reading interesting?"

"Why were the science books banned?" Sharna asked.

"Sorry, you should probably ask Teacher that in a few hours when you can ask questions," Trisha said apologetically as she reached the entrance to the library. "I haven't spent that much time in this part of the library."

Sharna immediately went to the location in the library she had found the books from before and began to pile a selection of new choices until she had enough to overflow her cart. She then pushed the cart back to her room, now knowing the path without help. Arriving there, she continued her consumption of the material she had gathered without taking time to sleep or take a break.

"You have been busy, Inquisitive," Teacher interrupted her reading.

Sharna barely heard Teacher's comment but then remembered she had questions that needed answered. "Why were these books banned?" she abruptly asked.

"The author of the book you have in your hand made the mistake of developing a technology that could increase the usage of overall energy consumption," Teacher answered. "The government thought she should have known better and was operating against the ideals of science. She was put in confinement and her work was suppressed. I think she is a general laborer now somewhere since she showed contrition during her confinement."

"And this one?" Sharna asked not liking hearing the answer she had been given.

"He uncovered a flaw in endorsed research conclusions on a major climate science study," Teacher continued. "He wasn't even against the report, he just wanted to make sure it was right. Didn't go well for him either."

"But these people were brilliant and were capable of doing so much to advance their fields," Sharna said with disbelief. "Why would we waste the valuable resource of their knowledge?"

"You could be next you know?" Teacher suggested. "Just because your research areas of focus are in favor right now, doesn't mean that you will stay in favor later. Especially since you are doing a deep study of religious practices. If the capitol succeeds in suppressing Xenon and the Way of the Lily, what do you think will happen to you?"

"There is so much to learn with the transport tubes and the mind energy model," Sharna stated. "They would be stupid to try to suppress that learning. It could be so much value."

"Just like the work of the two authors you just asked me about?" Teacher asked. "Tyranny, even in the name of science, cannot risk losing control of anything that could defeat it. To let go would be to surrender the very power that they crave. You will at some point be a risk they can no longer tolerate. If you take the time to consider it you will know it is true."

Sharna considered Teacher's words and didn't like thinking about their implications. And as much as she didn't want to admit it, he was likely correct in his assessment. A world where she was subjected to being a general laborer for daring to invent something that the government didn't want was a world she wanted no part of. Just because she was getting full discretion in her research now did not mean that would be a guarantee going forward under this form of government overreach.

"I see you haven't touched the books we left in the room for you as a place to start," Teacher stated. "I hope you will still consider reading them. I think you will find their content most enlightening to your goal of Lily meditation."

Sharna decided she would spend some time to glance through what was provided her, but she most wanted to continue consumption of the remainder of the science section in the library. She looked up to ask Teacher another question, but was no longer there. Sharna stared at the books she had avoided and after a brief delay decided she would start on them as soon as she had briefly slept.

CHAPTER 22

*D*espair closed in on Annabel Raelynn, repeating the daily dance. Each day she found a way to fight it off, holding on with a fleeting sense of hope that something better would happen. But that something still had not come. Nourishment at least was being provided at an increased level due to the appearing food items, but how long could she expect to be provided for this way? Whoever was getting food to her was taking a great risk to do so and may not be able to for much longer.

Those who were prisoners were slowly diminishing in number. She had already seen some die in the yard from injuries or side effects of the experiments being conducted on them. She had been subjected to few but thankfully nothing to the extent she had seen done to others. Hope was fleeting, but a flicker of it still remained. She had never given in to despair in her life and as tempting as it was to do so, she decided she would not begin today.

Annabel really missed being able to enter the dream state and as a result felt a certain emptiness that came from the lack. When you are in a continual state of calm and being centered in your internal spirit, it lifts up your outlook tremendously. But when you are used to this continual feeling of peace and it is forcefully taken away from you, it is like your entire support system is taken away. That coupled with the horrid conditions she was living in, made persevering not a guaranteed outcome even for the strongest.

Annabel cringed internally when she saw Joseph the guard walking up. He usually would strike any prisoner he came in contact with. And based on how he was looking at her, it looked like Annabel would have the misfortune of his attention today.

"No glare or rude comment today?" Joseph asked with a sound of mocking contempt in his voice.

Annabel stood silently, carefully keeping her eyes looking down at the ground. She was not sure she had the strength to endure the full measure of his attention.

"Nothing? Too good to speak to me now, eh?" he continued, clearly trying to intentionally create a reason to lash out at her.

"I don't mean you any trouble," Annabel replied with as much meekness as she could muster in her voice.

"You have been nothing but trouble," Joseph said. "You just are being good right now because you are afraid. I don't know how you are doing it, but I know you are stealing food from the locked stores somehow. That is going to stop!"

"Aren't all food stores monitored with surveillance?" Annabel asked carefully. "I have not been near that area at all. We have to stay far away or bad things happen."

"But yet you are not starving thin which you should be with what we have been feeding you. And our stocks are less than they should be," Joseph continued. "You are stealing or you know who is. And you are going to tell me now."

Annabel stood in a defeated posture, unable to come up with a suitable response. Joseph struck her with a strong backhand motion. As weak as she was, it knocked her immediately to the ground as her nose and mouth began to bleed.

"Do you know now?" Joseph asked with a baleful stare.

Annabel continued to be silent, not knowing the answer to his question and not wanting the source of food to be taken away.

"Nothing?" Joseph asked with contempt.

After a few moments without an answer, Joseph began to kick her as Annabel curled up in a protective ball, trying to dampen the effect of the beating.

"I am sure your memory will get better when I come back later to ask you," Joseph stated, seemingly looking bored with kicking a largely lifeless body lying on the ground.

Annabel barely registered him walking away as she writhed in pain on the ground. Struggling to breathe, she passed out into a comatose-like state.

∞ ∞ ∞

Gabriel watched with rising fury as he observed Raelynn's mistreatment. How could someone senselessly harm another for no visible reason? His anger grew to concern and worry when he saw her lying motionless on the ground covered in blood. She desperately needed medical care. She was already worn down and weak when she was beaten. Could she survive this?

"You seem bothered by something," Alaine interrupted his contemplation. "Is everything all right?"

"The camp is really mistreating its prisoners," Gabriel explained sadly. "I am worried we may get there too late."

"It is just a few hours more," Alaine tried to reassure. "We need to wait until it be late in the night when the guards are least watching. We will be ready, then you can help to save them."

Gabriel knew waiting was the best choice, but it was hard when he saw Raelynn lying there, barely clinging to life. Those few extra hours may be critical for her survival. But he also knew that she would want him to wait until they had the best chance to save everyone. So, he watched worried and waited. Waiting when you can do nothing is one of the most helpless feelings in the world. The hours passed at an excruciatingly slow pace, but they did pass.

"Our team is about to advance on the compound," Thorin walked up and quietly announced. "Are you two ready to do your part?"

"We will do what is needed," Gabriel answered. "Anything change that we should know about?"

"Something is bound to change once we get started," Thorin replied. "Always does. A plan is only good for the first few moments of battle, then you have to adapt. But everyone knows what their overall purpose is and we will keep the guard's attention. You just need to do your part; we will do ours."

"Let's get started then," Gabriel answered. "Give me the go hand signal we discussed when you are ready for me to start."

"I will, but I still don't understand how you will see it," Thorin replied before meeting back up with his team, leaving only Ara with Gabriel and Alaine.

"What does your grandfather look like?" Gabriel asked Ara.

Ara described his features as Gabriel scanned the compound looking for someone who matched his description. "I may have located someone that meets his description. He doesn't look well, but he is still alive."

"If you can get me to him like you said you can, I would really like to help him first," Ara asked.

"I'll get you to him as soon as it is safe," Gabriel promised. If we can't get the explosive containment field deactivated it won't really matter. We fix that first, then you can go to him."

Gabriel shifted his focus back to Thorin in his vision, watching for the go signal. It looked like they were nearly in position. It wouldn't be long now. Thorin gave the awaited go motion and proceeded to set off some makeshift explosives. There wasn't really any damage being done, but it was making a large racket, surely able to get the attention of those responsible for securing the prison.

Gabriel shifted his focus to the control room and quickly translocated the attending guard there out to the outside perimeter of the prison compound. Then keying in on Alaine and Ara, sent them back in the control room that he had just vacated. Ara was supposed to keep guard over the entrance and allow Alaine time to try to disable the system. Gabriel quickly translocated himself to where Raelynn was and did a quick assessment to make sure she was alive. She was, but did not look very stable. She needed some medical help and pretty quickly, but a few minutes more before taking action would likely not make a difference. Gabriel quickly located himself back to a safe and isolated place and began to translocate each reacting guard one at a time to the neutralization area that he had setup with Thorin. Once each guard was effectively disarmed and put into the makeshift prison area, Gabriel sent in the next one. The key was prioritizing who was the biggest perceived threat and sending them out of the compound first.

"There are too many at the control room door!" Ara called out, waving his arms in the signal to get Gabriel's attention.

Gabriel checked Thorin's team and they were not ready to receive more prisoners, so Gabriel instead translocated the squad of four attacking guards at the control room entrance outside the prison walls. They would be able to get back inside, but it would take time which he needed more of.

$$\infty \ \infty \ \infty$$

Thorin urgently directed his team members to use more speed to handle the prisoners being directed to the neutralization zone. So far, they had shot two of the guards who refused to drop their weapons fast enough but the rest had quickly surrendered. This was a new kind of battle where he could use overwhelming force, continually capitalizing on the confusion from the other side. Thorin would have just as soon as killed everyone Gabriel sent him, but Gabriel refused to follow this plan unless an attempt was first made to get them to surrender. And since Gabriel was somehow watching, he didn't think bending the agreement would be a good idea. Something about religion and being a peace with his actions was the stated reason.

"We need to move faster," Thorin yelled out to his team. "This can't even be a quarter of their available force."

"How are you doing this?" one of the captured prisoners called out. "This isn't even fair what you are doing. We didn't even have a chance."

"I know what you do to the prisoners inside," Thorin growled back. "I don't think you want to talk about what fair is right now."

"They are all going to die anyway," he replied back. "If the code isn't activated by the right person every hour, their collars all go off, then poof! I could help you with that though if that is why you are here to rescue them."

Thorin paused wondering if he could take this prisoner at his word. "How do you take the collars off safely?" Thorin asked.

"If you let me go, I'll help you," he replied. "There is a special tool we use in addition to a control-room release signal."

"What happens if we don't use the special tool?" Thorin asked.

"It will probably explode," the captured guard replied. "If you just get the signal release it makes it so other prisoners won't die if someone leaves, but without the tool, it will take a long time to figure out a way to bypass and if there isn't a continuous signal being sent from the control room, a timer will set it off also. You really do need my help. It is a new protocol to prevent the prisoners from escaping even if we are overrun."

"B-Team," Thorin called out loudly. "I need to pull you off and come with me. Detain this piece of scum and bring him with us. He may prove useful. If he is right, we don't have a lot of time and I am not sure our team inside understands."

∞ ∞ ∞

Alaine quickly worked her way through the console in the control room after setting up the equipment she brought along. Severing the link to Oversite, she quickly created a backdoor to get into the system to bring it under her control. There were two communication modules. She knew what the first one was she was pretty sure. It was configured from the console and it sent remote detonation signals best she could tell. It had a heartbeat signal that told the detonation collars that they were working correctly and if she understood the system right, there was a signal that could be sent to blow the prisoners up.

Alaine setup her own broadcasting array, quickly tying it into the existing infrastructure. Then with a synchronized switchover, she disabled the heartbeat signal and replaced it with her own generated signal which mimicked it but would not carry the risk of sending a detonation trigger. She breathed a sigh of relief when she did not see any evidence on the closed-circuit visual feed of prisoners that any collars had detonated. Then she spent some time trying to determine what that second communication module did.

Gabriel materialized beside her. "How close are you?" he asked.

"I pretty sure getting them collars off of one prisoner won't blow the rest now," she answered. "But I worried there is another trick with this second system. Some sort of keypad attached to it and there only be about ten minutes left till it wants a new code."

Gabriel quickly glazed over his eyes and just moments later he answered. "Looks like a guard enters a new code every hour into this based on the past few days. Some sort of validation eye scan which gives them the code, then they key it in."

"This console is already on lockdown, no way it will give a new code, even if guard was here to be forced to give it," Alaine answered. Need to hurry, or I bet we start losing some prisoners. I am done here if we can keep people out, I need to start taking collars off."

Gabriel nodded and made a quick action which found he and Alaine in front of her first prisoner. She quickly examined the collar and began the process of working to disable it. Alaine was moderately familiar with this technology and after about five minutes had the collar released and removed.

"Don't have time for this, before that timer goes off," Alaine said urgently.

"I may have help," Thorin offered coming up in a slow jog with several others from his unit while dragging a captured prison guard along. "He says there is a special tool that will disable the auto timing explosion on the collar. Says if code isn't entered hourly, they will blow within a few minutes of no code."

"That leaves us about four minutes until the time is out," Alaine said worryingly.

"You will get mercy if you help, as undeserving of it you are," Gabriel offered the guard with a pained expression on his face. "Where is this device we need?"

"In the storage locker by the control room," the guard answered. "But you will never get to it in time."

Gabriel and the guard disappeared from view for several seconds only to reappear holding a device with the guard in a very confused state.

"How do you do that?" he asked.

"Don't have time to explain. You will help Alaine and I and start releasing prisoners as fast as you can. If we get them all released before the collars blow, you will be set free. Understand?"

The guard nodded as he, Alaine and Gabriel were translocated to the next prisoner. Alaine approved of this approach. Sudden movements in location on the collars could set them off unexpectedly, even if they were in the prison. Working clumsily, the guard inserted the tool into the place and pressing a button release on the collar, removed it. No sooner had he done this, Gabriel moved them to the next prisoner. Gabriel had a worried expression on his face as they went one by one through the prisoners in the courtyard. Alaine noticed he seemed to show a lot more emotion on Annabel who she had met once before. But he did not spare her more time than the others, instead redirecting them quickly to the next prisoner to be released.

The medical experiment wing was the hardest to look at, but they kept disabling the collars one by one.

"Last one," Gabriel announced, "we need to hurry."

The guard fumbled with the release and just as was unclicking it, a sound emanated from the collar, forewarning a triggering. Gabriel quickly translocated the collar away, just as it was about to detonate.

"That was close," Gabriel stated, "but I think everyone has been saved."

"You said I could go if I helped you," the guard firmly reminded the group. "You promised to let me go."

Gabriel showed a pained look on his face once again at the sight of this person but then made a motion of forced acceptance. "I will land you far outside of the compound. If you come back toward it, you will forfeit your mercy." Then the guard was gone.

∞ ∞ ∞

Gabriel watched as the guard took off running in his far vision. In order to save Raelynn, he had to let the person go who had so badly injured her. And he still couldn't go to her yet, as they needed to finish neutralizing the remaining guards. Gabriel relocated himself back to Thorin's space.

"Focus on capturing the guards I send you and we need to provide medical help to as many as we can," Gabriel answered. "I am not sure how much time we will have until a ministry response force comes calling."

"That was something else you just did!" Thorin exclaimed. "Keep sending who you find to my crew where we have our makeshift holding cell setup. The team I have with me will start doing triage on those who have been detained here to give them medical care."

Gabriel nodded and began translocating those who were still at large, slowly sending them to be neutralized one at a time. When he completed his task, Gabriel sought out Raelynn's location and translocated himself quickly by her side. Gabriel took in the sight of her battered and bruised body. She did still seem to be alive but was only hanging on by a thread. He carefully touched her hand with his and lightly squeezed it.

"Hang on just a little bit longer, Raelynn," Gabriel implored. "We have saved everyone who was left. Just a bit longer and we will get you all out of this dreadful place."

Raelynn stirred slightly and the eye that was not puffed over, opened slightly. "We are really free?" Raelynn asked. "You came and rescued us like you said you would."

"I am here and you are free," Gabriel answered gently. "You are free again to dream."

"I think I will like that," she answered weakly showing a slight smile on her face. "Free to dream," she mumbled contentedly before closing her eyes to succumb to her desperate need for rest.

Gabriel smiled, the first he had experienced in quite some time. Then looking up, he caught Thorin's attention. "Let's gather everyone up. It is time to leave."

CHAPTER 23

Sharna did not understand why everyone wanted her to read books about philosophy and religion in order to master the Way of the Lily. A lot of talk about centering yourself and being a peace with the world around you consumed these books. They also talked a lot about some moral teachings, but she had picked up most of that in the books the ministry had captured.

"What is so important about me reading these books?" Sharna asked Trisha who had just entered the room. "All they talk about is making choices about how you live your life and what you feel inside. It's too fluffy and mushy if you ask me. I will take a research study any day over this drivel."

"I don't think there are many who would share your opinion on preferred reading material," Trisha said with a smile. "I tried reading through one of your books when I was putting them away and I didn't understand a thing in it. If all there was to life was technical jargon, I think it would be a very sad life."

"You didn't answer my question," Sharna stated directly and without pause.

"These books you are dismissing have been life changing for me," Trisha answered. "I had sort of hoped it could do the same for you."

"Why does everyone care so much about my life?" Sharna asked. "Everyone pretty much fears me or hates me anyway. If I wasn't so good at my research no one would put up with me."

"I don't even understand your research but I like being around you," Trisha said. "Inside I think there is something different you don't let out and I want to be part of you finding it."

"Ok, I will pretend to believe you," Sharna replied, wondering why she was having an actual conversation with someone. "But I don't think it is an accident that I was sought out. There is something you all want from me."

"Let me tell you a story," Trisha replied. "I think it may help you understand a bit more."

"If you must," Sharna answered, already regretting allowing this conversation to continue.

"I was still in school when the mass evacuation happened in Xenon a couple years back," Trisha continued. "But I was captured before someone could get to my house to translocate us out of there. They locked me up like a prisoner against my will and put me on a transport to Morfort to join a school there."

"My lab is in Morfort," Sharna stated wondering where this was going.

"When I was there, I was not a very compliant student," Trisha continued. "I am sure you don't know anything about that…."

Sharna couldn't help but cracking a small smile, remembering she was a terror to her teachers. "Perhaps," she answered.

"Anyway, a few of the students started listening to me when I spoke against the government sanctioned nonsense that was not clearly did not pass intellectual muster," Trisha continued. "I got into a lot of trouble for speaking out like that. But once my punishment was over, some started coming to me with questions and for quiet conversations. Eventually, I was able to share with them about the Lily and teach them what I could recite from memory. I was freed when the truce happened but I had made some friends there."

"What does that have to do with anything?" Sharna said, quickly losing what little interest she had in continuing in this conversation.

"Those friends and some they had influenced were all killed recently by the government," Trisha explained. "They were somehow caught learning about the Lily. I am told someone had succeeded in entering the dream Lily meditative state right before it happened."

Realization dawned quickly on Sharna that she was somehow responsible for this happening. "It was my technology development that caused them to be caught wasn't it?" she asked.

"It was, but I don't blame you for it," Trisha said. "You weren't the person who marched them out on a frozen pond to freeze to death because they wouldn't renounce their beliefs. Others did that, taking advantage of the technology you developed."

"I am clearly a threat to your religion," Sharna stated. "Logically, you should kill me so I don't do more damage. I don't understand why you are playing around with me and letting me learn instead? Access to your library just makes me more dangerous if you let me go, you know?"

"Yes, that is how the government would look at it if the situation was reversed," Trisha answered. "But those books you disdain teach a different way. That even though we may have differences, your life has value and we should seek to protect it, even if it risks us harm."

"You hope that by learning more, I will make different choices, don't you?" Sharna asked suddenly.

"From your standpoint, isn't that better than trying to kill you?" Trisha said with a chuckle.

"I suppose so," Sharna answered begrudgingly. "But that doesn't mean I am going to do what you want of me."

Sharna became engrossed in thought and didn't see Trisha finally leave the room. Even though Trisha had given her an absolution of sorts, could she absolve herself from the harm she had inflicted on others with her research? Was what she was working on something that she could reflect on later in life and be proud of? The ethics of her research had never been a consideration for her in pursuing it. If it was sanctioned by the government as an approved area, she felt freedom to pursue it. But since she had been here and been reading about this Lily religion, her absolute trust in the government guidance was admittedly shaken. If she didn't trust the bureaucrats to manage her research projects effectively, why then did she trust them to manage the endorsement of research and its direction. And that Teacher person had spoken about research getting suppressed. It could happen to her. She was not indispensable to them forever, even if she was in favor now.

"You seem deep in thought," Teacher interrupted Sharna's musing.

Sharna looked up, feeling unsure how long he had been standing there watching her. "I am ready to return," she answered.

"It will be arranged," Teacher replied. "Do you have any additional questions or requests before you leave?"

"No," Sharna answered. "But I do hope to come back here someday. I have been away too long already."

"You are always welcome, Inquisitive," Teacher answered. "Let your research assistant Aaliyah know when you want to return and we will provide a way. The guide who brought you will take you back now."

Sharna was honestly surprised that she was being allowed to leave without any objections or stalling. Trisha came to the door shortly thereafter and Sharna gathered her bag of belongings and followed her to the transport tube location. After depositing her robe and mask, she gathered her shielded electronics and took the journey back to the place of the waterfall with Trisha in the transport tube.

"I'll keep an eye on you to make sure you make it safely back to the protected path," Trisha said with a smile. "We don't want any wolves having you for lunch!"

"No, that would be unpleasant," Sharna said almost showing a smile. "I need to get back now."

Sharna walked through the nature preserve to the safety of the path. She didn't quite fully understand what had happened, but inside she felt something had changed. Her outlook was different as well as her priorities. No, she wasn't one of those religious adherents, but she also now had a realization that she had been doing some things that were not right and were causing others harm. It was time to make some of those wrongs right.

∞ ∞ ∞

Xavier tapped impatiently on the surface of his workstation as he tried to puzzle out an answer to his current problem. How could whole units of Covert Extraction Teams completely disappear? Oh, they definitely had the training to be able to do that, but why would they? Someone must have leaked or botched his orders to hold them out of the field until an investigation could be completed to ensure everyone's loyalty. How could they all be disloyal? That didn't make any sense.

"Those guards you wanted to see are here," Xavier's assistant messaged in.

"Ensure they are escorted then send them in," Xavier answered, not wanting to take any chances they would do something to harm his safety.

Two guards came in, looking somewhat cowed, escorted by four of his trusted bodyguards.

"You wanted to see us, Minister?" one of them finally had to courage to ask.

Xavier stared at them in silence for almost an entire minute before answering. The fear on their faces seemed to increase by the second for every amount of silence he offered. "The other day, I had you escort Stefan away until we could ensure his loyalty," Xavier began. "Yet when I had the surveillance logs reviewed, I find out that you disregarded my orders by using force on him and threatening to take him to general lockup where society's miscreants are housed?"

"I am sorry Minister," the nervous guard replied. "Normally, when we are told to contain someone, it is understood that it isn't supposed to be a pleasant experience for them. We were just trying to do our job."

"This is a valued CET soldier and a member of an important task force," Xavier said with frustration. "One, I hoped to have back into his role in a short period of time. But instead, since you idiots roughed him up and threatened his safety, he made an assumption that I planned to take out the whole CET community who happen to be the best soldiers we have. Something I think you both figured out the hard way from what I saw."

"I am so sorry mister Minister," the other guard said in a blubbering sort of way.

"And why wasn't I told when he escaped?" Xavier asked getting more worked up the longer he was talking to them.

"We filed a fugitive report on him when we became conscious," the first guard answered carefully. "And told our immediate supervisor of course. Oversite should locate him any time now."

"Of course you did," Xavier said. "And your supervisor was likely afraid to tell his supervisor and so forth. Bottom line is that we have a crisis on our hands right now, and it is all because of how you both screwed up. Get these two out of my sight. Let them rot in the lockup they were taking Stefan to."

Xavier watched as they were drug out of the room blubbering apologies and asking for mercy. It was hard to find good help and he clearly didn't have it with these two.

"Send Quintin in," Xavier called to his assistant.

Quintin walked in moments later. He was not projecting his recently found arrogance. It is easy to hold your head up high when things are going well. It is another to maintain it when it falls apart.

"Did we really lose all those lily adherents we previously captured to a military style raid? I thought you said they were fully secured?" Xavier asked opening the discussion.

"As usual, your information is on target," Quintin said nervously. "We were hit in the middle of the night. Somehow, they hacked into our system and managed to circumvent the fail-safes which should have terminated the lily adherents if a rescue or escape was happening. Some had already died in captivity but those who survived all escaped."

"And the guards who manned the prison?" Xavier asked. "I don't have a clear answer what happened to them."

"They were found secured outside the facility with some non-sensical stories," Quintin replied. "The footage we have indicates they were resisting the rescue then they just disappeared, one by one. Honestly, it reminded me of the mass exodus that happened in Xenon a couple years back."

"Did Oversite pickup any of the lily meditation signals at this time?" Xavier asked thoughtfully, sifting through the possibilities of what could have happened.

"It did," Quintin answered, "but not until after the prisoners were rescued. Do you think they have a way that isn't currently detectable?"

"It is possible," Xavier answered. "Have you presented your findings to that researcher, Sharna?"

"I plan to," Quintin answered. "She just reappeared in her lab. She has been away for a while."

"I'll send her a request to look at your data," Xavier offered. "She doesn't always take kindly to unsolicited requests from those without the highest authority."

"Thank you, that will help," Quintin answered.

"My other worry is how we lost control over the CET community," Xavier offered. "I saw that the CETs deployed to Xenon mostly all disappeared like have those stationed across the rest of the sectors?"

"Yes, we have lost track of our CET support," Quintin replied. "Something spooked them. They haven't been attacking anyone, mainly, just in hiding somehow I think."

"I think Stefan sent word out somehow that we planned to contain them to confirm their loyalty," Xavier stated. "Given the government's track record on doing that and what happens to those contained, I can see a desire to not go through that. We also sent a poor message with how Stefan was treated; against my wishes I will add."

"Is there anything you want me to do about them?" Quintin asked. "We have over half of the CETs in Xenon right now."

"No," Xavier answered. "We just need to keep sending reassurance to their audio channels hoping someone believes what is being said. We will probably have to end up fighting them in the field before we are done. Seems like a waste all over a misunderstanding."

"Minister," Quintin offered carefully, "I know I have had a couple of setbacks recently, but I really think we need a wholesale show of force in Xenon right now. The problem is, I don't have enough troops to do that. What I have is just trying to hold off these guerrilla insurgents who harry us at every turn."

"I was afraid you would ask that of me. Unfortunately, you are right to request that," Xavier answered. "From what I have read of the rail readiness, it will be hard to get troops there quickly even if I did deploy more forces."

"If we don't have the energy allotment to fly them in, then we will need to march them in," Quintin suggested. "But I need everything we have, or I am afraid we will lose Xenon forever and never take it back."

Xavier considered Quintin's request. This was just the sort of disaster that had cost his predecessor his title as Minister. He didn't think his position was that precarious, but at some point, there would be the need for someone to be saddled with the blame. No, he wasn't going to make this decision alone. This response would be reserved for the full Great Scientist Council. There did need to be a response and it needed to be overwhelming. No small group of non-trained rabble rousers was going to thwart the collective will of the capitol and the way of science.

This disease in Xenon needed to be cured and obliterating it would require strong and decisive action. But how to do it in a way that kept him blameless? He would not be wise to allow his enmity against the followers of the lily religion allow him to make poor judgements. No, some level of patience was required. To the one who is willing to wait, comes all good things. The present strategy of containing this religion was coming to the end of its usefulness. Discrediting it and creating a hostility toward religion had done so much until his predecessor had foolishly pushed too hard and too fast. Now would that be enough? Would he now instead be free to reach for older, more trusted remedies? The answer to his question lurked in the shadows. Was he ready to bring these ways into the open?

"Pull in the planners and provide me some scenarios by tomorrow," Xavier commanded after clearing his head from his musings. "I want to be able to present to the council at its meeting two days from now on our required response."

"I will get right on it," Quintin answered, with relief evident on his face that Xavier had shown willingness to provide extra support.

"We can't take half measures," Xavier said coldly. "We have already lost the battle for the hearts and minds of the residents of Xenon. All we have now is to keep this harmful ideology from spreading and then to forcefully stamp it out. If there is no one left in Xenon when we are done, then so be it. We can repopulate it later with those more flexible to the ways of science. Now that we have food redundancy in other sectors, they will not be able to hold us hostage anymore."

Quintin showed a surprised expression on his face, clearly not expecting this level of forcefulness from Xavier. But Xavier meant what he said. Sure, he would have much preferred the compliance route, but now that was ruled out, the only solution was overpowering those who fought. And you don't play to win by taking half measures.

CHAPTER 24

Stefan kept a low profile as he carefully made his way to the target coordinates. The heat-signature shielding body suit hampered his mobility somewhat, but it far outweighed the risk of being detected. Being on the run for this long should have taken a toll on him, but instead he rediscovered a rush he had not been able to replicate in his mostly desk role with the ministry.

"What do you think?" Stefan asked Jillian in a low whisper, hoping to not arise the suspicions of any automatic surveillance mechanisms. "Looks like there is an electronic perimeter but no actual defensive mechanisms."

"Looks the same to me," Jillian answered quietly not looking away from the target of her view to answer. "I'm going to circle around to check the other side. Meet me halfway?"

Stefan made an affirmative signal and began to make his way slowly around the sizable perimeter. If he didn't make any sudden movements, his suit would protect him from detection via a motion alert. The government put so much trust in automation to protect their critical infrastructure. Even an inexperienced team would have detected similar infiltration and surveillance actions but there were no people guarding here. All he had to do was trick out the automated systems. Somehow, this was viewed as more secure, but that fallacy was probably only justified since no people present made the human footprint less and thus didn't require a population quota contribution against the ecosystem.

Stefan never would have expected the overwhelming CET community response to his attempted arrest. Most went into hiding, but many responded to Jillian's eloquent speech and decided to join the resistance movement. Both choices helped the cause by taking the best troops from the government's disposal with some being successfully turned.

Stefan finally reached the other side and saw Jillian coming into view. He almost didn't see her, which spoke to the skill of her field craft. He made a subtle signal to gain her attention and they made towards each other.

"You see what you need to see?" Stefan asked in a low voice.

"No surprises that I saw," Jillian replied. "Let's talk it over with our team. I recommend a go on it."

Stefan nodded in agreement as they carefully made their way away from the target area. The government had such a foothold on their populace that the thought of someone making a serious attack on their infrastructure was unfathomable. But yet here they were about to strike a blow to the very heart of the capitol's ability to sustain their way of life.

Stefan and Jillian reached the rest their assembled unit. Technically, there were about three normal size units present but for the time being they were operating together to preserve strength in numbers. Jillian explained the target and risks to the team and quickly gained the agreement to proceed. They would attack at nightfall.

Stefan felt impatient as he watched the time, wishing the mission time would arrive already. There is a lot of idle time in warfare, but the wait before a known action in Stefan's mind was the worst. You knew there were risks of what was coming, but you had only so much you could do to prepare for them. Once you had checked the readiness of your weapons and equipment and gone over the plan with your teammates until all knew it, all you had left was time to contemplate your existence and prepare yourself for the risk that was to come. Stefan mind drifted to the Way of the Lily. One could find comfort in religion at a time like this. To believe in something greater than yourself. To believe that there could be something awaiting after death beyond just ceasing to exist.

"You seem caught up in deep thoughts," Jillian interrupted as she came by where Stefan was sitting.

"You know, the calm before the storm," Stefan answered. "It has always bothered me more than anything else."

"I think we are as ready as we can be," Jillian answered. "Just a couple more hours until we head out."

"I am glad you decided to help instead of just disappear," Stefan offered sincerely. "I wasn't sure my warning would be taken seriously when I escaped ministry custody."

"We knew something like this could happen once some of our team members starting disappearing in Xenon," Jillian answered. "I was just glad I wasn't deployed there. Called in a few favors to make that happen. Something about capturing the religion people like we were ordered didn't feel right to me. I wanted no part of being there."

"It has been hard for me also, being so close to the planning," Stefan replied. "I don't love being on the run and in hiding, but I feel so much freer than any time in my life – like I am doing something with real value and purpose."

"I know what you mean," Jillian replied. "Hang in there. Gotta check on the rest of the troops before we gear up and head out."

Stefan watched as she went and did final checks on the team. He wasn't sure he would be accepted back so quickly. Stefan felt grateful that Jillian had seemingly taken charge. Jillian had a way for command and this combination of units would follow her without hesitation.

The appointed departure time finally arrived and Stefan gathered up his gear and assembled with the remainder of the team.

"I know you are out of practice," Jillian announced, "but Stefan, I want you to lead the advance team. Your demolition skills are legendary in the CET. The rest of us will fan out to provide a protective perimeter. We expect to be detected with a response occurring within several minutes per government protocols. The quicker we can get in and out, the better. Any questions?"

Stefan looked around at his assigned unit once they reached the edge of the target perimeter. The quantity of explosives they were carrying was very heavy in their packs. But the number of targets was high as well.

"You all know what needs done," Stefan whispered to his standard size team. "Give me the signal when you are all clear. We need a large radius to be safe on this one."

Stefan carried his explosive charges and breached the entrance entering the protected perimeter. It would be a matter of moments until his team was detected and an automated signal would go out to the standby government quick response team. A normal reaction time would put personnel on the ground in less than thirty minutes. They had to work quickly.

Sirens and flashing lights sounded throughout the large solar power array. This provided power to nearly thirty percent of Preath and some additional to the surrounding sectors. It was by far, the largest such installation in all the sectors. It consisted of solar capturing shields and a large battery storage array to provide power consistency after daylight hours. The challenge was to cover all the space in time to lay the charges due to the distance between them.

Stefan immediately targeted the main power converter controllers and laid some initial charges there. After that was secured, he began supervising and helping lay the charges on the extensive solar shields that were spread throughout the land area. There was no way to complete this in time, he quickly realized, signaling a supporting group forward to aid in laying the charges as was a discussed backup plan. Minutes quickly went by and when he heard the sound of a likely government response being flown in, he realized he had only covered about three quarters of the planned target area.

"Clear the area!" Stefan yelled loudly while signaling the agreed signal to the remainder of his team. "Head toward the side not prepped," he called to those near him. We can throw charges near the targets on our way out. Put them on a time delay."

Stefan made sure everyone had started moving before he joined the charge to safety. Pressing the charge trigger transmitter, he enabled the explosive array which would begin its planned countdown. If he was killed or detained in his escape, the mission would still succeed.

"Charge enabled!" Stefan yelled trying to be heard over the sounds of the arriving troops.

The sound of weapons fire started to sound above the perimeter alarm. Stefan altered his path to run in a zig zag pattern, doing his best to keep his profile as small as possible. Passing another solar installation, he threw the charges he had in his hand, grunting with satisfaction as they landed at the base of the structure. He saw Jillian frantically waving them to safety while she was directing fire at the security response team the government had sent.

"What is the count on my team?" Stefan yelled to Jillian.

"You are the last, all are clear." Jillian yelled back in between firing her weapon.

"I set some charges on the way out," Stefan yelled. "We are still too close – we need to fall back!"

"Fall back!" Jillian yelled before she fired some shots. "Let's go!"

Stefan sprinted toward safety knowing it would not be long until the explosives blew. The government security response team landed in the middle of the explosives array and hadn't yet ascertained that charges had been set. Stefan glanced at the countdown timer on his wrist indicator.

"T minus ten seconds," Stefan yelled out. "Get to cover!"

Stefan quickly found something on the ground to get behind and put his hands to his ears anticipating a loud noise. The horizon lit up first but was quickly followed by a concussive shock wave and a loud series of explosions. One by one, blast after blast came, until finally all was quiet except for some lingering flames lighting up the horizon. Stefan felt slightly disorientated as was typical being so close to an explosive discharge, but knew it would pass in time.

"Everyone all right?" Stefan yelled to Jillian as he came up to check with him.

"We are," Jillian hollered back still suffering from some temporary hearing loss from the detonation. "The security response team looks wiped out though. That was some show you and your team just put on. I can see where you got your rep from."

"It feels good to be back in the action again," Stefan said with a growing grin. "How long do we have before they send another team?"

"We have time to get away if we hurry," Jillian answered before waving everyone to assemble. "Our next assembly point is three days march from here. You all know where to go. Break into groups of two to three and stay off the grid. Great job today but we have more to do. Let's go!"

Stefan watched as the team donned their anti-surveillance gear once again to aid in being hidden from the grid. Splitting up would make it harder to find them. Stefan paired up with Jillian and headed toward their next target which would likely have a lot more protection now that they had exposed a key weakness.

∞ ∞ ∞

"What was the Ministry of Energy Conservation thinking to leave our energy array so unguarded?" Xavier vented in Quintin's general direction. "Oh, we have a system to get a security team there in thirty minutes in the event of a breach he said. In thirty minutes, they destroyed the whole power generating grid just in time to come get destroyed with the station!"

"CET personnel destroyed it, sir," Quintin carefully interjected. "That isn't going to look good for us either."

"No, it isn't, but that can't be helped I guess," Xavier responded, calming himself slightly. It would do absolutely no good to be worked up going into the Great Scientist Council session. "That will impact our plans some I am sure, but there is no helping it now. Everything here?"

"Yes," Quintin replied. "This has our top three Xenon suppression scenarios that you asked for. I guess we can rule out the second one with less energy available."

"We will probably lose troop availability also if someone is smart and deploys personnel to guard our critical infrastructure," Xavier continued. "Can't be helped. Be ready in case I message you with any questions the council may have."

Xavier nodded to his security detail and made his way to the council meeting location. This meeting would be a rare in-person one. At least he was invited to it. When you don't know about the meeting is when you are most at risk based on what he had seen in the past.

Xavier arrived just as the meeting was being called to order. Trying to process the implications of the recent events on the energy grid were worth not being early as he usually was. This was not a topic to walk in unprepared for.

"Looks like we are all here," the head of the Great Scientist Council announced. "Let's get this session to order. Minister Alexandar, you asked for time to address the council on the insurgency in Xenon?"

Xavier stood up and looked at the assembled ministers. There was a look of nervousness, bordering on fear on their collective countenances. "You have all seen the content I sent ahead," Xavier opened. "Bottom line is that we need an overwhelming troop presence deployed to Xenon and we need them there yesterday. We don't have enough energy capacity to fly a meaningful amount in and the rail system to Xenon has been severely damaged. This situation is worse with the recent challenges to our energy generation capacity."

"Why isn't what is already in Xenon sufficient to put down some unarmed rabble rousers?" the Minister of Transportation asked.

"To say they are unarmed would be a mischaracterization of reality," Xavier explained. "Right now, there is a strong, armed insurgency who is only growing in capability. We need to put it down before they grow even stronger. If we move quickly with a lot more troops, we can do this. If we delay, it will require an even more overwhelming force."

"Ok," the Minister of Energy Conservation interjected, "say we give you your troops. How are we going to get them there in time? It will still take several weeks to get them into place in any of these options you gave us.

"You mean because any energy reserves we had just got blown up?" Xavier asked pointedly, knowing it would probably come back at him.

"I think I recall that some of your disgruntled troops are who did the damage," the Energy Conservation Minister replied tersely.

"This is getting us nowhere," the head of the council interjected. "Does anyone disagree we need more troops in Xenon?"

Xavier looked around the room and no one made a move to disagree.

"We also need to obviously improve our security on our infrastructure until we get this little rebellion put down," the council head continued. "Unless anyone objects, I think we need to deploy a solid defense presence to all critical infrastructure installations…real people, not this nonsense quick response team concept that clearly didn't work fast enough. Everyone else, we send north. How fast can we get them there?"

"By the time we get them deployed and sent up by rail transport, probably a week with the numbers I have in mind," Xenon offered. "And at least a week more to march them to where we want them inside Xenon. That is, unless we can spare some energy to fly some in."

"How long is it going to take to restore our energy levels, provided they don't hit other installations?" the council head asked the Minister of Energy Conversation.

"Our ability to manufacture new energy collectors and controllers is very limited since we recycle only from existing stocks. Mining operations have been shut down years ago and I don't think there is much we can salvage from the recent attack," the Energy Conversation

Minister replied. "This is well known. We set our population targets to fit within the energy footprint we have capacity for."

"So, we need to restart mining operations for more component materials?" the council head asked.

"That or revert to the stock of fossil fuels. Not that we have anything that is still equipped to use them," the Energy Conversation Minister answered.

How could this government be so shortsighted, Xavier wondered? All the rebels needed to do was cripple the energy grid and the ability to wage war would keep taking steps backwards. The government had boxed itself into place it would have trouble recovering from.

"It is clear we will have to wage our campaign without energy assistance," Xavier stated. "But we will bring overwhelming manpower like they have never seen. If we need to wipe out every person who lives there, then we will. The pursuit of victory will not allow us to stop and make excuses why we could not do what was necessary to prevail!"

"Well said," the council head answered. "We will need to solve these other problems later on, but for now, we need to put down this disease that is growing out of control in Xenon. The council approves your proposal, Minister Alexandar. Assemble whatever you require with the Great Scientist Council's blessing. Every able-bodied man, woman and child who can aid this effort is at your disposal. To victory!"

The head of the council's words reverberated through the chamber and were quickly drowned out by feet stamping and cheering. What was a fearful and tentative group was now united in single purpose – to put down the resistance and make Xenon into a new place, one fully committed to the ways of science. And somehow, Xavier had been handed the reigns to command this power – Something he did not plan to waste.

CHAPTER 25

Sharna looked around her lab, clearly not in the friendliest of her dispositions. Aaliyah didn't appear to have messed anything up while she was gone, which is more that could be said about most other so-called helpers she had gone through over the years. Her trip back from the nature preserve gave her time to reflect on the best course of action she could take to make things right. It was no longer a question of should she take action against the government, but more what she thought she could successfully get away with to maximize the impact.

"Welcome back!" Aaliyah said cheerfully walking through the door. "I had a feeling you may come back today. How was your trip?"

"Had a feeling?" Sharna said skeptically. "I suspect you had more direct suggestion than that."

"Perhaps," Aaliyah said this time more carefully. "I am still glad you are back. Anything I can help you with today?"

"Hold on, I need to test something," Sharna answered before enabling the surveillance scrambler she had developed. She did not want to be listened to now. If she only used it sparingly it didn't raise suspicions, as it could be assumed it was part of ongoing research.

"I may be able to use your help," Sharna answered. "I am scrambling right now so I don't think we can be spied on. If I asked you to help with something not quite within regulations, would you do it?"

Aaliyah looked at Sharna carefully to try to infer her motivations. Sharna was not one for subterfuge which made this exercise intriguing.

"If it has something to do with the trip you just took, I would very likely want to help," Aaliyah answered. "What do you need?"

The Teacher person seemed to think Aaliyah could be trusted. Trust did not come easily for Sharna. Beyond trusting in herself, everyone else in her life had let her down at some point. But here she was getting ready to put her life potentially in someone else's hands.

"I am not good at this, but I need help running fake experiments," Sharna finally answered.

"Fake experiments?" Aaliyah asked with confusion apparent on her face.

"Well, if I am going to do something I am not supposed to be, I need it to look like I am doing something else, don't I?" Sharna asked. "Everything I do gets a ton of surveillance since I have run off every ministry liaison they have sent to keep tabs on me. It is easier for them to assign someone to watch me remotely. The people who watch usually aren't very bright, but I don't want to take any chances."

"I can do whatever you need me to," Aaliyah answered. "Just need some good directions and I will follow them."

Sharna explained what she had in mind. She had better things to do with her time than conduct this ruse, but she now felt a bit paranoid and deemed it a necessary step, regardless of how ridiculous it made her feel to sanction it.

"That can be made more efficient," Sharna stated after turning off the scrambler device. "Make a note of the parameters used and reconfigure the machine to use the second setup I have documented here. We will try it again later after you have finished."

"I'll get right on it," Aaliyah said with seriousness as she took the device away and started performing the adjustments

That would give a periodic excuse to speak outside of being watched. Now she needed to start digging into Oversite. Some changes needed to be made there.

Sharna began to analyze the code she had written for the AI module for surveillance scanning. It was very good at finding new patterns which made moving around in a suspicious manner very difficult. This module was self-learning and seemed to have made some adjustments in its automatic detection algorithm following the energy array destruction. The self-adaptation was fascinating and seemed to already be tracking several parties following a suspicious pattern but had not yet passed the confidence threshold needed to initiate a response.

Sharna zoomed into the visual feed and recognized what looked like three soldiers moving in a covert manner.

Looking closer, she recognized one of the people as someone who used to be on a CET group supporting her research. Any missing CET members were priority targets from the communication she had received. The closer they got to a strategic asset, the algorithm would increase the response score and if it crossed the action threshold, an alert would be generated, even if face recognition couldn't determine who was there. Sharna quickly dismissed an idea that would help face recognition overcome the masks they were wearing. She needed to be thinking in ways to help Xenon and its allies, not hurt them.

A few keystrokes later, Sharna offered a rare smile. The escaped CET members would not be flagged. However, she did alter the suspicion parameters to target those who usually drove in a vehicle and were now walking. Changes in established behaviors would be a reasonable cause for suspicion. The fact that many more ministry personnel were having to walk than before after the energy grid was damaged would have to be investigated. That would keep everyone distracted while that was unraveled. She couldn't wait to see the reactions a bunch of midlevel bureaucrats would show when they were stopped and questioned in addition to having to walk to get to work.

Dreaming detection was also problematic. This would be more obvious to disable, but Sharna had some ideas on that also. What if some high-ranking ministers were detected to be dreaming? That would be interesting. It would probably be a bad idea to falsely flag her immediate protectors which left off the minister of her department in Scientific Innovation and the Minister of Scientific Compliance. The woman in charge of the Great Scientist Council wasn't well loved. That would be as good of a place to start as any. And after everyone piled on to condemn her, it would be hard to argue to accuracy of the technology when it later detected other ministers doing the same thing.

Sharna was pretty proud of herself for coming up with this action plan. Technology she could invent in her sleep but playing a high stakes game of kingmaker was another thing altogether. Was it right to do this she wondered? Probably not, but it would even things up.

∞ ∞ ∞

Aaliyah could hardly believe the apparent change that had come over Sharna since she had returned. Sure, the biting attitude and sharp intellect where still there but her focus had been clearly redirected as she moved with cunning and decisiveness. It was if Sharna's eyes had been opened and instead of being paralyzed with the knowledge of her prior actions, she was of a single-minded purpose to turn her energies toward a more noble purpose.

"Run that test now with the new parameters," Sharna instructed to Aaliyah. "I want to see if the new calibration increases the disruption range."

"Starting now," Aaliyah answered dutifully and pressed the button to initiate the scrambling of communication to disrupt any possible surveillance of the lab. Anyone who was watching should realize that the parameters that were being adjusted had nothing to do with the performance of the anti-surveillance mechanisms, even Aaliyah understood that much. But it would pass cursory oversight as long as no one dug too deep into the test data.

"You seem a lot different since you have come back," Aaliyah told Sharna.

"Don't try to get me to engage with all of that religion nonsense," Sharna replied tersely. "Just because I am doing some steps that will help those people doesn't mean I am one of them."

"Perhaps not," Aaliyah answered trying to suppress a smile. "I just like the change in you, is all I am saying."

"Well, don't get too used to it," Sharna said dismissively. "I still can't believe how much scientific research is getting suppressed. Some of the best minds of our generation are toiling as general laborers or in confinement – that is if they haven't been killed already."

"So, why don't we rescue them?" Aaliyah asked with a smile. "Wait, that would be too altruistic of you and someone might confuse you with someone who follows the Lily. Forget I suggested it."

Sharna sent a glare in Aaliyah's direction before shifting her expression to one of thoughtful contemplation. "How did you think of that before I did?" She replied with frustration. "I am clearly distracted right now."

"When there are so many choices to do good, it is impossible to do them all," Aaliyah reassured.

"That sounds like drivel excuse making to me," Sharna replied. "There are always ways to do more. I can make people invisible in Oversite but unless the target realizes it, they will never leave. I want you to go visit some disavowed scientists for me. Convince them to leave and head toward Xenon. With your ability to do the lily meditation, if you can get access to a transport tube, you may be able to get them to safety very quickly."

"I will gladly help with this mission," Aaliyah stated. "But only if you keep practicing trying to enter the Lily meditation while I am away. The more you grow at peace with yourself, the easier you will be able to enter it."

"Fine," Sharna said. "I will spend a few precious minutes on it every day while you are away. Here are your first five names and locations," Sharna said after a few moments of searching. "I will send you new ones after these are free."

∞ ∞ ∞

"How could you?" the Minister of Education exclaimed with an indignant tone. "The head of the Great Scientist Council engaging in religious superstitions!"

"I did no such thing!" the soon to be former council lead answered back forcefully.

"We have the evidence right here," the Minister of Transportation said calmly. "We have you sitting still in a chair and have sensors detecting the brain frequency that happens during that meditation the lily adherents do. This technology has never had a false positive. How long have you been a secret religion follower?"

"I am no such thing," she answered back angrily. "There must be some mistake or someone is trying to set me up falsely. I demand there to be an investigation."

"Oh, there will be an investigation all right," the Minister of Energy Conversation called out. We will question you and get to the bottom of this egregious breach of trust of your position on this council."

"The chair serves at the pleasure of the council. The council no longer has the pleasure," the Minister of Education called out. "Security, take her away!"

Xavier watched as she was pulled out of the room loudly protesting her innocence. Something didn't seem right about what had just happened, but he couldn't put his finger on it. She wasn't a very popular chair and the council would probably be better off without her as the lead, but something external could be at work. But without proof, there was no way Xavier was going to voice his suspicions for fear of joining her fate. The council devolved into loud murmuring and side conversations. Finally, Xavier become frustrated enough to speak out.

"While we are fighting amongst ourselves, the resistance is growing in Xenon," Xavier exclaimed loudly as the room suddenly went quiet. "Does anyone want to add something substantive to combating that?"

"Thank you for reminding us of our duty," the Minister of Education answered. "Without a new leader, we are going to struggle with unity. We have been through a lot these past few years and the only steady voice of calm and reason I have full trust in is you, Minister Alexandar. I know I am not the only one who shares this opinion. I ask the council's consent to install Xavier Alexandar as the new Chairman of the Great Scientist Council."

Xavier watched in surprised silence as each Minister in the room made a statement affirming him to this position. It was a role he was not actively seeking. But it was a role that was now his, as even rival ministers acclaimed their support of his elevation.

"Mister Chairman, this seat is now yours," the Minister of Education stated, as he directed Xavier to the head of the table while the assembled ministers clapped.

"I will accept this honor," Xavier said once he got into position. "But I will not accept our ongoing pattern of disunity. If we are divided, we will fall, but if we are united, we can overcome any adversity. And there will be adversity. We will lose before we will win. Already we are reeling from setbacks in our energy grid, setbacks in Xenon. It is a time for decisiveness, a time for strong measures and a time that we rally the people to defend an enlightened way of life. This may require some temporary compromises in our purity of actions. But if we do not adjust, we will fail. The enemy is growing in strength whether we believe it or not. They want to make their own nation with their own ways and it is imperative that we do all we can to stop this!"

Xavier looked around the assembled table and rotated his gaze to look each minister in the eye. Some showed fire in purpose and fortitude. Others showed fear and timidity. Those he would look to replace.

"I will appoint someone to replace me in the coming weeks. Until then, we have a lot of work to do. The troops are being transported and massed at the border of Xenon. We have enhanced security at our key infrastructure points. The time is coming for a reckoning. Be ready to be called upon."

Xavier looked around as the last of the Ministers filed out. Were they ready for what he planned to do? Xavier recited some strange sounding words then closed his eyes. The world was now open before him, ready for the taking. He had the vision, and if he was careful, now had the power to see it happen. Xavier opened his eyes and could not hide the formation of a smile on his lips. His eyes radiated with a dark intensity. Xavier stood up and slowly walked out of the room, all while eyeing his growing shadow.

CHAPTER 26

"ou are looking stronger every day," Gabriel said to Raelynn. "I was pretty worried you wouldn't pull through."

"You worry too much," Raelynn said with a smile looking up from her bed. "I am more worried about you. Don't think I don't hear rumors of what you are doing in between visits to see me."

"There is a lot that must be done to secure our freedom," Gabriel replied. "Capitol troops are massing and the people need all the help they can get to be ready."

"So much needless destruction," Raelynn said sadly. "We can't allow them to keep doing what they did to me and others, but there has to be another way to oppose this evil."

"Evil will always prevail unless righteous people stand in the gap to oppose its reach," Gabriel said with an intensity that he didn't usually show. "I've had a lot of time to think on this as I watched you suffer those long months."

"I had a lot of time to think as well," Raelynn answered back. "I decided to forgive them for they didn't know what they were doing. They are only following the false teaching that they have been taught. It isn't the people, it is the ideology, propagated by those who should know better but continue to do so anyway. We need to show them a different path. A way to redemption, not a way to destruction."

"Like they showed you and those with you?" Gabriel asked skeptically.

"No," Raelynn offered. "We need to be better than they were. We need to follow the Way of the Lily, even if it costs us dearly. Gabriel, promise me you will do all you can to find a better way."

Gabriel looked at Raelynn conflicted in his emotions. It was all he could do to fight the feeling of vengeance that flowed through his body. But in his heart, he knew she was right. If he became like them, he would be them. And that was something he could not abide.

"I will search for a way," Gabriel said finally. "But if there is no better way, I will do what I must."

"Thank you," Raelynn answered. "Please do not give up your search easily. The doctor says I should be up and around in a few days. When I do, maybe you can teach me the new dream way I have been hearing about?"

"You can count on it," Gabriel said with a much happier smile. "I should probably go now. Thorin gets impatient and cranky with me if I am away too long."

"I still haven't gotten over how you can translocate yourself without a transport tube over such great distances," Raelynn said. "You have really grown a lot since I first met you in your dreams."

Gabriel smiled and waved before translocating himself out of the underground area that Raelynn and the other escaped prisoners were recuperating in. He didn't exactly translocate himself straight from where he started to the finish but instead used a staggered approach that had several intermediate stops. By partially rematerializing himself in intermediate locations he could greatly reduce the draw it had on his energy. And now he had a new promise to keep. One that would probably require a visit to Teacher and the library. He had some ideas but needed more information.

"Nice of you to join us," Thorin said with an annoyed tone of voice. "Now that everyone is here, maybe we can begin our mission?"

"Sorry I am late," Gabriel said with a sheepish grin. "I needed to check up on the prisoners we rescued."

"Prisoners or prisoner?" Thorin asked with a twinkle in his eye. "Never mind, you are here now so shall we get started?"

"No plan changes since we last talked?" Gabriel asked.

"Not until it is changed for us," Thorin answered. "Let's move."

Gabriel entered his dual dream state probing ahead in his vision to identify potential risks. The area looked free of ministry personnel. It was becoming like this more and more frequently, the more incursions they had conducted.

"All looks clear," Gabriel whispered ahead to Thorin and the team with him. "Just the people we are supposed to meet."

Thorin gave Gabriel a nod to acknowledge his comment and still ordered his team to complete the countermeasures they would do if they were expecting someone to be lying in ambush. At least Thorin wasn't arguing with his information any more. He seemed to trust it, but still moved cautiously to verify it.

"Ok," Thorin whispered to his team as they came into position. "I know they act friendly to us, but it is always best to be sure. Gabriel, can you be ready to zap us out of there if it is a trap?

"You got it," Gabriel answered. "You want me with you or safely outside watching?"

This was relevant since in some areas of Xenon, Gabriel was known for what he did during the mass evacuation where he had helped rescue a boy from a school in the capital to reunite him with his mother. But this area was pretty far away from those who would know about that. Also, it was closer to where Ara and Dom would hold sway.

"Ara and Dom think they can handle this," Thorin replied. "Be ready in case they are wrong."

Gabriel agreed and proceeded to watch the approaches with the rest of the Nightstalker One grouping. Slightly shifting his vision, he watched Thorin, Ara and Dom proceed to the meeting location.

"Identify yourselves!" a nervous voice called from inside a building.

"I am Thorin from Nightstalker One," he replied. "You have heard of our work to oppose the unjust reach of the capitol. With me are two men from not far from here, Ara and Dom. We wish to seek your help if you will hear us out."

"I recognize the two young ones," came a voice from inside. I have seen them at the market in town before. They are local."

"Come inside and speak your piece," called the voice from inside.

Thorin, Ara and Dom proceeded slowly and carefully to the waiting room of the building. Inside the lighting was kept low to not give away who was present but everyone could likely see the three of them as they entered. Gabriel could barely make out those who were present and estimated the count to be about twenty people. For this lightly populated area, it likely represented every home or family in the area.

"We must fight or die," Thorin said simply to get their attention. "I know you are not trained soldiers and you would rather tend your crops than fight, but that is a choice you no longer have to make. The capitol is sending troops as we speak, to cleanse the Xenon sector of those who have a different vision for life and freedom so it can be repopulated with those who believe as the government does."

"I have lived in this area my whole life," Ara interjected above the murmuring. "I know the minds of those who live out here. We are a simple people who care about our fields and our families. But the government is against families. They would separate us all if they could, and now they have decided it is better to kill us all than to continue to fight to change our hearts and minds to their way of thinking. So, you can stay here and hope we are wrong, or you can take charge of your future and join us as we oppose this tyranny!"

"We have no weapons and we are few. They are many," came a skeptical voice in the darkness. "Why is now the time to fight?"

"Because they are coming now," Thorin said directly. "They will be massing at the border within a week's time. And we need every able-bodied person who is willing to fight for their families to join us. We have weapons and training and will teach you what we can in the next few days. If we do not, they will lay waste to your lands and destroy all you hold dear."

"How do you know this to be true?" a different voice asked.

"A representative from Kayden has told us," Ara answered. "They who saved us the last time the government tried to destroy our families. Now is the time for action and we need every one of you. Who will join us? Who will step into the light and be recognized as champion for freedom and be a defender of your families?"

"I will stand in the light," a voice answered as the outline of a middle-aged man became visible to all in the room.

"Welcome," Thorin replied meeting him with a strong embrace.

One by one, each person in the room stood forward, embracing the cause of freedom, exposing their countenance to the light so all could see they were ready to defend what they held dear.

"Gather a bag to get you by and meet back here in two hours. If there is anyone else who will join us, bring them also," Thorin said after greeting each person who promised their aid. "We will transport out then."

∞ ∞ ∞

"This one is going to be harder," Stefan said quietly to Jillian as they surveyed their next target.

"I had hoped that this location would not have changes in security yet," Jillian answered. "Not saying we can't hit it, but it is going to be harder to pull off."

"If we take out the control centers, it will be repairable but will likely take them a few weeks to do so. I don't think we can plant charges effectively on all the collectors in time," Stefan said while noticing that the security was more deployed on the perimeter of the compound than around the control centers. If they struck where the weakness in the defense was, they could still accomplish much of the desired mission, hopefully with few or no causalities.

Stefan and Jillian worked out an attack plan before moving back to join the rest of the CET group they had assembled.

"Distract and attack is the name of the game today," Jillian explained to the team. "There are three control centers in this compound. We take them out, then no energy will get out until they are brought back online, which will likely be weeks. Fortunately, these are not directly guarded. Unfortunately, the entire perimeter surrounding the compound is."

"We can't just drone the strikes in?" one of the CET members asked.

"These centers are reinforced," Stefan answered. "Not that we have drones anyway, but if we did, I would still say we need to plant the charges locally for maximum damage and effect."

"Same group as last time with Stefan," Jillian ordered. "The rest of you, let's make the biggest, loudest distraction you ever saw! Pack up, we leave in five."

Stefan quickly discussed the plan with his assigned team and made sure everyone had the demolition charges they needed and instructions on where to place them. Each two-person partnership would have an assigned control center to blow up.

"All right team," Stefan instructed. "This one will require stealth more than anything but if I give the signal, run as fast as you can to get out of there. There are a lot more guards present, and this time they are expecting trouble."

Stefan had each team of two split up and move slowly to the perimeter where it would be closest to get to their intended target.

Stefan moved quietly with his partner Abigail to the intended entry point. Once they arrived, they stayed hidden in the dark of night, waiting for the planned distraction to commence. Stefan checked the time and made the signal to Abigail that they had two minutes until they needed to be ready to go.

Abigail nodded confidently, indicating she was ready to do her job. She had shown out well in the last mission and reminded Stefan of himself when he was much younger with the precision which she placed the explosive charges.

Suddenly, the horizon lit up with an explosion and the sound of weaponry discharging.

"Fan out to cover the incursion point!" he heard over the firing. "We can't let them by."

As Stefan expected, security loosened near where he was at. Sensors would still probably detect them entering but with the alarms already going off for the other breach, he hoped not much attention would be paid to the silent spots. Stefan motioned to Abigail to come along and they quietly crept past into compound and made their way toward their assigned control center. Flash after flash went up and was almost blinding if he allowed his eyes to look in that direction. Jillian and the rest of the team were sure putting on a good show.

Abigail made a hand motion to request permission to set the charges which Stefan approved. The control center appeared to be locked and it would be more trouble than it was worth to try to break inside. But placing some explosives around the foundation and especially at the power entry and exit points should more than cover the destruction needed to dramatically hinder power generation at this facility. In just a few minutes they had placed all they had with them and set the fail-safe timer that would go off after enough time had passed to allow them to clear the radius.

"All ready?" Stefan asked in a whisper?

"Yes," Abigail replied confidently. "Ten-minute countdown from now just started."

"Ok, let's get back. We won't have much time," Stefan said while doing a quick double check of their work. "Standard meet up if we get separated.

Abigail nodded then proceeded to move at a fast clip toward the place they had entered. Stefan followed at a slightly slower pace while having the feeling that something didn't seem quite right. He had learned to trust these feelings over the years. Stefan looked around warily trying to identify the source of his discomfort. Not seeing anything, he continued to move toward the exit, mindful of the timed countdown being executed at his back.

"Well, what do we have here?" Stefan heard in front of him. "It looks like a saboteur to me."

Stefan looked around, determining quickly they were not talking about him. Abigail must be in trouble. Stefan wasn't carrying assault weaponry but did have his handheld weapon with him which he quickly reached for. He immediately slowed his pace and moved slowly and carefully approaching where he heard the voice ahead.

"What should we do with her?" a harsh voice asked.

Stefan moved slowly forward and saw Abigail crouched on the ground, her face bleeding and a weapon drawn on her. There appeared to be three guards surrounding her in her immediate vicinity. She looked mobile, but slightly roughed up overall. Stefan carefully raised his weapon and in quiet mode, fired at the first guard who had the weapon drawn on Abigail. He fell backwards with surprise as Abigail took her opportunity to leg kick one of the other guards to the ground and land a punch in the mouth of the third one who appeared momentarily stunned. Then with some visible pain took off running out of the light, to escape the compound. Stefan readied his weapon at the second guard but the weapon would not fire. What he would have given then for his own personal weapon versus this second-hand unreliable piece. At least it had gotten Abigail free.

The two remaining guards took a moment to recover their poise before radioing for help. Stefan cringed as he realized he was now on the wrong side of the guards who were now blocking his path to escape. On top of that, he was closer than he wanted to be to the blast radius. But to move forward now, would be certain death or capture. Stefan looked around and tried to find some terrain that would partially shield him from what he knew was coming.

Before he could fully situate himself, his body convulsed as a concussive wave shook the area he was in. A feeling of confusion and disorientation overtook him before his world went dark.

Stefan heard voices coming into focus.

"After all that, and we only caught this one traitor?"

Stefan slowly tried to move while he opened his eyes. He was somehow restrained.

"He lives," a voice spoke before planting a kick in the direction of Stefan's ribs.

Stefan grunted in pain. At least it sounded like Abigail had made it to safety.

∞ ∞ ∞

Quintin stood on the top of a hill, overlooking the assembled army that was spread out below him. Every military trained person in the surrounding sectors had been ordered to be here and were converging about twenty kilometers from the border with Xenon. Rail transport service was still working at this location and while it took from the dwindling energy reserves to transport troops in this manner, it was still way more energy efficient than using air transport to get them all here. From here, it would be approximately two days march to the border with Xenon from where they would put down any resistance that was still present.

The orders from above were to show no mercy. Those from Xenon who proactively surrendered and wanted to present themselves for analysis would be allowed to, but the threshold for passing was going to be very strict. Only those who were fully compliant to the ideals of science would be allowed to go on living. And if Oversite or some other feedback provided any doubts of that dedication, then a chance could not be taken on their survival.

Quintin walked down the hill and made his way to a holding area that had been specially setup. The troops here had begun to call him Acting Minister. He had not discouraged it and he was technically acting as the Minister of Scientific Compliance until Xavier made up his mind who should fill the role. Xavier had all but said if he performed well here, the job would be his permanently. He knew that, and the troops all but suspected it. But first he had a visit to make.

"Nice of you to join us, Stefan," Quintin said with fire in his eyes. "I always knew there was something about you I didn't like."

Stefan was badly bruised with cuts and welts all over his body. He was heavily restrained and equipped with multiple destruction mechanisms should he try to escape or someone rescue him.

"How is the energy situation?" Stefan asked with a smile which exposed a newly missing tooth.

"Yeah, I will give you credit for taking advantage of the incompetence of that ministry. But you are not going to take advantage of me anymore," Quintin threatened. "In fact, I have a very special plan for you."

"What? More forced beatings? More interrogation to determine why people you betrayed are not staying loyal?" Stefan asked defiantly.

"No," Quintin replied. "Something much more useful. It won't be long now. You will see when we get closer to Xenon."

CHAPTER 27

"**W**here to next?" Gabriel asked Thorin as soon as he had finished his latest recruiting pitch. Another thirty recruits were gathered. All by itself it would not make or break the cause, but great accomplishments are an accumulation of smaller ones.

"If what I am told is correct, the ministry is amassing an army just outside of the border of Xenon near where we destroyed the rail transport lines," Thorin replied with a strained look on his face. "I don't like our odds in a pitched battle but I like our odds even less if we let them swarm the countryside using their overwhelming numbers against us. We need to get everyone there for that confrontation and use every minute we have to train the volunteers what to do."

"You want everyone translocated to the border area then?" Gabriel asked.

"Yes," Thorin replied after a few second pause. "And we need all the other recruiting groups that have been gathered brought there also. Is that something you can do?"

"I will need some help to get it all done in time, but yes, that can happen," Gabriel answered. "I also need to look into some things that could maybe help us in our upcoming fight. Let me drop you and this group where you want to go, then I will work on making your other requests a reality."

"Your help has been amazing these last few weeks," Thorin replied with genuine gratitude. "I didn't trust you at all when you first came to us, but now I don't want to operate without you."

"We are not done yet," Gabriel answered with a smile as he looked over the assembled unit – one that had become a second family of sorts in the time he had spent with them. After a nod from Thorin, Gabriel entered his dual dream state and over the next few minutes translocated everyone to the other side of Xenon.

Once he was sure he had relocated everyone and passed on Thorin's request, Gabriel made his way to the library. He had some research to do if he was going to keep his promise to Raelynn.

∞ ∞ ∞

"I have that new test ready on the surveillance scrambler," Aaliyah interrupted Sharna's concentration.

Sharna looked up with an annoyed expression on her face and stopped herself before she questioned what test, quickly realizing that both Aaliyah had returned and that she likely wanted to discuss something without being heard.

"Took you long enough," Sharna said with feigned annoyance while motioning for her to begin the testing.

"So how did it go?" Sharna asked curiously, after Aaliyah had started the machine. "I haven't been able to pay as close of attention on the Oversite feeds as I planned to."

"I got three of them to safety," Aaliyah said carefully. "The other two were too skeptical to go along. I think they thought it was some sort of trap when I couldn't provide the right evidence. The others just suspended their disbelief and were willing to do anything to change their life situation. They are safe now."

"It is a shame on the remaining two," Sharna said. "They probably need more proof you didn't have. But why are you back? I could have just sent you more contacts remotely."

"Something came up that you needed to hear directly," Aaliyah answered. "Trisha has a request for you from the resistance if you are willing to help with it. They need someone to open up an access port in Oversite that can communicate to all handhelds in all the sectors. You have clearance levels to do something like that don't you?"

"Technically no, but that is just a small obstacle," Sharna replied knowing she could easily circumvent protocols she wasn't technically read into.

"I guess the government is already planning to broadcast something," Aaliyah explained. "Kayden just wants to enhance it a bit."

"I assume they have someone on their end that would know how to use a multi-socket encryption array if I give the right access key and address?" Sharna asked. "I can open it to them, but honestly, there are very few people I have ever seen who would be able to do anything with it."

"She seemed very confident they had someone who could," Aaliyah answered. "If you can give me the information, I will get it to them."

Sharna nearly smirked at her comment. "You are going to memorize a million-character encryption key and recite it to them?"

"I didn't say I understood it," Aaliyah answered. "She said something about a memory module being needed if that makes any sense."

"That is better," Sharna replied while generating the required information. "This will be good for the next three days. Beyond that, I will need to regenerate it, as the algorithm rotates the security protocols."

"Once this is used, it is just a matter of time before it is traced back to me," Sharna replied warily. "So, if they really want to use it, it needs to be for something more important than me being here."

"I understand," Aaliyah answered. "Trisha said they will make a plan for you to be extracted if they endanger you."

Sharna went back to looking at her console, once again absorbing herself in thought. Life would be different outside of her lab. That is, if she made it to safety. As much as she wanted to trust this resistance to look out for her wellbeing, it didn't hurt to put some safeguards in for herself.

∞ ∞ ∞

Stefan looked out of the metal barred cage he was held in. Something was clearly about to happen as there were people scurrying in and out of his holding area all morning long. A couple of his guards had jeered at him and said something about his upcoming trial and how they were going to enjoy making him confess.

He was surprised to still be alive. Being caught in the act of destroying an energy installation did not require a trial – it was punishable by death on the spot. The more he thought about it, the more he realized he was probably going to be subject a show trial of some sort. You always need to put a face to the enemy to rally the people, and that face was likely to be his.

A sudden calm overcame Stefan as he contemplated the fate that awaited him. Unpleasantness was surely waiting, but as he looked back on his recent choices and actions that precipitated his current predicament, he felt no regrets and was fully at peace within himself.

At this point a switch triggered in his mind. Instead of being uncommitted to the teachings of the Lily, he knew within the depth of his being that the teachings were true. Stefan gave up his remaining resistance to be directed by the Way of the Lily. And for the first time ever, knew with full certainty the path he should travel and what he was destined to do. He should have felt fear as to what was to come, but instead he grew with confidence, steeling himself, while concurrently opening himself to the coming suffering.

"I would look a lot more worried than you do, if I were in your position," Quintin stated with a malicious smile after appearing unannounced.

"The way of man fails, but the Way of the Lily brings hope," Stefan said with a serene calmness that clearly unnerved Quintin's cool demeanor.

"The only thing you should be hoping for is a quick death," Quintin responded without the same confidence he had just projected before quickly leaving Stefan's presence.

A few moments later, several guards came to remove Stefan from the holding cell and dragged him roughly to an assembled podium arrayed with broadcast equipment. He could see a vast host of soldiers assembled before him. This army would cause much harm. It had to be nearly every able-bodied person trained in public safety and defense. This many people would do who knows how much harm to Xenon.

Stefan turned and found seated in front of him what appeared to be various high-ranking officials from many ministries. Quintin was seated at the place of honor of those empaneled. Ursula stood in the position representing the lead prosecutor. They were going to subject him to a trial, and it was probably going to be broadcast far and wide.

He was to be made an example of. This was the only thing that made sense.

"Greetings to all the sectors watching," Quintin opened. "You may wonder why your energy quotas have been reduced recently. Today we will show the prosecution of someone who helped destroy two of our energy generation compounds."

Ursula stepped forward and began to lay out the evidence that had been collected. She showed video evidence of Stefan destroying energy installations and she went on to explain his elevated role both within the CET community and his special assignment in the Ministry of Scientific compliance. She called him an instigator and a ringleader. There was no denying that he had done the sabotage. The crowd below began to rise in anger. Stefan realized that he was being used to rile the soldiers up, to give motivation to the conflict that was coming.

"You have heard the charges and overwhelming evidence against you, Stefan," Quintin pronounced. "Do you have the gall to dispute it?"

Stefan adjusted his posture as straight as he could in the restraints he was still in and stared directly into the camera. His appearance was disheveled, his face was bloodied and bruised. But through all of that, he conveyed a radiance that could not be dismissed. It would do no good to show fear or doubt now. He was somehow being given an opportunity to speak with the whole nation listening and he did not plan to waste this chance.

"Dispute what?" Stefan asked defiantly, cognizant that he probably wasn't going to be given long to speak. "Dispute the fact that I rose to defend liberty and the rights of humanity? The question shouldn't be what actions I took, instead it should be why I took them. We are taught that the Scientific Reformation ushered in a new way of life, dedicated to the precepts of science. Anything that opposed the tenants of science was to be suppressed, lest it cause harm to our world and damage the future of our planet."

"I submit to you today that it is all a lie. We are not a nation of science. Science is the pursuit of knowledge wherever it leads. I served a long time in the Covert Extraction Teams. I arrested countless scientists for daring to discover something that was not approved. Those worried about the energy grids that I helped destroy? One innovation the government suppressed would have offset that power by a hundredfold. But the tyrants that be thought it was better to keep everyone controlled than allow humanity that benefit. No, we are not a nation of science. We are a nation of tyranny."

"We are a nation that rounds up people who believe a different way and tortures them, experiments on them and kills them, because we are cowards and we can. We say it is in the name of science. That is a lie. It is in the name of oppression, in the name of power. I used to believe as you do, but I have had my eyes opened. I have seen the world through a lens of truth and I have come to find the truth of the Lily. I am complacent no longer."

"I will do all I can with until my last breath to oppose this terrible regime. I serve the cause of freedom. I support the independence of Xenon, a place where people will be free to believe as they wish and not fear death or punishment if their thoughts do not conform to the endorsed way."

Quintin and those on the podium were fuming with visible anger. "You probably think you just broadcast all those lies," Quintin said finally into Stefan's ear. "I cut your feed about three sentences in. Oversite has edited your response which is playing now."

Quintin was given a motion from someone manning the camera. "You have admitted your guilt. The only punishment is death. Bring the honored execution squad."

A cross section of soldiers and ministry officials came forward holding stones and other heavy items.

"Let justice be served!" Quintin yelled to the riled-up masses of those watching below.

Stefan watched as they advanced on him and began to hurl projectiles at him. He felt each one as they hit his legs, his ribs and ultimately some shots in his head. Before he lost consciousness, he called out, "The Lily is arrayed in all its glory. The Way of the Lily is for all. You do not know what you do and the Way of the Lily will always be open for you."

The stones and projectiles continued to rain down. The crowd roared with approval. "For Justice! For Science! To Victory!" echoed in Stefan's ears before he took his final breath and expired.

Those who were watching remotely on their handhelds saw a slightly different scene than they were supposed to. They heard the entirety of Stefan's speech, they saw visuals of tyranny, and did not view the spectacle with the unrestrained glee as the soldiers had experienced.

The soldiers were ready to invade Xenon but behind them the seeds were planted for a different outlook. Stefan made his sacrifice and went to the beyond with no regrets, at peace in the choice he had freely made.

CHAPTER 28

$\mathcal{T}$horin stood with stoic calm which masked the fury battling inside of him. If he was going to die in a manner not in battle, he hoped he would have the courage to do what Stefan had just done. To stand tall to the tyranny and to proclaim it unabashed, knowing certain death is near – that was the true measure that anyone could aspire to.

And he was not alone in his torment for what he just witnessed. Stefan deserved so much better. Gabriel may have been able to save him if he was here, but with the explosive collar on Stefan's neck and likely other deterrents…no, there was nothing that could have been done. His sacrifice would not be in vain.

"What do you think?" Jillian asked Thorin, interrupting his thoughts. "Do we have a chance? There are a lot of troops they have staged."

"Yes we do, but that chance is not large," Thorin quietly acknowledged. "But it will be even less if we do not make a stand together."

"Going to be a lot of people who die today," Jillian said grimly. "Did we do the right thing by fighting the government?"

"After what I just saw with Stefan, there is no doubt in my mind," Thorin answered. "Freedom is worth dying for, even the hope of it."

"Well, let's not go out of our way to prove that today," Jillian said with a nervous laugh. "I think the troops would appreciate if you were to address them. You know, commanding general and all."

"I am not going to forgive you for getting that title attached to me," Thorin said with annoyance. "But I will return the favor by making your my second in command, General."

Jillian rolled her eyes in jest. "I suppose I had that coming, more superior General."

"Let's get this speech over with," Thorin replied. "We have untested troops and they will need to be motivated properly."

Thorin walked to an area he could be seen by most of the assembled troops. Some engineer type named Alaine had setup a projection system that would broadcast his message and commands to all those in range.

"Patriots of Xenon," Thorin began. "Today we fight to survive. The capitol troops only want to serve their masters and wipe us from the face of the earth. They are motivated by hate, distrust and lies. But make no mistake, they will grant no mercy. Not to anyone fighting or to those who don't. Xenon and all who live here are a disease in their mind that must be eradicated."

Thorin looked around and those he could see he had their attention in full. He saw anxiety and fear in their faces. He was not giving a message of hope, but instead one of hardship and trials.

"You do not have to act as they do, but you must defend that which you hold dear," Thorin continued. "Your section leaders have all taught you your roles. Trust them. Follow them as you would follow me. The armies of the capitol are massing and we must be ready. For if we fail, all that we hold dear will be no more. Defend your families, your lands and rise up to achieve Xenon's freedom and independence!"

The roars of the cheering needed no amplification for Thorin to hear them fully. The people of Xenon were ready and Thorin was now confident they would stand in the face of oppression, no matter what would befall them.

∞ ∞ ∞

Quintin oversaw his armies marching forward in unison as they approached the border with Xenon. Scouts had informed him that Xenon had massed thousands of troops, mostly irregular, just over the border.

"Even without air support, we can make quick work of this rabble sir," his commanding general offered. "Permission to engage the skirmishers sir to see what they are capable of?"

"If you think that is necessary," Quintin answered. "Permission granted."

His general made some orders and a few minutes later they began a fast attack of some encampments across the border. Weapons fire broke out in attempt to repel the invaders, including some high-tech weaponry that was not expected to be available to the rebels.

"They aren't supposed to have that are they?" Quintin asked.

"That is why we are sending in probes before committing our full force," the general answered. "They have some good weaponry, but I doubt they have enough to sustain a prolonged engagement. They only have what they stole, where we can keep getting more to replenish from the central armory."

"Now what?" Gabriel asked impatiently. "Chairman Alexandar is not going to be pleased with us just sending skirmishers."

"Now we pull the skirmishers back and bombard them with projectile weapons. Once we wear them down a bit, we will bring the whole force forward."

"Better," Quintin answered. "I want to get this first battle over with today. We need to break their spirit hard before we annihilate them."

∞ ∞ ∞

"We are taking causalities, General Thorin," Ara reported breathlessly. "We are holding, but so far they haven't sent many troops at us yet."

"Skirmishers to take our measure," Thorin assessed to Jillian. "Probably going to start sending explosive charges at us next since they seem to be without air support or at least don't have enough to use unless it is super critical to the fighting."

"Dig in?" Jillian asked.

"Send orders to withdrawal to the dug in positions as soon as the skirmishers leave the field," Thorin commanded to Ara who quickly proceeded to run away to pass the orders. "Where is Gabriel at and all those dreamers? I know that they aren't crazy about violence, but we could really use their help right now!"

∞ ∞ ∞

Gabriel watched with concern as the battle began. People were getting injured but it didn't look like the capitol had committed its full forces yet.

"I feel like I should be down there with them right now," Gabriel lamented to Raelynn. "The odds of what we are about to do seem low at best."

"I asked you to find another possible way, and this is it," Raelynn replied with steadfast conviction. "And this is our best chance to do the most good for Xenon."

"Then we best be getting started," Gabriel answered as he looked around the assembled room. Every dreamer who had a moderate and above level of dream gifts in Xenon had assembled here.

"Alaine, can you remind everyone what you need them to do?" Gabriel asked as he tried to calm his mind for what was about to come.

"You all know how a transport tube works," Alaine explained. "It has a way of multiplying the power coming out when you dreaming. When Gabriel is ready, I need you all to do your dream thing and this device will hopefully give us some extra options if Gabriel can figure out how to use them."

Gabriel wasn't really sure he would be capable of what was about to be attempted. He had seen some references to it in some of his research but time was fleeting and many lives were in danger.

"Let's try it now," Gabriel asked the group. "Dream as long as you are safely able, but break off when it gets to be too much for your strength."

Gabriel shifted himself into the dual dream state he had grown accustomed to using. There was a sense of growing energy and power in the air, a tension that was begging him to do something. If only he had the knowledge of how to do what he wanted to do. Gabriel tried to reach out to that energy in the air but as much as he tried, it seemed to be just out of his grasp. Something did not seem right with his approach.

He knew his grandmother's dreaming tone and reached out to her like he would if he wanted to talk with her. He saw her watching and looking at the battle unfolding below.

"The devastation will be horrific," she said sadly. "So much waste and loss."

"I wish I knew what to do to stop it," Gabriel said with growing frustration in his voice. "I am trying to mesh with the dream energy but I seem to just be bouncing off of it whenever I try to embrace it."

"Maybe you aren't supposed to wield it," Isabella answered. "Sometimes we need to just act and know that we have the support of others behind us, uplifting us in their dreams. They are all dreaming with their focus directed for you. Step forward in faith and trust in the Lily."

This was an approach that Gabriel had not considered. This may be just the answer he was looking for.

"Thank you, grandmother," he said gratefully. "I think I know what I need to do."

Gabriel separated himself from his grandmother's dreaming and suspended himself high above the raging battle. Explosions were flying through the sky and raining devastation on the Xenon first ranks. Xenon could not reply in kind, or at least with enough explosives to do similar damage. Instead they were just trying to weather what was coming their way. They were trying to hold on until it was done. This could not stand.

Gabriel set himself down next to Thorin and Jillian's command post. This was within range of explosive ordinance, although not where it was hitting most strongly.

"Gabriel, get down, you will get killed standing in the open like that!" Ara yelled when he saw Gabriel materialize.

Gabriel resisted Ara's attempt to pull him into the bunker and continued to make himself visible above the fray of the battle.

"Xenon will be saved this day," Gabriel said with a cold intensity that caused Ara to back off on his demands. His proclamation could somehow be heard over the din of the battle. It radiated strength and calm in the midst of the blood and chaos.

Gabriel raised his hands and began to meet each projectile charge in the air with his will, causing it to be smothered before it could detonate on the ground. It was like there was an unseen shield protecting the airspace of Xenon.

"Your weapons have no strength here!" Gabriel yelled in a way that those attacking could hear as they watched in disbelief as their bombs bounced harmlessly in the air and were made useless before falling to the ground.

The intensity of the projectiles suddenly increased and altered from being concentrated in one place to being spread all across the horizon. They were probing for weak spots but none were to be found. Gabriel continued to feel himself growing in strength and not feeling any of the expected energy drain he would expect with this sort of action.

∞ ∞ ∞

"What is happening?" Quintin yelled to his general.

"They must have a new weapon that stops projectiles," the general answered.

"Then send in the troops!" Quintin yelled. "They can't possibly have a special weapon to stop that."

"Is that Gabriel?" Ursula asked Quintin when he had finished yelling at his general. She had pulled up a feed that showed Gabriel standing tall in the midst of the attempted bombing. "Could he be somehow in charge of whatever that weapon is?"

∞ ∞ ∞

Gabriel continued to swat down projectiles until they stopped being shot.

"Nice of you to join us," Thorin said once it seemed safe to come out of the bunker. "I don't know what you just did, but thank you for doing it. Now all we need to do is hold off a force that probably outnumbers us ten to one."

"Just as the bombs did not get through, neither will their troops," Gabriel said with a faraway look in his eyes. "Bring your troops in the open so they can look their enemy straight in the eye and stand tall."

"But won't that make them an easier target?" Jillian asked skeptically.

"Gabriel is right," Thorin answered relying on his trust he had developed with Gabriel. "We will show fear no longer and stand as one to oppose whatever is sent our way. Ara, relay the order."

Ara scrambled off to make sure everyone came into the open to meet the charge the capitol troops were about to execute. Not long after,

Gabriel began to see Xenon troops tentatively making themselves visible, acting against their best instincts and training.

"Do not cross the border into Xenon! This land is not and will never by yours!" Gabriel projected across the battle lines into the troops of the enemy.

Despite his warning, the capitol troops still massed and began their charge. As they got closer, they starting firing their weapons at the exposed Xenon defenders but just as Gabriel had blocked the bombs, he also blocked the discharge from the smaller weapons so they did not cause damage. As the first wave of advancing troops reached the border with Xenon, Gabriel reached out to them with his mind and translocated them in mass, scattered them across all across the sectors except Xenon, all while leaving their weapons abandoned on the battlefield. They just disappeared from the battle to find themselves in the middle of the desert, in nature preserves, back in the capital and on abandoned roads all throughout capitol-controlled territory. They were now separated and alone and most importantly no longer attacking the troops who just wanted to protect their freedom.

The yells on the Xenon side went up when the first wave disappeared from view and was quickly followed with tension as the second wave advanced. A whole mass of soldiers could not just disappear, so wave after wave was sent and all disappeared. Gabriel kept his focus until the advancing army was no more. All that remained was the command post and those who were attending to the wounded.

"Freedom is upon us!" Gabriel projected so all could hear. "You have all stood in the face of tyranny. You have fought to defend your families, your loved ones, and your way of life – Your right to practice religion, to advance in science. But most of all, we have fought for each other. Stand tall, be proud. While we have won this great battle, the enemy is not yet ready to surrender and rest."

Thorin stepped up beside Gabriel putting his arm around him and providing him a strong embrace. "Do we advance and go across the border?"

"For now, we only defend," Gabriel replied. "But a time will come where we must root out the evil that exists across that line. Maintain a defense line and be diligent, for the enemy will not abandon their desire to cause us harm. I must now take care of one more thing."

Gabriel reached out in his mind and quickly scanned the capitol until he found Xavier watching the battle transpire on an array of monitors. Even though the distance was great, Gabriel took in his features and caused him to materialize in the command post with Quintin across the border. Once he had Xavier in place, Gabriel translocated himself to join him. He had one more task to accomplish.

∞ ∞ ∞

Xavier looked up in surprise at his sudden change of scenery. He sensed some sort of pull on his body and had not resisted it. Something of importance was about to happen. The battle had clearly gone badly for Quintin and he was now somehow looking at Quintin who was in a state of denial and disbelief on what had just occurred.

"How did you get here?" Quintin said nervously as he stumbled over his words.

"Probably the same way you lost my army," Xavier replied in a cutting manner.

"What kind of weaponry do they have? I have never seen anything like it," Quintin said still in a state of disbelief.

"The kind that will protect our freedom," Gabriel announced having just materialized in front of them.

Xavier looked at Gabriel and saw something in him he had never seen before. There was a sense of immense power in his eyes that caused a shudder down Xavier's spine. Gone was the underling who cherished every crumb Xavier dropped for him. Gabriel was now his own man and was not here to beg for mercy but to set his terms.

"That was you, wasn't it?" Xavier asked thoughtfully. "The action doesn't honestly surprise me, but that it was you who did it does. I really misjudged you."

"This is my home, even though you tried to take it from me," Gabriel answered. "And now I aim to see it be free. Your troops are scattered across the wind, you need to sue for peace. Xenon's troops are mostly unscathed and thanks to all the weaponry your troops left on the field, are armed more than you realize them to be. Leave us in peace, recognize our independence and my reach will stay content."

Xavier began to laugh in a way that was unsettling. "You can have your freedom for a while. You will find out it is not all it is cracked up to be. You will rue this day. Gabriel, I thank you."

"Thank me?" Gabriel asked.

"Oh yes," Xavier replied as he directed a very disquieting and penetrating look toward Gabriel. "You have given me what I need to change the path of a nation. Sure, we tried to stamp out your Order in the name of science to make people believe that religion is for the weak and is outdated. It almost worked. But that time is past. Now, we can return to the old ways. Ways where we battled the weaklings of the Lily. Oh yes, my Order was always stronger."

"Your Order?" Gabriel asked, not believing and understanding what he was being told.

"You think your Lily is all powerful because you can do your dreams and make things different around you?" Xavier continued. "True power is not in the weak Way of the Lily. It is in the Way of Nature Rising where the shadow arts have triumphed over your Order for generations. Check your precious histories in the areas no one is allowed to go. You will find it to be true. Enjoy your small victory. We didn't extinguish your Order through the Scientific Reformation but we will extinguish it now. I will give answers to your display of power and use them for my purposes. So yes, thank you."

Gabriel and Quintin stared at Xavier with a confused expression on their faces. Ursula on the other hand, well, she didn't seem to have any confusion. She knew.

"Are you through with your weak attempt at power in pulling me here?" Xavier asked. "You know, I let you bring me. I could have blocked that clumsy attempt."

"I will send you back when I am ready or I may make you walk all the way back," Gabriel answered, not quite as confident as he was a few minutes before.

Xavier chuckled at Gabriel's statement and begin to recite some strange sounding words. "Until we meet again, Gabriel. Ursula, are you coming? I need a Minister I can trust."

Xavier raised his hands and then he and Ursula were gone.

Xavier smiled as he watched the confusion on Gabriel's face from his console in the capitol. The game was going to be much more interesting now.

EPILOGUE

$\mathcal{G}$abriel returned to the place where all the dreamers had been lending support and collapsed on the ground in exhaustion. "Xenon is saved but great danger lies ahead," he rasped to those who could hear.

"You did it," Raelynn said happily as she lightly caressed Gabriel's face. "You found another way."

"He needs to rest now," Isabella said to those surrounding him, hoping to hear his account of what had happened. "We must let him gather his strength. He will need it in the days to come."

∞ ∞ ∞

Sharna watched her security feed with a passive disdain. There were several armed security agents approaching her lab and she didn't think it was to say hello. Granted, it would take a bit of time for them to circumvent the high-tech reinforced security perimeter that protected her lab but that would not last forever. Sharna took a moment to make her peace with her current situation. And the odd thing about it was she had no regrets.

If she was going to be arrested for something, helping to undermine that horrid show trial was a worthy reason. And that Stefan had stood up for true science was the best part of it. There was no long-term safety and helping to support what was right superseded all other considerations. Sharna looked at her handheld and a message from Aaliyah popped up.

"A7435 is the code if you dare to dream your way out. If you can't, be ready and keep strength and someone will come for you as soon as they can. – A"

Realization dawned on Sharna what was being suggested. She had already prepared a quick exit bag fearing this outcome and grabbed it quickly including all the research she had records of in portable memory. She then picked up the lily plant on her workstation and brought it over to the transport tube. With some quick manipulation, she restored the electronics to its original condition and entered in the location code that Aaliyah had sent her.

"Open up in the name of Science!" she heard yelled through the secured partition entrance.

Sharna had to muffle a small laugh. It would take a lot of effort to get through that door, especially after she had scrambled the controls. Oh, they would get through eventually, but she had ample time. Sharna tuned out the noise, situating herself by putting her hands on the controls that enabled transport.

Sharna sat motionless staring at the lily plant. For the first time since she could remember, her mind was calm and in a unique sort of focus. She knew in her heart she was doing right and had a peace with it. The Lily reflected that peace, that serenity and that focus. Then without any warning she saw a bright flash of light and found herself in a place she had been before – The place where the library and Teacher resided. She was where she most wanted to be.

THE END

COMING SOON

Book 3 of the Dreamer Series

The hum of melodic chanting echoed across the chamber. A small flicker of light permeated through an otherwise dark enclosure casting long and ominous shadows. The form of a person came within view of the emanating light. It was shrouded in a black hooded robe obscured with a mask which took the form of a serpent's head. In the person's hand was a staff of intricate designs. The staff was raised and all went quiet.

The silence lasted for but a moment, but it could have been an eternity. Xavier looked through the eye holes of his mask as he surveyed the devotees arrayed in front of him. Their passion cut through the façade of their adornment. The ceremony was ready, awaiting just his assent to begin.

Xavier raised his arms and called forth words of power. *"Eleem al Forakin!"*

Smoke began to rise from the floor in response to Xavier's command. Those watching began to pound their staffs into the ground in a rhythmic cadence while repeating the words that Xavier had so strongly intoned.

"Behold the power of Nature Rising!" Xavier yelled out above the repeating chants and pounding of staffs. The chanters increased their volume of the incantation and intensity of their cadence. Louder and louder the sounds grew. And by some unspoken or choreographed command, they all stopped in unison and once again stillness consumed the chamber, now further obscured in smoke.

"Bring forth the sacrifice," Xavier called out as he watched three bound and gagged adherents of the Lily brought in and placed on an ornate altar isolated from the mass of congregants. A veil was raised showing several pacing but contained tigers. They were hungry, Xavier had seen to that.

Awareness slowly dawned on those who were placed on the altar. Yes, they expected death, that much was not a surprise, but a level of fear now showed on their faces as they comprehended the essence of their impending demise.

Another robed adherent called out in her feminine but hardened voice. Ursula took the place at the right hand of Xavier. Her eyes were piercing, even through the mask she wore, daring the most courageous in the room to meet her gaze. She turned her eyes toward those destined for sacrifice.

"The Way of the Lily is weak!" she yelled. "Let us drain them of their power that ours may increase. And from nature we emerged and to nature must we pay the price for our ascendance. Feed that which acts against nature into the mouths of those who have been so harmed."

Ursula then unsheathed a decorated curved knife and created cuts to draw blood on all three people who were prepped on the altar. The pacing tigers began to make noises, smelling the blood in the air. Ursula swiftly walked out of the sacrificial area before releasing the gate that restrained the wild animals to their cages.

The tigers came out tentatively at first, being distracted by all those watching who had again resumed the pounding of their staffs. But slowly they approached the persons on the altar and began to first lick the flowing blood before becoming impatient, clamping their jaws down on the bodies, first dismembering them, before ultimately killing them with aims to consume them.

Xavier began to feel an inrush of energy as did those around him. He raised his arms to receive it, then it ceased. Xavier looked around, observing the ecstasy by others in the room. It was one thing to order a life taken, it was another to observe it so personally in such a raw way.

One small step. Xavier thought to himself. It would not be long now until ceremonies such as this could come into the open. A new power had arisen in the north – one that threatened their very existence. He had tried to eradicate this Way of the Lily to no avail. And it has risen up in power and had come into the open in such a display of power that even more would flock to its ways. His student had become a master and now a formidable enemy. No, this was a good first step, but more groundwork still needed to be placed.

Xenon would still fall. The Lily would fall with all those who followed it. He was the Master of Shadows. He could not fail.